"You finally have a horse."

She stood slowly and looked up at him. "Because of you," she said and unexpectedly reached out and hugged him.

He froze for a second, and when he finally realized he wanted to hug her back, she was moving away. "What was that for?"

She actually blushed. "I'm just happy and you made it happen. I can't wait for tomorrow to go to your ranch to ride him."

What he needed right then was to leave, to go out into the cold air and think straight. To be a friend to Grace was his goal, but he wasn't stepping over the line. He was there to try to show her the lodge as Marty saw it, with the hope she'd end up staying. He knew the odds of that happening were low to nonexistent. "Get some rest and come by in the morning when you're ready to ride."

Dear Reader,

Two broken people, Grace Bennet and Max Donovan, have been hurt by life, and both have decided to do whatever it takes to never be hurt again. Then Grace gets a notification that the uncle she never knew existed has passed and left her land and a lodge near the small Wyoming town of Eclipse. Fate brings Grace, a city girl raised in Las Vegas, and Max, the county sheriff and one of the famous sons in the Donovan rodeo family, together in Eclipse. Instant attraction between them is strong, but neither one wants to go beyond friendship. They can't take that chance. But sometimes taking a leap of faith can be the safest thing to help you find where you really belong.

Writing *Grace and the Cowboy*, the last book in the Flaming Sky Ranch series, was a joy for me, and I hope that you enjoy reading it.

Mary Anne

HEARTWARMING

Grace and the Cowboy

Mary Anne Wilson

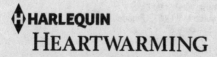

HHARLEQUIN
HEARTWARMING

H HARLEQUIN®
HEARTWARMING™

Recycling programs
for this product may
not exist in your area.

ISBN-13: 978-1-335-47559-6

Grace and the Cowboy

Harlequin Enterprises ULC
22 Adelaide St. West, 41st Floor
Toronto, Ontario M5H 4E3, Canada
www.Harlequin.com

Printed in U.S.A.

Mary Anne Wilson is a Canadian transplanted to California, where her life changed dramatically. She found her happily-ever-after with her husband, Tom, and their family. She always loved writing, reading and has a passion for anything Jane Austen. She's had over fifty novels published with Harlequin, been nominated for a RITA® Award, won Reviewers' Choice Awards and received RWA's Career Achievement Award in Romantic Suspense.

Books by Mary Anne Wilson

Harlequin Heartwarming

Flaming Sky Ranch

A Cowboy's Christmas Joy
A Cowboy Summer

Eclipse Ridge Ranch

Under a Christmas Moon
Her Wyoming Hero
A Cowboy's Hope

The Carsons of Wolf Lake

A Question of Honor
Flying Home
A Father's Stake

Visit the Author Profile page
at Harlequin.com for more titles.

For Deborah Leisher:

My dear friend who's willingly tackled
the impossible for me and made it
a win for both of us.

I love you.

CHAPTER ONE

ON A BRIGHT mid-November day, Grace Bennet stood alone by a private hangar at the airport outside of Tucson, Arizona, scanning the northern sky. Finally, a sleek private jet came into view and started its descent toward the main landing strip. As it touched down, Grace shielded her eyes with her hand to block the noon-hour sun and tried to ignore the knots in her stomach. She hadn't seen her father, Walter Bennet, founder and CEO of the Las Vegas–based Golden Mountain Corporation, for at least six months. After her mother had passed a year ago, what had always been a tenuous link between father and daughter had almost ceased to exist.

Now her father was begrudgingly making a brief stopover on his way to Japan on corporate business. She hadn't actually begged him to meet her prior to leaving, but she'd come close before he'd finally agreed to it. Grace needed a legitimate face-to-face moment with him, not a phone call or a video call. She needed to ask him one question that no one else could answer for her. She really needed the truth.

Walter Bennet might be a lot of things, including domineering, controlling and a bully at times, but he wasn't a liar. He was brutally frank, never editing his words to spare anyone's feelings, not even hers.

The plane with the glittering Golden Mountain logo on its tail section slowed and taxied over to a stop about thirty feet from where she stood. The cabin door lifted up, the steps dropped down to the tarmac, then Sawyer Bakker, her father's executive assistant, motioned for her to come on board.

"Come on, Grace," he shouted over the whine of the idling engines.

The man was dressed in an immaculate three-piece navy suit, and he was smiling at her. He was fifty-eight to her father's sixty but looked ten years younger. Grace figured that might be because Sawyer was given to freely passing out genuine smiles, making up for the profound lack of warmth from her father.

"You're going with Walter to Japan?" she asked as she took the steps up into the plane.

She'd called her father Walter all of her life. He'd insisted on it. Her mother had always been Marianna. No Mommy and Daddy.

"He wants me there for the investors' meeting in Brussels after we finalize the expansion plans in Tokyo." He motioned her past him into the cabin. "Sorry to rush you, but we're on a tight schedule."

"How is he?" Grace asked in a lower voice.

"Impatient. I'd say you're looking at a ten-minute window before he gives takeoff orders."

"Got it," she murmured and went farther into the eight-passenger cabin, a space that looked like a well-appointed study with its rich dark woods and leather finishes. Walter was sitting at a round table by the closed door to his sleeping quarters in the back. A crystal decanter that she knew held his special whiskey blend was to his right. Some of the amber liquid was in the glass in front of him.

Walter didn't stand and greet his only child as she approached him but motioned her to a captain's chair directly across the table from him. "Sit," he said abruptly before he pointedly glanced at his wristwatch. He looked at her and his ice blue eyes narrowed. "You said you were in a hurry for this, so let's get to it."

He tossed back his drink while Grace took

her seat, feeling as uncomfortable as she always did around him. When she finally met his gaze again, she was taken back to see how much older he looked at that moment. What had once been thick brown hair was thinning and streaked with gray. The lines at his eyes and the brackets at his mouth seemed deeper. It looked as if the last year hadn't been kind to him. Clasping her hands in her lap, she tried to focus past a sudden sadness that came out of nowhere.

Quickly she said, "I need you to answer a question. That's all."

He shrugged. "If it's not about you coming to work with me, I'm just losing time and money sitting here."

He hadn't changed. His time was valuable to him, and he rationed it out to the last minute. He poured more whiskey. "So, *are* you coming to claim your spot at the Mountain?" Walter had called his corporate headquarters in Las Vegas "the Mountain" for as long as she could remember. His eyes narrowed when she didn't answer. "Why do I sense you're going to disappoint me again, Grace?"

She wouldn't be baited to go down that rabbit hole and let him control the conversation.

She kept eye contact and said simply, "That's not my plan."

His exhale of air was a low hiss. "You really are Marianna's daughter. She was beautiful and passed her looks down to you, along with her ability to make me miserable without even trying."

Her parents had met when Marianna had been a top international runway model, and Walter had already made a name for himself and a lot of money in his business ventures. Grace had inherited her mother's height at five-ten, the same ebony black hair and striking violet eyes. But her mother had drawn attention wherever she went and loved it immensely. Grace hated being noticed unless she wanted to be. She hadn't been born to be a model, not any more than she'd been born to take over her father's empire when the time came.

"Marianna was always beautiful," she half whispered.

"She never looked like some thrift store reject," Walter said before he downed his drink.

Her outfit—a gold silk blouse, black leather pants and black wedge sandals—had been a real find in the consignment shop she ran with her former college roommate near their apartment in Tucson. She liked the style and the fact she hadn't had to spend a week's pay for it. Walter would have preferred she wear sharp business suits—the female version of his style—with her hair styled in a short bob and brushed sleekly back from her face. She'd never dressed like that and preferred to wear her natural curls loose, falling just past her shoulders from a center part. She didn't respond to his critique.

"There was just one Marianna," Walter finally murmured as he stared down at the now empty glass in his hand.

Grace felt her throat tightening, thinking about her mother. Taking a breath, she swallowed hard, then tried to steer their conversation back on track. "The question I need answered is—"

He abruptly cut her off. "Is this where you ask for money?"

She looked right at him. "No. I don't need your money."

His sarcasm grew sharper. "Did some guy with tattoos and a Harley get you in some trouble, and you need a lawyer?"

"What? No," she said more sharply than she'd meant to. "I'm here about a letter I received from an attorney in Wyoming."

That caught his interest. "Was it a job offer?"

"No," she said again. "I have a job I'm happy with."

"Of course you are. Who wouldn't want to spend their life selling used clothes and coffee after getting an expensive degree in business and marketing?" He sat back, looking so in control that it made Grace feel slightly nauseous. She braced herself for what she knew was coming in his attempt to intimidate her. He didn't disappoint.

"Obviously you don't appreciate the life my work has made possible for you. I've indulged you at every step, letting you take your time settling down, leaving it up to you to tell me when you were ready to become part of the company. You're going to be twenty-seven years old in a few months. I was twenty-one when I bought into my first investment. You've had a lot of time to do nothing except indulge your need to be some ridiculous free spirit."

His words hurt, but she tried to at least give the appearance that they didn't. "I did what you asked me to do, including carrying a 4.0 GPA all throughout college. While doing that, I was working, and I haven't asked for anything from you since my freshman year." Her tone became more defensive than she'd wanted it to be, so she made herself finish as evenly as she could. "I have friends and a life that I like in Tucson. That's all that matters to me right now."

"Do you want me to applaud you?" He chuckled roughly. "You're a fool, Grace."

She'd had enough, and she'd end this now on her terms. She got right to the point. "The letter from the attorney in Wyoming was about him settling the will of a man from a small town in the northern part of the state. I was named as his sole heir."

Walter looked surprised. "Who is this guy?"

This was it, and she spoke carefully to get it out before he cut her off. "Martin Roberts. His will says I'm his niece. All I want from you is to tell me if this Martin Roberts really was my uncle."

Her father's expression hardened. The only sound in the cabin was the muted whine of the plane's engines idling until he said, "Martin Roberts used to be Martin Robert Bennet, my older brother."

She hardly knew how to process what he'd admitted so easily. "Your...your brother? I had an uncle and you never told me about him. Why?"

That brought a scoffing exhale from Walter. "Martin was a waste and not worth anything." He waved his hand dismissively. "Now you know. Forget about that letter and a man who doesn't deserve to be remembered."

Grace was stunned. "Your brother—my uncle—is dead."

He shook his head. "He's been dead to me for almost thirty years. You contact the attorney for a full monetary assessment of the inheritance. No, don't bother with that. I'll make this all go away. Leave it to me."

Walter was throwing out orders that he expected her to follow without question, and for most of her life, she had done as he'd told her to do. But after she'd left to go to college, she'd realized she was capable of making her own decisions. "No, this is my inheritance and I'll handle it."

It seemed to take a second for her answer to sink in with him. When it did, he didn't explode. She remembered his rules for winning: *Get your adversary angry and when they get emotional and start yelling, you keep control and make them look like a fool, then you win.* He stared at her, holding eye contact, another tip he'd given her: *Never look away.* "I'm offering to help so you don't get tangled up with some yahoo who calls himself an attorney."

"I have what I came for, so I'll leave and let you go to Tokyo," she said. She wasn't going to play his game.

"Listen to me," he said, his voice tight. "Uncle or not, Martin was a no-good born loser."

"But he *was* your brother," she allowed herself to say.

"It was his choice to walk away and give up the Bennet name." He smiled at her, a totally humorless expression that he used to keep an adversary off balance. It only made her more determined to not back down. "In hindsight, it was probably the only good thing Martin ever did, to get out of here and leave us alone."

Grace flinched inside, and she had to fight to keep her tone calm when she responded. "He's dead, Walter, and I never even knew he existed. How could you keep that from me?"

"It wasn't any of your business," he said without hesitation as if that justified and explained everything.

"He was part of my family, and I deserved

to know him. Why did he walk away? What did you do to him?"

"Nothing." His single word was hard and flat.

Grace almost sagged from the weight of sadness she felt. "I can't believe you don't care your own brother died."

He shrugged. "Martin's whole life was a mess and it's over. We won't talk about this again. Ever. I'll make it go away. Am I making myself clear?"

What was clear to her was Martin Roberts had been her uncle. He'd been family, and his own brother didn't care about what happened to him. She'd stepped inside the corporate jet expecting one of two possible outcomes: either the attorney had the wrong person, or by some twist of fate, the man really had been her uncle. Maybe she'd been naive enough to think that she and Walter could share the shock and grief of his loss if the attorney had been right.

"Yes, I understand," she murmured. But she wouldn't agree to anything with him. Her world had changed. Instead of what Walter wanted, she would go to the place her uncle had called home, and she'd find out the truth for herself.

She stood abruptly to end the meeting. "You

can bill me for your time, Walter. I'll leave you to mourn Uncle Martin." She turned away as Sawyer appeared from the cockpit and went to raise the door and lower the stairs for her.

Before she could get outside, her father called after her, "I don't need you to tell me to mourn anyone. You call the attorney, or, trust me, I will!"

She looked back at him. "Don't you dare. It's not your business."

For a moment she thought he was going to break his own rules and yell at her, but he didn't. He kept his voice level, but he spoke slowly, enunciating each word clearly. "Listen to me—if you decide to head out to the Wild West, you are on your own." A smugness entered his tone. "You'd probably fit right in at some run-down motel in some jerkwater town in the middle of nowhere."

She bit her lip hard to keep from saying something that would only make things worse. She settled for, "Whatever it is, it's my life and my choice. It's got nothing to do with you."

He waved her away with a dismissive motion of his big hand. "Go and do whatever you want to do, but if you fall on your face, I won't help you get up. If you need money, get a second job. See how that works out for you."

Grace knew if she left then, she'd pay a price. Maybe banishment from Walter Bennet's world. If so, she'd pay it. "Go to Japan. I'm heading to Wyoming!" she called back to him as she took the first step down.

He threw out one last verbal volley. "Regrettably, it looks as if you've inherited some of Martin's stupidity."

She didn't look back this time as she hurried down onto the tarmac and over to where she'd been allowed to park by the hangar. She tried to let go of a wild mixture of pain, anger and disbelief as she slipped behind the steering wheel of her old green Jeep. She didn't drive away immediately but stayed to watch the corporate jet taxi back onto the main runway. When its wheels lifted off the ground and the plane climbed into the heavens, she finally felt as if she could breathe again.

It was done. She was going alone to Wyoming to see where her uncle had lived and find out all she could about a man she'd never heard of until two days ago, a man she'd never be able to meet.

CHAPTER TWO

One week later, Wyoming

IT WAS ALMOST MIDNIGHT, and Sheriff Max Donovan was worn-out. He was on his way home after spending twelve hours driving around the southern section of Clayton County, trying to track down thieves who'd been stealing irrigation system components. He was frustrated that he'd come up empty-handed again. He was heading north toward the town of Eclipse and debating if he should sleep in the back room of the sheriff's substation in town or tough out the extra twenty miles to make it to the Flaming Sky Ranch his family owned and ran.

But when he drove onto the main street of the town, Clayton Way, he remembered he did have another option just over two miles north of the town limit: Split Creek Lodge. A couch there was more comfortable than the cot that was too short to accommodate his

full six feet two inches. The Lodge had been
shut down since the owner had passed away,
a man who had been a good friend to Max.
Marty Roberts was a quiet man who'd shown
an uncanny understanding of what Max had
gone through during a low point in his life
three years earlier.

He drove past the station and kept going,
envisioning the huge sectional couch in front
of the double-sided firebox in the rock fireplace in the great room of the Lodge. He
could stretch out there and not worry about
his feet hanging off the end. He only wished
that Marty could've been there to greet him,
grinning and offering great coffee and a game
of chess.

As he drove, he rotated his head to try to
loosen his neck and shoulder muscles. Other
vehicles were few and far between at this time
of night. He slowed when he caught sight of
the Lodge sign ahead. The only part of the
ten-foot-tall electric sign that was still lit up
was a two-word advisory: "No Vacancy." The
Lodge was empty, but at least no unsuspect-
ing traveler would pull in and try to get a
room.

Max pulled up to the double gate. A sign
above the keypad set in a rocky pillar read

"Welcome to Split Creek Lodge." He put in the security code, and once the gates opened, he drove through and onto a packed dirt drive half-buried under the dead leaves from the trees that formed a canopy overheard. He'd only driven halfway up to the Lodge itself when he stopped the truck abruptly and flipped off the headlights. The lights were on inside the reception area and the great room to the right of it. He'd locked up tight two days ago when he'd made his last security check.

He cautiously drove forward in the shadows until he was able to make out the sprawling log-and-stone single-story structure with its central peaked roof. Suddenly the light in the great room went out. With it being a moonless night, Max couldn't make out much from the top of the drive where it merged into the cobbled parking area that ran along the front of the Lodge.

Only one parking slot was occupied. An old canvas-topped Jeep sat in front of the steps leading up to the porch. Taking his night vision binoculars from the console, he focused them on the back of the lone vehicle. Its license had been issued in Arizona.

He entered the number in his dash computer and kept watching the Lodge as he waited for a response. He wasn't going inside without some clue about what he might be facing, especially without any backup. A high-pitched beep signaled that the data was loading, and he watched the information on the Jeep come up on the screen.

The 1982 Jeep was registered to a Marianna Grace Bennet in Tucson. She was twenty-six with blue eyes, black hair and was five feet ten inches tall. She had valid insurance and two speeding tickets that had been settled with a fine. Most people hated their pictures on their driving license, but Ms. Bennet had no reason to complain. By any standard, she was strikingly attractive. If he ended up having to arrest her, she'd definitely be the best-looking criminal he'd ever handcuffed.

He called the dispatcher covering the northern section of the county overnight and when Lillian Shaw picked up the call, he was surprised. She'd worked at the substation in town for the past twenty years, and her time off the clock began at nine in the evening. "Lillian, what are you doing there?"

"You were gone and there wasn't anyone to cover until Denton takes over at two. Now, cowboy, what's your 911?"

The tiny middle-aged lady had more energy

than a kid. She'd been a real plus for Max when he'd taken over as sheriff six years ago. Thankfully, she wasn't showing any signs of winding down to retirement. "I'm at Marty's place. Someone's inside and I'm going to check it out. Give me fifteen?"

She responded briskly. "You got it, cowboy. Be safe."

He eased the truck slowly forward, rolling to a stop behind the Jeep to block anyone leaving in a hurry. He wasn't in the mood or the condition for a car chase tonight. Killing the engine, he tossed his hat onto the passenger seat, then undid the front of his brown suede jacket.

He got out as quietly as possible and approached the Jeep, trying to see inside. All that was visible was a wrapper from a candy bar on the passenger seat and a take-out coffee cup sitting in what had probably been meant to be an ashtray. He stepped back and took the stairs up to the wraparound porch in two strides, then ducked down as he moved closer to the door to keep from being seen through the windows. Once he was at the wall between the last window and the doorjamb, he straightened up and inched closer to the heavy wooden doors with frosted glass inserts. One thin strip of glass was clear, but as the lights in the reception area flashed on, all he could see was a narrow section of the long check-in desk directly across from the door. Nothing moved.

He pushed back the right side of his jacket to have access to his radio and his weapon in its hip holster, unsnapped the guard, then rested his hand on the butt of the gun. He listened for movement inside. He was tired but angry that someone had broken into the Lodge, and he wouldn't let it go any further, no matter who was in there.

A dragging sound suddenly came from within, then a jarring crash that he could feel vibrate in the wooden floor of the porch. He reached for the door latch, felt it disengage, then kicked the barrier back hard enough to hear it impact against the interior wall.

"Police!" he yelled with his gun half-drawn as he rushed inside. He barely managed to stop before he'd trip over a woman sitting on the hard floor with a heavy metal display rack overturned by her side. The brochures that had been in its pockets were scattered all over the dusty wooden floor.

Her hands were up in surrender, and she

looked horrified. "Stop! Stop! Don't shoot, please."

"Don't move," he ordered. "Who else is in here?"

"No one. I'm alone. I swear."

He wasn't about to trust her and quickly scanned the area but saw nothing and heard nothing except her rapid breathing. As he secured his gun, he stared down at her. Dark shoulder-length curls tangled around her face as she sat there, awkwardly on the floor with her hands up. Dressed in a well-worn black leather motorcycle jacket, jeans with rips at the knees and totally out of place black-strapped sandals, she watched him with eyes that were more lavender than the blue her driver's license had claimed. They were wide from the shock and fear of someone bursting into the Lodge with a gun and screaming at her.

Her pale lips worked silently before she actually spoke in a breathless voice. "Are…are you really the police?"

He pushed back his jacket again to expose his badge and gun. "Yes, ma'am."

She frowned up at him. "You could have bought that stuff online."

"Ma'am, I'm the sheriff of Clayton County. Who are you?"

"Marianna Grace Bennet, but… I go by Grace."

"Okay, Grace. Now I need to know why you broke in here."

"I did not break in here," she said quickly.

Pretty or not, she was in the wrong place at midnight and lying to him on top of that. He hunkered down in front of her to make serious eye contact. "The gates by the highway were locked when I left here after my last security check two days ago. Inside lights were off. The entry door was locked." He reached behind himself to feel for the door, then swung it shut as the wind began to grow outside. "The back door was locked, and the cellar doors were double locked. How do you explain that? And please don't lie to me. I'm not in a good mood."

She surprised him when she sat up a bit straighter. "I want my one phone call a prisoner's entitled to."

This wasn't going to be easy. "Ma'am, you aren't my prisoner, not yet."

"Then I want to call 911 to make sure you are who you say you are."

"Okay," he said. "Call 911, but the thing

is, at this time of night, I *am* 911. Your call will go to central dispatch at headquarters in Two Horns, where they'll track the call then contact the closest substation and it's sent to the officer on patrol to respond. Your call will be forwarded to *my* cell that's in *my* jacket pocket since I'm the only one on duty around here. Believe it or not, even with all the rerouting, it only takes a minute to get to my phone."

She looked up at him with narrowed eyes, and he could tell whatever shock and fear he'd generated in her with his sudden appearance was almost gone. Unfortunately, his adrenaline was waning, too, and his weariness was making a comeback. "I'm not saying you're lying, but I'm alone out here in the middle of nowhere and you broke in, slamming that door into the wall, not to mention the gun, and I can't take your word for anything."

She was right, and he wanted to get this over with. "Okay, do what you need to do, but the landline phones here are shut off."

"I have a cell phone," she said and fumbled getting it out of her jacket pocket. When she held it up so he could see it, her hand was slightly unsteady.

"Okay. Go for it."

Max watched Grace Bennet put in the call and a minute later, his phone rang in his jacket pocket. He guessed the main unit had bypassed Lillian completely. He took it out and held it up so she could see the screen. "My phone, your call." He put in the code that stood for "no episode," then looked at Grace.

With a roll of her eyes, she exhaled, then said, "So, you really are 911, huh?"

"Yes, ma'am, and I'm at the end of a very long day." He stood up. "I want to go home, but I can't leave until you answer my questions so I can sort this all out."

"Okay. I'll make this as clear as I can. I got here fifteen minutes before you showed up and scared me almost to death."

"How did you get on the property?"

"Through the gates, once I put in the code, and I shut them behind me. Then I drove up that long drive. I thought when I got inside I could warm up." That admission was followed by a scoffing sound. "Sure, get in here, warm up. It's probably colder in here than it is outside." She extended her hand to him. "Speaking of cold, this floor is freezing. Can you help me get up?"

He reached to grasp her hand and helped leverage her to her feet. Once she was standing, she pulled free of his hold, but that didn't keep him from feeling how cold her hand had been. He was very aware of her height, not quite eye to eye with him, but a lot closer to it than most women he knew.

"Now, let me get this straight," he said. "You had access to the gate code somehow, and you came up here to break in?"

"I told you I didn't break in. I have the gate code, but I used the keys to open the door. I put them down somewhere and I was looking for them. I thought they might have fallen under that stupid rack that I tried to move and knocked over. The owner's attorney left the keys behind a pot on the porch, and he sent me a text with the gate code."

That took him back. "What attorney?"

"Mr. Burris Addison. He's the executor for my uncle's will, and he said that my uncle left this place to me. This lodge is mine…which, I guess, makes you the trespasser here."

So, the possible heir Burr had mentioned to him weeks ago had been found, and he was looking right at her. He couldn't see much of Marty in her beyond her height, but he knew Burr would have had her thoroughly vetted before giving her the key.

"Marty was your uncle?"

"His name was Martin Robert Bennet, but it seems he went by Martin Roberts around here."

"He went by Marty, not Martin, and although he was a good friend of mine, he never mentioned having any family."

She exhaled. "Then we're even. I never knew I had an uncle until a week ago."

His cell phone sounded again, and with one glance at the screen, he knew that Lillian had counted down the fifteen minutes from his last call. When he connected, she immediately asked, "What do you need to tell me, cowboy?"

He rattled off his army serial number to let her know he was in a safe situation. "I'm inside here and everything's under control."

That wasn't enough of an explanation for her. "Who or what did you find in there?"

He kept his eyes on Marianna Grace Bennet, who never looked away from him. "I found Marty's heir, a niece."

"Oh, my goodness," Lillian said. "So, he did have family?"

"It looks that way."

"Tell me you didn't draw your gun on her."

"We're both in one piece. Burr apparently forgot to mention he'd found her and—"

Grace cut him off. "He wasn't expecting me until the beginning of next week. I'm early."

Lillian obviously heard that explanation. "I'll give him a call and let him know she's already at the Lodge."

"Aces," Max said.

"Are you coming here or heading home when you finish?" Lillian asked.

It looked like he was going to be sleeping on the cot at the substation since Ms. Bennet appeared to be staying at the Lodge overnight. "I'll be going to the station," he said.

"Okay, just one last question. There was a rerouted emergency call from an unknown number that was cleared. What was that about?"

"That was a mistake."

"Okay. Safe ride, cowboy," she said and hung up.

Max put his phone away and found a smile for the woman in front of him. "Ms. Bennet, I want to officially welcome you to Eclipse and the Split Creek Lodge. People around here just call it the Lodge—capital *L*—or Marty's place."

GRACE NEVER LOOKED away from the sheriff, a tall man who didn't look much like the law, except for what she saw when his jacket was open. His deep brown hair was trimmed and combed straight back from strong features and dark hazel eyes. His black jeans were faded, and his Western boots were scuffed and dusty. She caught the cowboy vibe he gave off, even if there was no fancy Stetson in sight.

"Thank you," she said and looked down at the messy floor. "I went into town first to see about a hotel or a room of some sort. Everything was pretty much shut down except a place called the Golden Fleece Saloon. I figured there wouldn't be any rooms available there."

"You figured right. Everything shuts down early around here."

"I guess I'm stuck here at least for tonight." Even keeping her jacket on hadn't made her a speck warmer. Her sandals were the worst; her feet were so cold she expected them to turn blue any second.

The sheriff's phone rang again, and he pulled it back out. "What now, Lil?" He nodded, said, "I'll pass it on to her," then put his phone away. "Lillian called Burr, and he'd like you to come into town in the morning and meet up with him at his office. He'll be there from nine until noon."

"Good grief. This Lillian person called the attorney at midnight to tell him I was here?"

He shrugged. "Burr's up late all the time. The man never sleeps. I'm going to leave and get off your property, but I'd like to ask you something first."

"Of course."

"Why didn't you know about your uncle?"

She spontaneously shivered and wrapped her arms around herself. "My parents never told me my father had a brother who left before I was born." She shrugged, bitterness she couldn't shake caught in those words. "I don't even know why Uncle Martin walked away from the family. I sure can't ask him now, so it is what it is."

He nodded. "It sure is. So, you're okay staying here for the night?"

Finally, he'd asked exactly what she needed to talk about. "I will be, but it's freezing and the heaters I tried don't work. On top of that, a lot of the light bulbs are burned-out." She glanced up at the deer antler chandelier hanging from the high, heavily beamed ceiling over the desk. Only five bulbs out of a dozen were lit. "I like both light and heat."

He smiled ruefully. "Marty had a thing

about not replacing light bulbs until he had no choice, and the heaters are useless without fuel. The propane tanks were shut down a few months ago, and the earliest you can get a propane delivery is tomorrow, if you're lucky. The water pipes are wrapped, so you should have water."

She glanced through the archway into the shadowy room beyond it, where she could make out a massive see-through fireplace in the middle of the space. If it was safe to use, it could be her answer for heat. Before she could ask the sheriff if it worked, he made her an unexpected offer.

"Listen, I live just north of here, and we have plenty of room at the family ranch. You're welcome to stay there for a couple of nights until you can get this place livable."

That had come out of the blue. She'd been brought up in Las Vegas in a penthouse on the top floor of the first hotel and casino her father had built, and this was way too small-town for her. The man seemed nice enough now that he knew she wasn't a burglar, but going to his house wasn't an option. He was still a stranger, sheriff or not, and she couldn't trust him like that.

"Don't take this personally, but I don't know

you and you don't know me, so I'll stay here and hope the fireplace in that big room works. You go home to your family. I'll be just fine here."

"I guess there isn't any point in telling you that Marty and I were close friends and he'd vouch for me, since you know nothing about your uncle."

She sure didn't. "Yeah, that wouldn't impress me," she said with bit of a smile. "The fireplace does work, doesn't it?"

"Yep, it does, and it gives off good heat. But it won't heat more than one room."

That was good news. "That's all I need. I can sleep in there, and even if half the bulbs are burned-out, there'll be light. I'd imagine there's a couch in there somewhere under those dust sheets."

"There are big sectionals in there that face either side of the hearth."

"That's great," she said. "And thank you for the offer. I'm kind of surprised with you being a cop and all, that you'd take a stranger into your home with a wife and kids there."

He shook his head. "I'm not—"

She cut him off. "I'm sorry. I didn't think that through before I said it out loud."

He shrugged. "No problem."

She had a thought, maybe a better idea for where she'd spend the night. "Did Uncle Martin live in this building, or did he have a place off-site? Maybe a house close by?"

"Marty lived behind the desk."

"He what?"

"In his living quarters, a room behind the desk at the back," the sheriff said, gesturing. "That way he would always be close by to greet guests when they came in, especially those who showed up well beyond check-in time. He never wanted guests to feel they were imposing on him."

Grace turned to look past the desk that butted up against the side wall by the archway and stopped at a wide hallway on the other side of it. A large-faced clock that had stopped at three o'clock sometime in the past was hung beside an old-fashioned cubbyhole structure with room keys dangling under the room numbers. A closed door to the right of that had a brass plaque on it: "Office. Ring Bell for Assistance." She hadn't noticed that before. "He lived in his office?"

"Technically, I guess you could say that, but the office is only part of what's back there. It's more like a studio apartment with a kitchenette, sleeping area and double doors that lead out onto a raised deck." As if he knew she was thinking about staying in there, he said, "There's lights in there, but no fuel for the heater."

She shrugged that away. "Then I'll stick with the couch for tonight."

"Come on and I'll get the fire going for you before I leave," he said as he turned and started toward the archway. Grace hurried after him, forgetting all about the brochures scattered on the floor until her foot slipped on one. She frantically reached out and managed to grab the edge of the desk with one hand—relieved until her grip failed and she lost her footing completely. In a blur she was falling until she wasn't because the sheriff had caught her under her arms before she hit the floor. As she found her footing, he let her go and they stood facing each other.

"Wow, I didn't expect that," she said. "Thank you. I don't fall, not usually, but..." She frowned at the brochures under their feet. "Those pamphlets are slippery."

"Are you okay?"

She was embarrassed and tired. Her right wrist stung from hitting something, most likely the edge of the desk, but for some reason she found herself able to smile ruefully at the big man. "I'm fine, unless embarrassment's fatal. It isn't, is it?"

His expression morphed into a crooked grin. "Not that I know of."

"That's a relief." She crouched down and started picking up the leaflets as quickly as she could while the sheriff righted the metal rack. Then he hunkered down by her and started gathering up the scattered travel brochures along with her.

"You don't need to do that," Grace said. "This is all my fault. I can do it myself."

"It's not a problem," he murmured as he slipped the brochures he'd already picked up into one of the empty rack pockets.

Grace put those she'd retrieved in another pocket as she asked, "What do people call you besides Sheriff?"

He was starting to make another stack. "My name's Max."

"Okay, Max, can you describe Mr. Burris Addison for me?"

He kept clearing the floor. "Well, he's about five-ten or eleven, midsixties, partial to flannel shirts, jeans and boots. Got a full head of hair that's been gray for as long as I've known him."

She liked what he was telling her, but that

wasn't what she really needed to know. "What about his character?"

"He's exceptionally good at what he does. He genuinely likes people, and he makes himself available at any time." More brochures went into another pocket. "You can trust him to do right by you."

"He sounds almost too good to be true. Most attorneys I've known I wouldn't trust with anything except to do whatever it takes to win." She really disliked her father's head counsel, Fredrick Moore. The man reveled in reducing his opponents to rubble.

"Well, Burr's for real. An honest man who chooses his battles, in and out of court," Max said as he straightened and put the last of the brochures where they belonged. He towered over her. "I'll put the rack back."

As he pushed the now full rack into the corner where the desk met the sidewall, Grace said, "Thank you."

He turned, headed to the archway and disappeared into the shadowy space beyond. A moment later, lights flashed on overhead, and what bulbs hadn't burned out in the massive wagon-wheel fixtures hanging from the ceiling gave off enough light for her to be fine.

When she stepped into the great room, Max

was standing in front of the massive stone fireplace. Crouching down to open the screen on their side, he said, "Marty always kept split logs and kindling in here, so you're in luck. You've got fuel for more than a few fires."

Grace saw what he meant. A large square niche cut into the rock face was stacked neatly with logs and kindling. "Please, Max, I'll do that. I'm really good at making a fire, and you need to get home. You said you were tired."

He glanced up at her and motioned to the covered furniture beside her. "That's the couch under there. It's good for sleeping on—I've done it before." He turned back to the hearth as if he hadn't heard what she said about the fire-making and reached for two logs.

She didn't like that, him taking over and telling her how things would be. It reminded her too much of the way her father played at being a father: telling her what she needed, what she wanted and how he'd make it happen. "Honestly, I can make the fire."

"Of course you can. It's not brain surgery," he said without looking back at her.

Well, I guess that's that, then. Short of being rude and telling him to leave, he'd be making the fire. She moved to reach for the dust cover and tugged on the corner, and the sheet slid off onto the floor exposing a black leather sectional couch. It wasn't old and saggy as she had expected it to be, and the long center section looked as if she'd be able to stretch out on it comfortably. It was definitely doable for the night with the fire to keep her cozy.

Max spoke while he laid the logs in the hearth along with kindling. "If you didn't already bring your things inside, why don't you go and get them while I try to get it warmed up in here."

The man was just trying to be helpful, but he was getting on her nerves issuing orders. She wished she wasn't getting edgy from it. She picked up the dust sheet and tossed it to the far end of the couch. "I'm glad Uncle Martin kept wood in here for the fire. I would have hated to have to break apart the furniture to burn for heat."

Grace was surprised when Max stood abruptly and turned to her, frowning. "You were going to chop up the furniture?"

"Oh, no. I was kidding, just kidding," she assured him quickly. "Sorry."

He shrugged it off. "Forget it. It's been a long day."

"I guess breaking up any of this furniture and burning it would be a felony."

"No. This is all yours, so legally you could grind it up into sawdust if you wanted to, but that'd be a real shame. Most of the wood furniture in here and in the rest of the Lodge was handmade by Marty. This building isn't the only thing he left to you. It's everything he had in his world, really."

The impact of that statement blindsided Grace. She'd been so wound up from the meeting with her father and the decision to come to Wyoming on her own, that it overrode everything else. Now she faced the reality that the man who had left her everything he'd valued in his life hadn't tried to contact her while he was still alive. "He was a furniture maker?"

"Among his many gifts," Max said as he turned and crouched by the hearth. He struck a match, and moments later there was a pop and the first flame leapt to life. "He made my dad a chess table, a duplicate of the one he'd made for himself."

She didn't think her dad had ever made anything with his own hands. All he did was sign contracts and boost his bottom line. The fire was obviously all the sheriff's, so she headed toward the door. "I'll get my things," she said.

By the time Grace brought her luggage inside, Max had the fire roaring, its heat starting to defeat the cold. He was staring down into the leaping flames with his back to her. Grace moved over beside him to hold her hands out to the lovely warmth and sighed with pleasure. "That feels wonderful."

He seemed startled when she spoke, as if he'd forgotten she was even there. "What?" he asked as he turned toward her.

"I just said the heat feels so good. Thank you for making the fire even if I could have done it myself."

"So you said, and you're welcome," he said, then went to the far end of the fireplace and disappeared for a moment.

Grace heard a dragging sound then a solid click before Max came back into sight. "I closed the other side to send the heat in this direction." He went past her around the couch to a low bank of cabinets under the windows that took up the entire front length of the room. He opened up the first door and pulled out a couple of blue blankets and two pillows. He set them on the end section of the couch by the crumpled dust sheet. "There's more in there if you need them."

"Thanks," she said.

He pointed to a door on the other side of the room. "There's a bathroom through there to the left. It's small, but it's functional. Is there anything else I can do before I take off?"

When the fire flared and shot embers up into the chimney, Grace was close enough to see the tiredness in Max's eyes. She figured he really was a nice guy, probably with a beautiful wife and adorable kids and that's where he should be, not here doing what she could have done for herself. "I'm all set, thanks to you," she said. "I do have one more question. If I take a shower, will there be hot water?"

He grimaced slightly at that. "There won't be any hot water until you get the propane tanks filled. That can't happen until you call the propane company. Put that at the top of your list of things to do in the morning."

This man wasn't like any cop who had ever crossed her path before. "Is it part of your job description to aid and abet total strangers you come across in abandoned lodges while you're obviously dead tired?"

Max grinned. "I am tired, for sure, but you're one hundred percent within your rights to be here, and I'm being hospitable to an old friend's niece. You can get a long way in this town on the goodwill Marty Roberts built up here over the years."

She'd never heard her father spoken about

like that. "I wish I'd met him, even just once." She bit her lip to stop saying any more. Her problems weren't his.

"He was worth knowing. In a way you'll get to know him by just being here and seeing the life he lived." He motioned vaguely around the space. "He loved this place, and when he got too sick, he had to shut it down and it broke his heart." He hesitated before he said, "I guess I should warn you that the same people who cared about Marty are expecting you to bring the Lodge back to life."

She'd assumed she'd sell once she found out what she wanted to know about her uncle. "You mean, they'll be angry with me if I sell it?"

"No, just disappointed. The Lodge has been a home of sorts for out-of-towners, even a few locals over the years. There was an old-timer in town who lived in one of the rooms here after his wife passed. His name was Laz, and he was here for six years. It's a special place and sort of a landmark, too. I guess it's only natural to expect that they'd want Marty's only relative to pick up where he left off."

"I'm glad you warned me, but I'm here to take care of the estate before I head back to Tucson, where I live. I'm not here to take over this place and run it." When he frowned at her words, she quickly tried to explain it to him. "I mean, I inherited it out of the blue. I can't live here." She was still building her new life in Tucson piece by piece. "I'm sorry if that's not what you and the others would want from me, but I'll only be here for as long as it takes to put this up for sale."

He surprised her by passing that off with a shrug. "Well, you do what you need to do." Max pushed his hands into the pockets of his jacket. "When I was a kid the LeRoy-Toney family ran it. Then I came back from the army and Marty was here catering to new families and helping people who needed a break. This place was solid and peaceful, the same way Marty was."

There was no suggestion from the sheriff that her uncle had been any bit the "loser" her dad had claimed he was. That eased something in Grace, and she decided to ask Max a question that had come to her while he'd been talking. "Why don't you buy it and bring it back to its old glory? You obviously care about it so much."

She could tell she'd surprised him, but he didn't hesitate too long before he gave her his answer. "Maybe in another life I would have done just that, but my reality is working around the clock as sheriff. I'm up for reelection soon, and that's going to take up whatever downtime I might have had. Then there's my family and our ranch. There's always something that needs doing or some event to plan for. So, if anyone wants to resurrect this place, I'll help in any way I can, but it can't be me taking it over."

Grace knew it had been a long shot, but she was still disappointed. "I understand. Of course you have your life and family. It was just a thought."

"Okay, then," Max said. "Sleep well and stay warm."

Grace followed him to the front door and as he reached for the latch, she said, "It was nice meeting you, despite the way it happened."

He glanced back at her. "Nice meeting you, Ms. Bennet," he said.

"Please, call me Grace."

"Grace. You sure you don't need anything else?"

"Do you think Uncle Martin was happy here?"

He didn't look annoyed, but she didn't miss the slight sigh that came before his response. "Maybe *satisfied* is more the operative word.

He took life as it came, you know, one day at a time, and it worked for him." He was doing up his jacket while he spoke. "Marty said once that he'd found the real Marty out here, the one who finally understood who he wanted to be—the man who rode the Split Creek land to ease his heart, and he said his past was what had made him appreciate what he'd found here."

The more she heard about her uncle, the more her regrets grew. "Thank you for telling me that," she said softly.

Max narrowed his eyes on her. "The propane," he said, totally out of context for her.

"Pardon?"

"Sorry, but as soon as you get up in the morning, call Van Duren Propane Services. Try to set up something for tomorrow. Don't forget," he said before he opened the door and stepped outside and closed it behind him.

The fact that he had to get in one last order before he left irritated her, but it was done. Max was heading back to his family, and as she heard his truck start up, she looked around at a strange place that seemed sad in its emptiness. The least she could do was leave it more welcoming to strangers. Kind of a tip of her hat to her uncle and how he'd welcomed strangers every day. The thought made her smile.

CHAPTER THREE

MAX WOKE IN his office at the substation just after dawn, a bit stiff from sleeping on the cot. Grace Bennet had been an unexpected midnight surprise, a woman who looked as if she could have been a model, tall and slender, and she'd be called beautiful by anyone with functional eyes—man or woman.

So, Marty hadn't been alone after all but apparently chose to make no contact with what family he'd had. Max didn't understand that, but then again, he didn't have to. Marty had to have had his reasons. All that mattered now was that Grace had shown up, even though Max held little to no hope she'd stick around.

He stood, stretched his arms over his head, then grabbed fresh clothes out of his locker and went into the small bathroom to shower. He needed to get ready for a planned meeting at the mayor's office, and he hoped a shower might just take the edge off him having only five hours of sleep. When he stepped out of the shower, feeling vaguely restored, there was a knock on the office door.

"Hey, cowboy," Lillian called through the barrier.

He was startled to hear Lillian was there after working so late the night before. "What are you doing here?"

"I forgot my wallet last night and came back to get it before making Clint's breakfast. Are you decent?"

"Nope, haven't been for a long time." Lillian laughed at his answer to the same question she always asked him when he was in the shower. It never got old for her. "Did you find your wallet?" he called back.

"Yep, but I was wondering how it went with Marty's niece."

He briskly dried off while he talked. "His niece slept over there last night. That's why I'm here trying to get my mind working again." He glanced in the small mirror over the sink and decided not to bother shaving.

"And?" Lillian nudged him for more information.

"She's going to see Burr this morning." He ran a towel roughly over his hair, then reached for his clean clothes and dressed quickly in black jeans along with a fresh beige uniform shirt. Lillian was standing not two feet from him when he opened the door.

"What does she look like? Is she nice? Does she have someone with her, a husband or kids or anything?"

"Hey, slow down. She's tall, black hair, violet eyes and I have no idea if she has a husband or kids. She came alone and didn't mention anyone joining her."

"Did you say *violet* eyes?"

"Her license says blue eyes, but they're a shade of violet."

"Call me surprised that you're making a distinction between a woman's eye color."

"They were just unique," he said.

Lillian, dressed in the beige shirt and black slacks she wore every day, crossed her arms over her ample chest. "Pretty?"

"This is not the time for this discussion. I'm due at Leo's office soon, and I'm foggy enough from sleep deprivation. But, yes, she's very pretty."

"Hmm, interesting," she said and kept asking questions. "How did she explain not being here for poor Marty all these years, especially toward the end?"

"Because she never knew she had an uncle,"

he said. "Seems her parents kept that from her for some reason."

"You tell her she'd better ask them why. Marty didn't deserve to be alone at the end when he had family."

"That's her business, not ours."

"What about the Lodge. Did she say what she plans to do with it?"

Max sat on the single chair in front of the corner desk to pull on his boots. "She indicated to me that she's only going to be here long enough to get the conditions of the will settled. When that's done, she'll head back to Arizona, where she came from."

"Oh, no," Lillian said on a groan. "We'll have to figure this out."

"There's nothing for us to figure out. It's all up to her, no matter what we'd like to see happen."

"I guess you're right, Max. But it wouldn't hurt to make her feel real welcome and let her see how much the Lodge means to people around here. If she's Marty's flesh and blood, she might just come around and stay."

He was almost certain—niece or no niece—Grace was going to leave sooner rather than later. "Who knows?" he said, barely covering a yawn. "I'm getting too old for double shifts and always being shorthanded."

"Nonsense, you're a kid," she said.

"On what planet does a thirty-seven-year-old pass for a kid?"

"You need time off, cowboy," she said. "You also need to have a life away from here."

He had a life, and after the election at the end of the month, that life would change completely if he lost. For now, he did what he needed to do and was thankful for his job. "You're starting to sound like my mom," he said.

"You ought to listen to your mother." He put on his belt and holster before he walked with Lillian up to the front to get his hat and jacket and see her out to get back to her husband.

A call came in on the nonemergency line and Lillian took it. He was doing up his jacket when she finished the call. "Forget the meeting. Leo's youngest had a fall and broke his wrist. He'll reschedule for later this week."

So he got up at the crack of dawn for nothing. "Okay," he said, putting on his hat. "I'll head home, then. I'm craving Mom's huevos rancheros."

"Lucky you. Maybe drop in on Marty's niece today to make sure she's doing okay." The phone rang again, and Lillian took it. She smiled, then simply said, "On my way." She turned to Max. "Clint's hungry," she explained. "I'll be back around nine." Then she left.

ONCE MAX WAS in the pickup heading home with the heater blasting full force, he considered Lillian's suggestion. He would check in on Grace on his way back from the ranch before he went down to Two Horns for his shift. When he was barely a mile from town, his attention was caught by someone walking on the gravel shoulder of the highway with their back to the traffic. Not a smart move, even on a highway that wasn't usually busy. A car could be coming right at them, and they wouldn't know it until it was too late.

He slowed, then realized the not-so-smart pedestrian was Grace Bennet, her dark hair blowing back in the breeze. She was wearing her motorcycle jacket and jeans and was seemingly staring at her feet as she walked briskly. Thankfully, she had on bright red running shoes instead of sandals today.

He eased onto the shoulder, checked that it was safe to do a U-turn and pulled up behind her, then tapped his horn to get her attention. She stopped abruptly about a car's length from the truck and turned. He motioned her toward the passenger door to keep her away from the passing vehicles.

She jogged over as he slid down the window. "What's going on?" he asked.

She smiled in at him, her cheeks rosy from the cold. "I'm walking as fast as I can to get to town. It's freezing outside!"

"Is there something wrong with your Jeep?" he asked.

She groaned. "I hate to admit this, but after you left I went back out to the Jeep to get the charger for my cell phone, and I couldn't find it. So, I went inside, and the charger was in my bag, but my phone wasn't in my pocket or anywhere I looked for it, but eventually I just gave up. Anyway, I accidentally left the key in the ignition after I'd used the interior light to hunt for my charger. My Jeep doesn't warn you when the door's open and the key's still in the ignition." She turned both hands palms up. "So, no car. I knew the town couldn't be too far and I could walk to it, then get a burner phone and call a taxi or use Uber to get back to the Lodge after I met with Burris Addison. I didn't want to be late."

She jumped when a bright red muscle car zoomed by, shaking the truck in its wake.

"The town is 2.1 miles from the Lodge," Max told her.

Her shrug was breezy. "Not a problem. I do more than that in the gym most days." She shivered. "I have to admit, though—it's a lot balmier in the gym than it is out here!"

"Climb in and get warmed up," he said.

She shook her head. "Oh, no, I can't keep you from your appointed rounds. The walk will do me good."

"That's the Postal Service motto. But I'm not asking, I'm *telling* you to get in here."

Her smile died at his tone. "Is this, like, a police order?"

"I protect and serve, and I'm protecting you. We not only don't want people walking on the side of the highway unless it's an emergency, but there are laws against performing dangerous actions while walking on a major thoroughfare."

"Dangerous... What are you talking about? I was doing fine."

"You were walking with your back to oncoming traffic, so you'll never know a car's coming at you until it hits you."

"So, what's the penalty?"

"No penalty. Just please get in."

She still didn't move as he unlocked the

passenger door for her. Then she finally said, "Okay, fine," as she opened the door, stepped up into the cab and settled back to do up her seat belt.

Before he drove back onto the highway, he took his phone out of the charging slot on the console. "There's a local mechanic who's really great with cars, Henry Lodge. Let me call him and put him on speaker."

"Can't you give me a jump start?" she asked.

"That Jeep of yours is pretty old, isn't it?"

"It's a 1982 Renegade."

"I gave an old truck a jump start last year and totally fried the wiring. I really don't want to be sued for killing your Jeep."

"I wouldn't sue you, but I'd be pretty ticked off," she said on a soft laugh that he found he liked a lot more than the frown she'd given him moments before.

"We don't want that," he said. "If Henry says I can jump start it safely, problem solved."

Max put in the call, and Henry Lodge's deep voice came over the speaker. "Max, I'm on a job by the mill, so if you need help, you'll have to check in with Donny Boudreaux."

"I don't need that, Henry. This is about a dead battery, but it's in an older vehicle, and I'm worried about trying to jump it in case

I fry the wiring the way I did with Kenny's old truck."

"What's the year, make and model?"

"The owner's on this call. She can give you the details."

Grace gave him the information and explained the situation.

"I don't think you should take the risk of trying to jump it," Henry replied.

"So how soon can you get over to the Lodge to figure it out for Grace?"

"I could maybe meet up with her around two."

Max glanced at Grace, who nodded her approval. "Okay, two it is."

After Max put his phone back in the charging slot, he pulled back onto the highway. "So, I said I wasn't going to issue you a ticket, but I was serious when I told you it was against the law to be hitchhiking on the side of the highway."

"Hitchhiking? I wasn't hitchhiking," she said. "I didn't have my thumb out, and I didn't ask you to stop."

"No, but you had no idea if any cars were coming that could have easily swerved and hit you. Protect and serve. I swore to do that six years ago."

"Okay, I get that, and I won't do it again. Just drop me here," she said at the town limits. "I have to point out that there are no cars around us." She twisted to look behind them. "Just one truck waaaaaaaaay back in the other lane."

He kept driving. Burr's office was five blocks ahead on the left side. "Okay, point taken."

"So, can you stop and let me out now?" she asked, her gaze burning a hole into the side of his face.

"Of course," he conceded and slowed, and kind of wished there were at least a few cars coming toward them. But the street was almost empty as he cut across and slipped nose first into a parking space right in front of the attorney's office.

He left the truck idling and turned to Grace halfway. "You're here. There's no ticket and I apologize for lecturing you. If you ever have to walk on the highway again, face the traffic."

SHERIFF MAX DONOVAN sure knew how to annoy Grace, but she found she couldn't work up any anger toward him. "Oh, I'll remember. I guess I should thank you for bringing me here."

"You don't have to thank me," he said when

she looked over at him. His expression had softened and there was a teasing glint in his hazel eyes. "But it's nice to be appreciated once in a while."

He certainly didn't resemble any of the police she'd dealt with over the years. And for whatever reason, she was having trouble holding on to being annoyed by him. Instead, she found herself almost smiling. She'd been nervous about facing the attorney, actually hoping the hike into town would help settle her. But Max had distracted her to the point that she'd forgotten about the meeting.

"Then, thank you again," she said as she looked at him, realizing his cowboy image was complete now that he was wearing a real Western hat, black with a band of braided leather around the crown, along with black jeans and his jacket. "I won't bother you again. I can figure things out from here."

All he said was, "It's no bother."

Grace looked around at the town from where she sat comfortably in the warmth coming out of the truck's vents. The stores lining the main street were eclectic, from a gourmet chocolate shop to one that specialized in Western wear. There were only a few cars around, along with a man on a horse coming from the opposite direction toward them.

She was delaying going inside, and she realized why. She was worried about the reaction she'd get when the attorney found out she wanted to sell the Lodge. Hopefully he wouldn't hate her.

Just when she was about to open the door, Max spoke up. "You obviously couldn't have called for propane this morning, so you really should do that now." He picked up his cell phone and scrolled through his contacts before he handed it over to her. "That's the number for the propane company. Make sure you let whoever you talk to know that you're Marty's niece."

"I... I... Yes, of course," she said, and took the phone from Max. She looked down at the screen and the name that went with the contact's phone number. "Little Albert?" she asked. "Is he tiny? Or just short? Or really skinny or really fat?"

"He's big and strong and irritating as heck. He's little because he's the son of Albert Van Duren Sr., who's called Big Albert. The truth is I beat out Big Albert for sheriff six years ago, and he's running against me this election. He's serious about kicking me out. So, don't mention me when you call, just Marty."

"Okay," she said, her head swimming a bit from all the information. She made the call and by the time she got through and dropped her uncle Martin's name, Little Albert had given her a slot for line maintenance and tank servicing at four o'clock. When she ended the call, she looked at Max. "Okay, four o'clock sharp. Little Albert said and I quote, 'I'd do anything for Marty's family.' So I'm all set as long as I'm back at the Lodge by two for the mechanic, then four to meet Little Albert."

"Please, forget you ever heard that nickname from me," Max said while the truck still idled.

"Of course. What's said in this truck, stays in this truck."

He grinned at her. "You bet."

"Cool," Grace said as she opened the door and got out. She swung it shut, but not before she heard Max's quiet chuckle behind her.

MAX HAD BEEN right about Burr Addison being good at what he did. But he'd failed to mention the attorney was a bear of a man with an impressive mustache that he slowly stroked with his forefinger as he listened to her. His office had a set of steer horns on the wall behind where he sat and a golden horseshoe lying on top of a stack of folders in front of him. After he'd gone over the section of the will that mentioned Grace, he settled back in his chair, a touch of sadness in his blue eyes.

"Marty did things his own way, so I can't give you your copy of the will until I take care of some loose ends. When that's done, I'll give you the full version and get the grant deed finalized in your name. I'm sorry for any delay."

"That's okay," she said. "You knew my uncle well?"

"He was a good friend. I met him just after I came down from Montana and set up this office. He'd been here three or four months and was just starting on renovating the Lodge."

"I don't know much about my uncle. Actually, I just know what the sheriff's told me."

Burr smiled at her. "Let me contribute a totally random story about Marty. Ten years ago he won a contest to rename Tipsy's Pool Emporium. They wanted to change the name of their business and held a contest to see who could come up with the best one. Marty won with One Q-Ball. Clever, huh?"

"That's a great name. What did he win?" she asked.

"A custom pool cue complete with a leather case. Also, a free game every day for a year and no entry fees for tournaments in perpetuity."

She was fascinated by what he was telling her. "Was he a pool shark or something?"

There was a twinkle in Burr's blue eyes now as he stroked his mustache. "With all due respect to Marty, honestly, he was horrible, the worst. I can't tell you how many times he'd sink the cue ball on the break." Burr looked almost wistful. "But he loved playing. No matter what Marty did, he had fun."

The more she heard about her uncle, the more she knew he and his brother had to have been polar opposites. Walter Bennet's definition of fun was making money and sparring with his opponents in the business world. "He sounds like a great guy."

"He was indeed." Burr sat back. "You come on up to the diner sometime and we'll talk some more about Marty."

Grace had no idea she was tearing up until Burr passed a box of tissues over to her. Grateful, she took a couple and wiped her eyes. "I wish that I could have helped him when he needed it."

"If wishes were horses..." Burr said on a deep sigh. "But you're here now, and you're getting to see where he lived and where he built a good life."

"Do you know why he left the Lodge to me and not to someone else, like Max?"

"I don't try to second-guess my clients. Besides, Max has his own life. He's doing well as sheriff, and he has his family and the ranch to consider. He couldn't run the Lodge, too. Logic says he left it to you because you were all the family Marty had. Now, you take all the time you need to decide what you're going to do with the Lodge. Whatever you decide, whether you decide to keep it or sell it, I'll be there to help."

Max had been right. Burr Addison was making the whole process as easy on her as possible. She definitely felt that she could trust him. "Thank you so much."

A rap sounded on the door and Burr called out, "Come in!"

The door swung open, and Max was there. "Hey, Burr, I don't mean to break up your meeting," he said from the doorway, "but Anna called and told me you wanted to talk to me. I'll just wait outside until you're done." He looked at Grace. "Sorry for intruding."

"Hold on there, Max," Burr said. "We're pretty much done here, and I won't keep you more than a few minutes."

Grace stood. "I'll leave and let you and the sheriff do your business."

She hitched the strap of her purse over her shoulder, ready to leave, but Burr stopped her. "I actually need to talk to the both of you together."

She slowly sat back down, glancing at Max, who hadn't moved. "What's this about, Burr?" he asked.

Burr leaned forward and picked up two blue envelopes that were beside his folders, then stood and came around the desk and held out an envelope to each of them. "Marty left directions that after you two had the chance to meet, I was to hand these to you."

Grace took hers and looked down at her first name written on it by an unsteady hand. "Thank you," she said and pushed it into her purse before turning to Max, who was staring down at his.

He took a breath, then asked, "Do you know what this is?"

Burr shook his head. "I don't. Marty just stipulated when I was to give them to you. Why don't you two go down to the diner and grab an early lunch and maybe figure this out between the two of you? My treat. Just tell Elaine I sent you."

Max turned to Grace. "If you want to go, we should get there before the noon rush takes over."

The lure of the blue envelope and Max maybe being able to clear up why they each had one made her agree. Besides, she was starving.

"Okay," she said and watched him push his envelope into his jacket pocket.

When they were outside, Max started down the stairs toward his truck and Grace followed, then climbed in on the passenger side. As they pulled onto the main street, she looked over at him. "You don't have a guess as to what the letters are about?"

He exhaled. "Not any more than you do. I don't want to open mine at the restaurant, but you can open yours if you want when we get there, and we can discuss it, I guess."

She didn't particularly want to open it with people around. "No, I think I'll wait, too."

Within minutes, they were pulling into a parking space in front of the Over the Moon Diner. After he shut down the engine, Max turned to Grace. "You need to know that Marty never did anything without a clear reason behind it."

"Did he like to meddle?"

"Not really. He was always up for a good conversation and liked to debate things. He talked me through something around three years ago, but not by meddling—he was just helping me."

He stopped her from asking any questions she might have wanted to ask him by saying, "I'll make this easy. If you don't want to go to lunch, just say so."

Oddly, she didn't want to be alone right then. And there was little to no food back at the Lodge. "I'm starving."

"Then you're at the right place. Their food truly is over the moon," he said.

"Cool," she said as she opened her door and stepped out, then went around to meet Max at the front of the truck. His hazel eyes met hers,

and he gave a crooked grin. "Way cool," he
said then started up the stairs. Grace smiled
to herself as she followed him.

CHAPTER FOUR

MAX HAD BEEN eating at the Over the Moon Diner for as long as he could remember. When he was around seven, he helped his mom deliver handmade tamales and salsa to the original owner, Elaine's father. Even though that had been thirty years ago, when he stepped inside with Grace by his side, he almost felt as if it was his first time setting foot in the place.

The red-and-white-checked tablecloths matched the uniform shirts worn by the servers. The booths that lined most of the walls had red Formica tops and black faux leather seats. A photo wall opposite the front windows included black-and-whites of lunar and solar eclipses, along with stunning color photographs of meteor showers labeled "Flaming Skies." The place had the vibe of a 1950s diner and Burr's wife, Elaine, ran it with friendly ease.

When she spotted them, the petite woman

with silver curls came over and greeted them with a bright smile. "Welcome, welcome! Burr just called and told me to expect y'all." She looked at Grace, her smile fading as sympathy showed in her eyes. "I'm deeply sorry Marty's gone. He's really missed around here in so many ways."

"Thank you," Grace said. "It makes me feel better to know that he wasn't alone here."

"Oh, he sure wasn't," she said. "That man was a real people person." She glanced at Max, then said, "You two sit wherever you want."

The diner was about half-full and country music played in the background. "Table or booth?" Max asked Grace.

She scanned the room, then turned to Max. "Whatever you prefer."

Elaine pointed to the booth by the door. "Your regular booth is available, Max, if y'all want to sit there."

"Sounds good to me," Grace said and crossed to slide in with her back to the door. Max sat across from her. "You can watch the world go by out the window and catch any lawbreakers," she teased.

Elaine smiled at that. "Now, I already know

what the good sheriff wants, but what can I get you to drink?" she asked Grace.

Grace ordered tea, and after Elaine disappeared back into the kitchen, she reached for the menu. "What's good here?" she asked Max.

"Honestly, everything," Max said. "I usually just get the breakfast special."

"'Two eggs, bacon or sausage, a side of home fries and toast'?" Grace read out loud. "Sounds delicious," she said, then put the menu back in its metal stand.

"How did it go with Burr?" Max asked her.

"Great," Grace said. When Max raised his eyebrows, she amended, "I really like Burr. He's pretty awesome, actually."

"Never tell him that," Max said, shaking his head, a smile playing at the corner of his lips.

Elaine returned with Max's coffee and Grace's tea. "Never tell who what?" she asked.

"Never tell your husband that he's awesome," Max said.

"Oh, I tell him that he's awesome all the time," Elaine said, chuckling.

"Oh, you two are married?" Grace asked.

"Yes we are, and Burr is well aware of his

awesomeness. Now, have you two decided what you'd like to order?"

After they'd relayed their breakfast special preferences, Grace studied the wall opposite their booth. "Are those photographs of meteor showers from around here? They look incredible."

"Yeah. I've learned to love them, but dang, they sure used to scare me when I was little," Max said.

Grace leaned back to look across the table at him. "It could be scary, I guess. All I've seen are a few shooting stars, but nothing close to that kind of a show."

"Up at the original Donovan ranch my grandpa built in the high foothills before the family moved down to the bigger property in the valley, we used to watch them all the time. The old ranch is still the place to watch meteor showers. You feel as if you're in the middle of a firestorm, or the most amazing pyrotechnic display ever. Back when I was in my teens, that was *the* place for a guy to take a date."

Elaine came with their food, and Grace ignored the heaping plate of scrambled eggs, bacon and potatoes as she cocked her head and eyed Max. "So, who did you take to watch the meteor showers?"

"A girl I was dating in high school. I just remember it being freezing cold. Meteor showers are at their best from December to January. Although sometimes they show up earlier or later."

"But was it romantic?"

He shrugged, not much wanting to talk about those nights. "Yeah, some, but it was hard to do anything when all of my family and neighbors were right there."

She smiled. "I bet that was awkward."

He hadn't thought about those nights for a very long time. The world had been so different back then. He'd been so different. "Yeah, it sure was," he said and nodded toward her food. "I thought you were starving."

"Yes, yes, I am." She picked up her fork and speared a home fry. She chewed and swallowed then smiled over at him. "Good, very good."

They ate in silence for a while and then she asked Max, "Did Uncle Martin go watch the meteor showers?"

"Most of the time he viewed them from his back deck at the Lodge, but he'd come up to the old ranch, too."

"Can I ask you something a bit personal about him?"

"I guess so," he said with a touch of discomfort. There were a lot of things Marty and he talked about that they both understood would remain between them.

"Did Uncle Martin bring dates up there? I mean, was there, you know, any special woman in his life? I don't even know if he was ever married." Max watched a faint blush creep over her cheeks.

He could answer that. "He dated once in a while, but none of the women stuck around. Before I came back from the army, I heard he was dating a woman named Angie. Some thought they were serious, but I never met her."

"What happened to her?"

"I don't know. He never mentioned her to me, so I didn't ask."

"There was no one else?"

"No marriage as far as I know, but he told me he'd once found a woman he thought he could love. Unfortunately, it didn't work out."

"What did he say about his life before he came here?"

They'd joked about their talks being like therapy for both of them. For Max, there had been real truth in that, and one of those talks had led him to running for sheriff at Marty's urging. But all Max understood about Marty's past was that whatever had happened before had been painful for him, and that he'd had an alcohol problem that almost destroyed him. He never went further than admitting to that.

"Not a lot," he said in response to Grace's question. "I got the impression he had it rough, but the Marty I knew wasn't a complainer, and he wasn't a man who looked back very often. He lived in the moment."

"He…never talked about any family?"

Max knew what he could share that might help Grace. "Marty told me that about twenty years ago, he was driving through on his way up north to Montana and stopped at the Lodge for the night. When he woke the next morning and saw the view from the Lodge in the light of day, he knew he didn't want to leave. He loved to joke that he checked in, but he didn't check out."

"So buying the Lodge was an impulse?"

"Maybe. The owners were thinking of selling, and he made them an offer right there and then. If it helps, he told me he never once regretted coming here and staying, but he did regret past things that he couldn't fix."

Grace reached for her mug to have a drink of tea, then changed subjects abruptly. "Burr's so nice. He treated me as if I was a friend."

He smiled at that. "People around here are friendly, and they help each other."

"That's small-town stuff, isn't it?"

"It's the way it is. I remember when I was maybe ten years old and a neighbor's barn burned down. All the locals showed up to help him rebuild. The first day, they'd cleaned up and finished the framework. The next day they came back and finished the outer walls and the roof." That was the day he'd noticed Freeman Lee's daughter, Claire, for the first time. He hadn't thought about that for what seemed like forever, and he was mad at himself for remembering. "They soon had their barn fully back."

Her violet eyes widened slightly. "I've never known anyone who was at a real barn raising."

"You do now. It was fun until I started showing off my roping skills on a fence post and ended up pulling down a small section of Freeman's back perimeter fencing." Claire had hurried over to help him push the post back in the ground. Another memory. He finished his coffee, then added, "The moral of that little story is, if you need help, ask."

"Speaking of help," Grace said, "I appreciate everything you've done for me, but I'm pretty good on my own once I'm up and running. I've already taken up way too much of your time."

"Well, I needed to eat, too," he said, reluctant to just finish up eating and drop her off at the Lodge. She needed exposure to the town and its people to appreciate what Marty gave her. Maybe it wouldn't make a difference in her selling and leaving, but he had to try. He owed Marty that much. "You mentioned you wouldn't be staying here too long. How long is not too long?"

"I don't know yet. Maybe a few weeks. I'm not sure how much time I can be away from work."

He'd never asked what she did in Tucson. "Work's calling?"

"Yes and no. I work at a combined consignment and coffee shop. I'm covered for now, but I don't want to push my luck and find out I don't have a job when I get home, either."

"Can I ask why you're here alone? Aren't your parents curious to see what you've inherited?"

Grace stared at him blankly for a minute, then said, "Oh, my parents, no, no... They... they're both gone."

Max hadn't expected that and found himself apologizing for bringing them up. "I shouldn't have asked. It's a side effect of my work, and I work too much. My social skills need attention. I apologize." She was too young to be alone like that, unless there was a boyfriend she hadn't mentioned.

"No apology needed. I was an only child, and my grandparents died before I was old enough to really know them. So it was just me and my parents. Then I... I found myself on my own, building a new life in Tucson."

"There's no other family?"

"No, not that I know of. Then again, I never knew I had an uncle."

She didn't look sad, but maybe a bit lost. "I'm sorry that's the way it's worked out for you."

"Me, too," she said.

"Since we're here, and you wanted to get that burner phone, why don't I show you around town on the way to the electronics store? I'll make sure you get back in time for Henry."

She looked down at her empty plate, and he

could almost see her thinking of how to refuse his offer. "Sure," she said finally. "That would be great."

Elaine showed up right then, smiling as usual. "How was everything?"

"Very good," Grace said, "thank you." As Elaine began to clear their table, Grace slid out of the booth and stood up. "I'll be right back."

Max watched as she headed toward the short hallway that led to the restrooms. Before Elaine could take off, he caught her attention. "Can I talk to you for a minute?"

"What a coincidence," she said, pausing with the plates stacked on her arm. "I wanted to talk to you, too."

"About what?"

"Grace. The word is, she's going to sell the Lodge."

"She's figuring out what to do, but she probably will. She's got her own life in Arizona."

"If she's not sure…" Elaine leaned closer toward Max. "Maybe she can be persuaded to stick around and keep the Lodge."

"I hope she'll stay, but it's not up to me. It's her choice."

Elaine grinned at him. "How about you turning on the Donovan charm?"

"That ran out a long time back," he murmured. "But her feeling comfortable here wouldn't hurt."

She looked past his shoulder and nodded. "Sure glad you stopped by!" she said as Grace approached the table. "Maybe I could run out to see you sometime and show you around the kitchen at the Lodge. I did some cooking for Marty and filled in when he was short on help."

"That would be really nice of you," Grace said. "But I wouldn't want to take up your time."

"No worries. I own this place. I can take off any time I want to, and I'd love to talk to you more about Marty and the Lodge."

"I'd like that," Grace said.

"See you soon," Elaine said, then turned to cross to a table where a couple was just sitting down.

"Nice lady. As nice as her husband, it seems," Grace said as she settled into the booth again.

"Elaine was wondering what you've decided to do about the Lodge."

She glanced down at the table, then back at Max. "I haven't even been here a full twenty-four hours, so I don't have a clue, but I appreciate her offer to come out and show me what my uncle was doing out there. If I sell, I'll need all of that information to pass on to the new buyer."

"It couldn't hurt."

"I should freshen it up, but that means more time away from Tucson. If I just sell it as is, it's going to minimize how much I can get for it. Maybe the best I can do is find someone to buy it who wants to work on it and won't just tear it down." A sad smile touched her lips. "I'm pretty certain from what I've learned about him from you and Burr, Uncle Martin wouldn't have wanted the Lodge to be torn down to make room for some new development."

It took Max back that Grace understood what some people would want to do with the land. A large ranch in the area had almost been taken away from a family that had owned it for years by an underhanded development company. They wanted it to be split into luxury ranches. The Eclipse Ridge Ranch was safe now, but that didn't mean that developers wouldn't set their sights on the land the Lodge sat on. He knew they would, but he also knew now that Grace understood what Marty had wanted, even if she didn't stay. "Did Marty put any restrictions in the will on what you could do with the Lodge?" he asked.

"Oh, no, none. Maybe he mentioned something in the letter Burr gave me." He could see her eyes glisten slightly as if she was close to tears. She reached for her napkin, and he thought she was going to dab at her eyes, but she simply held it bunched in her hand and stared down at it. "I'm sorry. I just want to do the right thing."

"Hey," Max said. "It's okay. You might not have known Marty, but he was family." He added something that he'd found out the hard way. "They say you can't miss what you never had, but that's wrong. That can hurt more than anything."

She raised her eyes to meet his. Moisture clung to her dark lashes but didn't fall on her cheeks before she swiped it away with the napkin.

Max checked his watch. They had two hours before Grace needed to be back at the Lodge. "Ready to go?"

Grace put her purse over her shoulder and stood. "Yes."

Once outside, Max walked north on the

raised sidewalk, intending to do a loop at the end before coming back to where he'd parked so Grace could get an overall look at the town. She walked to his right and seemed to be enjoying looking in the display windows of the shops. As they approached the town's consignment shop, Gabby's Vintage Treasures, Grace slowed, then stopped to look at the display. "Lovely," he heard her half whisper before she glanced at him. "I'd like to go in and look around. Professional curiosity."

"Go for it. When you're ready to head back to the Lodge, you can call me."

"I don't have a phone yet."

"You said you wanted a burner, so go back by Burr's and four doors down—there's an electronics shop. Herb can set you up for now. You can also ask him to tell you where the substation is so you can go there and ask a tiny lady with a huge smile and gray hair in a tight knot to contact me. Lillian always knows where I am."

"The famous Lillian. I'd love to meet her, but I can't pull you away from your work again."

"You can't walk back on the highway, either.

Just call me. If you're late getting back in time for Henry, he'll leave for his next job."

"Okay, okay," she said reluctantly. "I don't have a number for you that isn't 911."

"Have Herb put in the nonemergency number for the station."

"Okay."

Right then, Gabby Brookes, the owner, came out onto the walkway. Gabby was in her midtwenties and given to wearing jeans and fussy tops that seemed to match the character of the Grand Lady B&B she ran out of a beautifully maintained Victorian house on River View Drive. She had opened the consignment shop a few months ago.

"Sheriff Max," Gabby said as she came toward them. "You haven't been in here since… Oh, I remember." She grinned at him. "Since never."

"I'd say that's about right." He grinned back and cleared his throat. "Gabby, meet Grace Bennet. She's Marty's niece. She's staying out at the Lodge."

"Oh, my gosh," Gabby said to Grace, her smile slipping. "I'm so sorry about Marty. I just loved him."

"Thank you," Grace said. "Your store looks

lovely. I work at a consignment shop in Tucson."

Gabby moved closer, seemingly studying Grace's leather jacket. "Is that an authentic Harley-Davidson?"

"Yes! Would you believe I found it in a donation bag? The owner of the store wanted to tag it for fifty dollars. I told her I'd like to buy it. I felt guilty for a hot second, then thought that I'd never sell it, so it wasn't like I was going to make a five hundred percent profit on it or anything."

"What a find," Gabby said and touched the sleeve almost reverently. "It's in great shape. It must be from the sixties or early seventies."

"You've got a good eye—1968."

Gabby and Grace hit it off right away and Max took his leave. The time he'd had to kill earlier had been filled by Grace Bennet. She was pleasant, pretty determined not to bother anyone and had repeatedly declared that she could handle things on her own. He smiled to himself as he headed to the substation to get some paperwork out of the way. He couldn't help but think that despite her insistence that she could take care of herself, she could use a helping hand for the time that she was in Eclipse.

WHEN GRACE FINALLY left Gabby's shop, Gabby walked her out. She'd enjoyed her time talking business with Gabby and had given the other woman a few ideas to increase foot traffic for her store. She was pretty sure that if she wasn't leaving, she and Gabby would become good friends.

When she turned to say goodbye, Gabby surprised Grace by hugging her. "I'm so glad you stopped by here. It's fun to talk to someone who knows the business."

After they parted ways, Grace went down to the electronics store, and she left with a basic flip phone ready to use. She had asked Herb for the nonemergency number for the station, and he had put it and Max's cell number in the phone's contacts for her. Once out on the street she almost called Max but reconsidered. In spite of Max's warning, the Lodge was an easy two-mile walk from town, and she could be back in plenty of time for the mechanic. She crossed to the other side of the street, avoiding the only traffic—a kid on horseback—then started toward the highway.

She'd barely started walking on the southbound shoulder facing the traffic when she was startled by a blaring horn. She looked up and saw Max's white pickup slow down, then make a U-turn across the vacant lanes and pull in front of her. She felt guilty for being caught but was taken back when Max opened his door and yelled at her.

"Get in! Now!"

Everything in her wanted to dig in her heels and wave him off, but she got the feeling that the insistence in his voice wasn't just about her going against his orders; something else was happening. She approached the truck and climbed inside. "I was facing the traffic and staying back from the road. It wasn't—"

"We'll deal with that later," he said abruptly. "Buckle up."

"This is ridiculous," she said, only to have her words cut off when he pulled across both lanes to head north and put on his siren and lights.

"Seat belt," he said over the noise.

"Yes, sir," she said tightly and did it up.

"Sorry, I'm on a call and didn't expect to see you on the highway again." He quickly explained about a possible sighting of the thieves who'd been looting ranches for irrigation equipment. A ranch hand had called in about two men who could be the culprits. "I'll drop you off at the Lodge."

"Oh, okay," she said, feeling just a bit foolish for her reaction to the man who was clearly doing her a favor. She smiled wryly and spoke loud enough to be heard over the noise around them. "I've always wanted to ride in a police car or a fire truck with the siren going and lights flashing."

They were quickly approaching the Lodge when Max slowed the truck and drove off the highway then came to a sharp stop in front of the gates. "Okay, out," he said.

"Yes, sir!" she said, unsnapping her belt.

WHEN GRACE WAS out of the truck, she turned to look in the open door at Max. "That was incredible!" she exclaimed, her eyes shining.

Max wouldn't have expected her to react like a kid, but it seemed as if she was completely over being angry with him and had thoroughly enjoyed the ride.

"Thanks, Max. Seriously, that was so cool!"

She shifted emotions so quickly; he felt a bit dizzy. "Dang, I was going for awesome," he said.

"Maybe next time you'll get there," she called over the siren's screech, then her smile faltered. "Stay safe," she said just before she pushed the door shut and went to open the gates.

After searching the area around the ranch where the flatbed truck had been spotted, Max found two men parked near a culvert close to the sign for Wolf Bridge, eating sack lunches. They were from Montana and looking for work—not irrigation systems. After he checked them out, he let them go, then drove to headquarters in Two Horns to cover for Lawson, one of his deputies.

It was nearing six o'clock when he left. When he neared the Lodge, he spotted the Van Duren propane truck near the open gates, and he kept going. As he approached the town limits, he slowed and pulled off into the empty dirt parking lot adjacent to the Grange Hall, which had closed down months ago for renovation. Positioning himself where he had a clear view in both directions of the highway, he let the truck idle.

He took Marty's letter out of his pocket and stared at his name written on the front of it. Blowing out a breath, he carefully worked his forefinger under the sealed flap to get the letter out: a single sheet of lined paper with unsteady writing on both sides. As he read the note, he could almost hear Marty saying the words.

Max, my dear friend,
If you're reading this, I'm gone, but I couldn't leave without thanking you for being such a special part of my life and for all your help and support over the years. You always understood how important the Lodge was to me, giving me a life I never dared hoped for before arriving in Eclipse. A simple stop to rest from my wanderings for one night and I found my home.

You've done more for me than I could have ever have imagined, yet I find myself in the position of needing to ask one last favor of you. If a girl named Grace Bennet comes to town to see about the Lodge sometime in the future, I would appreciate it if you would do for her what you did for me and be her friend. If Grace does come, you'll understand why I'm asking you to be there when she needs you, to watch out for her and make sure she's on the right track with a friend by her side.

One thing I leave up to your discre-

tion: Rebel. If Grace does show up and sticks around, I want her to have Rebel, but only if you think she'll really care for him. If not, please keep him at the Flaming Sky and tell him I miss him. You make that call.

If Grace never gets there, which is very possible, I've left Burr contingent instructions for the disposition of the land and buildings.

Have a wonderful life, my friend, and never live in the past. Face your life head-on and know the best is yet to come. Find your easy heart, and don't doubt yourself. I have never doubted you.

Marty

A sigh caught in his throat as he put the letter back in his pocket. "I'll do what I can for Grace and for you, Marty," he whispered into the space around him. He hoped against hope that Grace could be the right person to keep Marty's dreams alive one way or another.

His phone rang and a glance down at the

screen showed a number that wasn't local. He answered it. "Sheriff Donovan."

"Hello, Sheriff Donovan. This is Grace Bennet."

CHAPTER FIVE

Max HAD BEEN thinking about Grace since he dropped her off at the Lodge, and now she was calling him. He sat back, his eyes on the few cars passing by on the highway. "Is this a 911 call?"

"Well, no, I didn't dial 911. I got a phone and Herb put your cell number in it for me."

"Good. What can I do for you?"

"First, did everything work out okay on your emergency?"

"False alarm." He closed his eyes. "Did Henry get there?"

"Yes, right on time, but he couldn't fix it. He needed some parts he'll have to hunt down because the Jeep's older. He needs to rewire it and he said he'll be back tomorrow as soon as he has the parts."

"What about the propane?"

"Albert tested the tanks, filled them, got the furnace going, and I now have hot water and a stove that works. You won't believe what else he did." She didn't give him a chance to even guess. "He found my phone caught in a broken part of the desk's kick plate in reception. It must have flown out of my pocket and lodged there when I almost fell the second time. He also mentioned something about a dance celebrating the grand opening of the Grange Hall, and I thought he was going to ask me to go with him. I don't even know what a Grange Hall is, and I sure as heck don't know him."

"Did he ask?"

Grace made a scoffing sound over the phone. "No, not directly. He just said something like he thought I'd have a great time there."

Max opened his eyes and glanced in the rearview mirror at the newly painted building some thirty feet behind him.

"He also talked about Uncle Martin and how he was a really nice guy. That made me happy—that and having heat and getting my phone back."

Max knew the truth about most people in the small town: the good, the bad and the ugly. He knew a lot about the ugly side of Albert Jr. as a kid in school, and about his marriage that he'd destroyed by cheating. Now he was going through a bad divorce. "I'm glad he got you heat in the Lodge."

"Me, too, and Henry said that the wiring only takes a couple of hours, so I should have transportation tomorrow. That's kind of what I called you for."

"What's that?"

"I totally forgot about needing food out here. Could you give me the number of a store that delivers groceries?"

Max could almost hear Marty's words from the letter. *I would appreciate it if you would do for her what you did for me and be her friend.* A friend would make sure Grace had food at the Lodge, even if there never had been an official food delivery service in town.

"Sorry, there isn't much of that around here, but tell you what, if you send me a list of what you need, I can go by the general store, get it filled and drop your order off on my way up to the ranch."

"Oh, gosh, no. I can't have the sheriff delivering my food when he's supposed to be out keeping the town safe. I have some cashew nuts, and there's hot water for a shower. I can survive until tomorrow."

"I'll have you know that I'm capable of doing more than just going after the bad guys.

I can also catch runaway steers, help old la-
dies cross our busy streets, start fires when I
need to, and I can deliver food."

Her laugh over the phone eased something in
him that had felt heavy since reading Marty's
letter.

"Wow, skills, huh?" Grace said.

"Unbelievable skills." He stopped that patter
right there. "I wanted to come by there anyway, so I can kill two birds with one stone."

"Why?"

"To talk to you about that stunt you pulled
today. So, text me what you need, and I'll
see to it that you get it within an hour. How's
that?"

She didn't like the idea of them "having a
talk." She hesitated. "Okay. Can I give you
my credit card number to pay for the food? I
have a bit of cash, so if I keep the list short,
I should have enough for a day or two until I
can get to the bank."

"Don't worry about it. You can pay me
then," he said.

He could tell she didn't want to do that or
have him lecture her about her being back on
the highway, but she finally caved.

"Okay, but I'll pay you as soon as I can get
to town."

"Of course, and I know where you live so I can do a collection if I have to."

"I guess I can run, but I can't hide?"

"Nope. I'll see you soon."

AN HOUR LATER when Grace opened the front door, Max stood there, taller than she remembered, wearing his leather coat and black Stetson, and holding two full bags of groceries in his arms. He went past her to set the bags on the desk. "Farley didn't have those small jellybeans you wanted, so he put regular ones in the order, and he saw you wanted a coffee grind he's temporarily out of, so he substituted the grind Marty used to get. He didn't put it on the bill," he said as he handed her the receipt. "He said it's a housewarming gift, and if you don't like it, take it back and he'll find you one you'll love."

"That's sure nice of him," she said. "And thank you for making the delivery."

"No problem," he said.

"So, what do I do with the huge can of roasted cashews I found on top of the fridge?"

"Eat them. Marty loved them. His idea of the perfect afternoon was relaxing with a coffee and a bowl of cashews."

She loved learning that about her uncle, but

her nerves were making her uncomfortable as she waited for Max to lecture her about walking on the highway after his firm warning not to do it again.

"I'll try that," she said, then found herself blurting out, "Max, I'll make this easier for both of us."

"Make what easier?"

"I owe you an apology for what I did today. I shouldn't have even thought about walking back here after you warned me not to, but I didn't want to take up more of your time, and it's not a long walk. I stayed well over on the shoulder and walked facing traffic."

He studied her, then shrugged. "I don't remember the last time someone apologized to me for doing something as utterly foolish as walking on the side of a highway and endangering themselves *and* the lives of others. I told you that the only time you should ever be doing that is in an emergency."

This was worse than she thought it would be. "For Pete's sake, I wasn't robbing a bank. I just didn't want to bother you again and take you away from your work. Now I'm foolish?" she asked, accompanied by an eye roll.

Max took off his hat, laid it crown down on the desktop by the groceries, then instead of being mad at her, he picked up the bags. He looked at her then said in a very even voice, "If you're done confessing to your wrong-doing, how about we put these things away before the mint-chocolate-chip ice cream melts?"

"I apologized to you. I didn't confess anything," she said.

"Oh, I thought that's what you did. I was going to go easy on you because I didn't want to have to lock you up for ten days."

"What?" she gasped. "No, no, no, no. You can't do that. I apologized even though I don't believe that there's any law against trying to get home."

"Yes, you apologized, and I appreciate it. I don't get apologized to that often, you know. I'll just forget your confession and keep it between us, then you'll only get a ticket."

"That's not legal, is it?"

"No, it's not, and I wouldn't do it anyway. The truth is, you were stranded and refused to take my offer of a ride, which you ended up having to accept anyway. Being stubborn isn't breaking any law."

She exhaled. "Then why did you tell me all that in the first place?"

He broke out in a huge grin. "I'm sorry for making you sweat."

She reluctantly smiled back at him. "I don't sweat," she said, "I glow, and for what it's worth I only apologized so you wouldn't scold me first. You're so mean."

"That hurts something awful," he said, then laughed.

Grace stared at Max, knowing her face had to be beet red. He was teasing, and she fell for it. "That was all a joke, wasn't it?"

"Yeah, but a bad one. I apologize, really I do. I was going to talk to you about being stubborn and about not taking help from people. But I wanted to see how far you'd go apologizing. I let the rope out too far," he said, still holding the grocery bags. "Now that's over with, let's put this stuff away."

She followed him into the kitchen, which had surprised her when she'd seen it for the first time that morning. The appliances were all stainless steel and the refrigerator was huge. The dishwasher was a double—something she'd never seen before—and the stove had six burners and a central double grill. Max crossed to the counter by the fridge and pantry and put the contents of the bags away, then washed his hands in the extra wide farmhouse sink. An old microwave by the sink was the only thing that wasn't restaurant quality.

The rest was simple: white cupboards, dark wood floors and six windows along the back wall that overlooked the large deck and the land beyond. The dining room shared the same view from a table that looked as if it could seat sixteen people at least.

Max closed the fridge and turned to Grace. "If you're up for it, as a way of making up for my unfortunately horrible sense of humor, how about I make us breakfast for dinner, and add a cup of Uncle Martin's coffee?"

Before she could answer, his phone rang. "Hold on." He retrieved his cell from his pocket and glanced at the screen then took the call. "Hi there," he said, looking out the window over the sink at the view. "I'm in the middle of something."

He listened, then shrugged. "No, I'm off unless they really need me."

More listening before he said, "Okay, okay, I'll be there. Give me half an hour. Love you, too," he murmured, then stopped the call and put his phone away before he looked back at Grace. "I'll have to pass on dinner. I'm supposed to be back at the ranch, and I…" He exhaled. "I'm sorry."

Of course. She'd thought he was married, probably with kids, but even so, she was disappointed to find out it really was true. "It's got to be hard having a family and doing the job you do."

"Yes, it is," he said on a sigh. "You enjoy your dinner, and I'll head out." He grabbed his hat off the desktop on his way out.

She followed him back into the lobby. "I've told you I'm sorry for taking up your time. Would you please tell your wife that I won't do it again?"

That stopped him and he turned, his eyes narrowed on her. "What?"

"Your wife, or your significant other. I'm sorry I had you delivering my food when you were supposed to be at home."

He stared at her for a long moment, then he actually chuckled. "You're on the wrong end of that lasso."

"What does that mean?"

"I'm not married. My mom and dad are waiting for me."

"You aren't married?"

For some reason he frowned at that. "No."

She was surprised and a part of her was kind of pleased. "Oh, I assumed… I'm sorry. So, you live with your parents?"

He grimaced at her words. "Now that sounds bad, doesn't it, living with Mommy and Daddy at my age?"

"I didn't say that." She spoke quickly. "I was just asking."

He cut her off, holding up his hand as he said, "Whoa, there!"

She knew she was blushing. "I wasn't making fun of you."

He moved closer to her, the frown gone, but he wasn't smiling. "Grace, please. I'm kidding."

It took her a second to get what he said. "Really?"

"Really," he repeated as he tipped his hat slightly back with a forefinger to the brim. "This is my 'I'm kidding' face. Okay?"

"Okay," she breathed. "I guess I'm feeling a little overwhelmed by everything that's happened in the last twenty-four hours. I'm sorry, I'm not usually like this. That was foolish." She stopped talking the moment she realized she was reacting to Max the way she used to with her father when she'd make a mistake. From what she'd seen so far, no man could be more different from her dad than Max, except for his penchant for telling her what to do.

"You've gone through a lot, and I promise to tell you when I'm joking from now on. Okay?"

She exhaled. "Yes, please."

"For your information, my parents live in the main house on the ranch, and when I came back from the army, I didn't want to be around a lot of people. The foreman's house was empty, so I took it over." She noticed a vague tightness in his expression as he explained that to her.

"You live alone out there?"

"When I'm there, I'm alone." He abruptly changed the course of their discussion. "Have you had time to check out Marty's apartment yet?"

"No, I haven't. I wanted to take my time and…" She shrugged, at a loss for words to describe why she hadn't walked through the door to see where he'd lived. "Maybe tomorrow after the Jeep's fixed."

"I just think you'd be more comfortable in there than on the couch."

Maybe she would be, but she was staying on the couch for now. "The couch is comfortable and now that I have heat, I'll be just fine wherever I choose to sleep."

"Okay, good, then I'll be going. By the way, I never would have lived in my parents' basement…if they'd had one."

She smiled. "That's a joke, isn't it? You're funny."

"Good, you're a fast learner. I won't have to raise my hand every time and say, 'Just kidding.' That makes life simpler."

She promised herself that she'd do better around Max. She didn't want him getting tired of Grace Bennet, the new girl in town with no sense of humor. "You said before that Uncle Martin liked life to be simple. I believe I do, too."

He nodded. "That makes three of us. Sleep well," he said, then left.

Her phone chimed as the sound of his truck engine faded away and she glanced at the screen. It was from the sheriff's office.

Checking in to make sure all is well at Marty's. Hope grocery delivery was successful.
Lillian Shaw, dispatcher, Clayton County Sheriff's Office.

A well-being check on her from the sheriff's dispatcher. That must be a small-town thing, too. She typed back:

Delivery perfect. Great service. Thanks. Have a good evening!

She went into the great room to set up the couch for her bed again. No fire was needed tonight with the heaters doing their job, but she missed the snap, crackle, pop and the smell of the wood burning. She made herself a dinner of tomato soup and a grilled cheese sandwich and ate it alone sitting on the couch. She kind of wished Max had been able to stay. She wasn't used to being alone so much. In Tucson, her roommate, Zoey, was always around, and before that, there were people paid to tend to her every need by Walter.

Her eyes fell on the square blue envelope she'd put on the coffee table when she'd arrived back at the Lodge after her siren-and-lights ride. She was almost afraid to read it. "Just do it," she muttered to herself as she reached to pick it up. She made herself open it and found a single sheet of lined paper inside it. She tossed the envelope onto the coffee table, then opened the note with shaky writing on both sides.

My dearest Grace:
I'm not sure you even know who I am,
so let me introduce myself. I am Martin
Robert Bennet, your uncle. Even though
I never met you, you've been on my mind

ever since I found out about you on your sixth birthday. I don't regret much of my life, but one thing that hurts to think about is the loss of you ever being in my life. But that was never possible.

Since you're reading this letter, I know you came to see the Lodge. If you want to sell it, that's your decision. But if you keep it, a good friend of mine, Max Donovan, the county sheriff, can tell you all about it and why it's been so dear to me. I hope you will stay, at least for a while, to get to know the Lodge and people in the town of Eclipse. They have been my lifeline, friends that I never expected to make. I came to love the people and this place.

I can say I love you because I know I would have under different circumstances, but I think it's more that I've loved the idea of you, something good coming from Walter and Marianna. I promise you, if you stay, you'll never regret it. But I understand that you have your own life to live, the way I chose to live mine on my own terms. I do have a wish for you, that you find an easy heart. I found mine on a piece of

land that called to me, a building that
wrapped around me, and a town that
accepted me. I wish for you to find your
easy heart, too.
Love,
Uncle Martin

At first, Grace couldn't even figure out how to react to the letter, then tears came—tears for lost years and time that could never be reclaimed. She'd never been a crier, but she curled up on the couch and cried until she couldn't anymore. Exhausted and overwhelmed, she closed her eyes. *An easy heart.* She had a vague idea what that could mean, but she had no idea how a person found it.

IT SEEMED NO time had passed when Grace woke up to a hard pounding sound, and she realized someone was at the front door. Shifting on the couch, she glanced out the window and saw the thin light of dawn creeping into the room. She'd slept all night. Scrambling to her feet, she hurried to the door so the pounding would stop. When she pulled it open, she found herself face-to-face with Henry Lodge, the mechanic she'd met the day before.

He was a short man, wearing a heavy jacket

and black rubber boots, his dark hair in a braid that hung halfway down his back. The cold air flooding in cut through the sweater and jeans she'd slept in.

"Good morning, Miss Grace. I'm sorry for being so early, but I can't get the piece I need until later this morning. Just wanted you to know."

"Thank you."

"Just be here at noon. My time's real tight today."

"I'll be here," she said.

After Henry left, Grace went into the washroom and made herself presentable. She brushed her hair, then dressed in a vintage red sweatshirt, one of her finds at the consignment shop. The logo on the front was for a college she'd never heard of. Putting on her jeans along with her red running shoes, she looked around for cleaning materials, but there were none. So she grabbed a towel and started dusting in the lobby, making her way to the great room after she found a broom to clear the dust that had accumulated on the fireplace stones.

When she looked at the time on her phone, she was surprised it was almost eleven o'clock. She needed warm clothes, but she couldn't get them until the Jeep was fixed. Dropping down on the couch to relax for a few minutes, she looked around the room that she'd freed of the dustcovers earlier. Now she could appreciate the size of the space and the way her uncle had laid out the furniture.

Along the front wall were the couch and easy chairs where guests could sit and visit, read the books that were stacked neatly on a bookshelf, or just rest. The back area was totally different. The space in the far corner held several small, round tables. Board games and toys sat among them in wicker baskets, and a large chalkboard took up most of the end wall. No TV, but there were speakers in the corners. The remaining part of the room was taken up by a few tables that she figured were meant for guests to sit at while they drank coffee or hot cocoa and enjoyed the beautiful view out the back windows. It was family oriented, and she liked that. She also loved the view out the back windows.

She moved to pick up the dustcovers she'd left by the archway but hesitated when she spotted something white between the black cushions of the sofa she'd slept on. When she tugged it out, she found herself holding a small photograph that she recognized immediately, even if she'd never seen it before.

She remembered the day it was taken twenty years ago at the exclusive restaurant on the top floor of the first hotel/casino her dad had built in Las Vegas. She sat across from her father at a private table, her mother sitting to the side between them. Marianna had always seemed to hover between father and daughter. A Mylar balloon was attached to her chair back with an oversize pink bow, and a fancy pink cake sat in the middle of the table with a large silver number-six candle on top of it.

Her sixth birthday. She'd asked for a pony again, something most kids asked for during their younger years, and she'd received a plethora of presents that circled the cake and hadn't been opened when the photo had been taken. There had been no horse, not even a stuffed version. But she did get a charm bracelet from Tiffany's that she'd lost the next day. The clothes she got had some big-name designer labels that thrilled her mother, at least.

The only toy among those presents had been a fashion-model doll in her mother's image from when Marianna had been at the height of her career. Grace had never opened the box the doll came in because she wasn't allowed. "It's a collector's item and worth a

lot of money," her father had told her. So she'd
been afraid to even touch it.

She turned the photo over and saw "Grace,
6TH BP" scrawled on the back and she recognized a stronger version of Uncle Martin's
handwriting. She stared at the picture of three
people at a celebration and none of them smiling. The photograph had either fallen in between the couch cushions sometime in the
past or it had slipped out of the envelope without her noticing it last night. Frowning, she
put it in with the letter from her uncle and
laid the blue envelope back on the table. She
wished she knew the story about how that
picture had ended up with Uncle Martin. Just
one more thing no one was left to explain to
her.

She stood and decided that it was time she
checked out Uncle Martin's private quarters,
a place she figured would put her as close as
she'd ever get to him. Before she could over-
think it, she reached for the brass doorknob
and let herself into the apartment.

She wasn't sure what she'd expected, but
the room could have been anyone's. It had
been stripped, the way the rest of the Lodge
had been, and she didn't know if she was
disappointed or relieved that she didn't see

anything that would tell her more about her uncle. It was exactly as Max had told her. It amounted to a studio apartment with an office area near the door, a wrought iron bed, a kitchenette and an easy chair placed near the back wall in front of a set of sliding glass doors. The brown corduroy chair was turned toward the view and looked well used.

She breathed in the musty air tinged with a faint lemon scent, then crossed to stand in the center of the space, not certain what to do first. Then the view caught her eye: the land beyond the raised deck seemed to go on forever toward distant mountains. No wonder the corduroy chair was so worn; what a view to wake up to and to go to sleep by. It would be the perfect place to watch eclipses and meteor showers.

There was a straight line of trees running north and south, off in the distance past a sea of dried grass and scrub brush. Beyond that were the foothills, then the mountains that rose into the true blue Wyoming sky.

She walked over to the chair and sat down. She'd been wrong. Uncle Martin had left his stamp on the room in the form of an easy chair turned to the view he'd loved. She had no doubt that what she saw was what had drawn him to stay and never leave.

She was startled when someone called out, "Miss Grace?"

Henry was back. "Yes, yes, I'm coming!" she called as she got up and hurried out of the room. Henry stood in the open doorway.

"I'm so glad you're here," she said. "Did you get the part?"

"Yep. I'll get right on it. It shouldn't take more than a couple of hours."

"I have coffee made. Would you like some?"

"Thanks, I sure would," he said, then headed down to the Jeep.

After she'd delivered the coffee to Henry, Grace went back inside and into her uncle's room. Before she'd actually been in the room, she'd thought it might be smart to repurpose the space and turn it into a business office. Now she knew she wouldn't do that. In fact, she'd do as little as she could so she could stay in it while she was at the Lodge. Just standing there, she finally felt a connection with her uncle that she didn't want to lose.

In exactly two hours, Henry was at the door with the good news that the Jeep was fixed. "She's ready to go," he said. "Come on out and I'll show you."

After bundling up, Grace followed him out and he got in behind the wheel. When he turned the key, the car started right away. "That's terrific!"

"She's all yours," he said, and he slipped out, leaving the Jeep idling. As she slid behind the wheel, she heard Henry say, "Ah, the good sheriff."

Grace turned to see Max pulling up to park beside Henry's tow truck. She hadn't heard the pickup arriving because the Jeep was pretty noisy.

Max got out and strode toward them, his black hat pulled low against the glare of the afternoon sun. "Howdy, there," he said, his smile welcoming.

"I heard about the steer that's jamming traffic down south on the highway, and I'm surprised that you aren't roping the critter." Henry's tone was edged with teasing. "I mean, that situation had Max Donovan written all over it."

Max shook his head. "I do enough of that on the ranch. Lawson owed me, so he's down there taking care of the steer." He looked over at Grace. "It sounds as if Henry worked his magic."

"He sure did."

The mechanic crossed to his truck, reached inside and took out a clipboard. He wrote on it and tore off the top sheet of paper before he came back to hand it to Grace. "Here you go. All new wiring, a new fuse box and I hooked up your heater. It had been disconnected. It's perfectly good now—no frayed wires or any possibility of a fire."

"A fire?" Grace asked as she looked up from the paper in her hand.

"The wiring was frayed, and you could have had an engine fire."

That kind of unnerved her. "I guess the battery going dead was a good thing."

"It was great timing," Henry said as she looked down at the bill again.

The price on the invoice seemed reasonable to Grace for all the work he'd done. "You do take credit cards, right?"

"Usually," he said. "But the thing is my handheld card reader isn't working today for some reason. I take checks or cash."

Grace grimaced. She hadn't brought much cash on the trip, didn't use checks and had depended on her credit cards. All the cash she had was barely a hundred dollars. "Would it be okay if I came to your shop today after I go to the bank and get cash?"

"The yard's shut down. I'm running up to Big Horn territory to watch my boys compete in a roping contest. I'll be there a few days. I'm running short and I need to get on the road."

"Call me when you're back, and I'll bring the money," she said.

Max had been quiet up until then. "Why not simplify this, Henry?" he said. "Grace has an awful lot to do around here, so how about I settle with you now, and she can settle with me when she gets the money?" He looked at Grace, waiting for her to agree.

She could see that Henry was anxious to leave, but she didn't want Max to pay for her, even if it was a short-term loan. There was that horrible feeling of her control slipping away, and she didn't want that. But she didn't want to make things harder for the mechanic. "How about I wire the money to your account when I get it from the bank?"

"You know, don't worry about it. When I get back, I'll let Max know and we can take care of it," Henry suggested.

He didn't know her except that she was Uncle Martin's niece, yet he'd let her pay when she could. "If you're okay with that," she said.

"No problem. Now, I need to get out of

here and head north. Great to meet you, Miss Grace. And Max, safe ride."

"You too and tell your boys I can't wait to see them at the rodeo."

"Will do," Henry said, then got in the tow truck and headed off with a wave.

"I'll get the money out of the bank today, so I have it ready when Henry comes back," she said.

"If you're going to do that today, why don't I meet you at the bank and introduce you to the manager?"

That wouldn't hurt. "Oh, sure," she said.

"How about I meet you there in an hour?"

She found herself saying, "Two hours," just to feel she had some control over the situation. Petty, but it made her feel a bit better.

Max didn't blink or try to talk her into meeting sooner but said, "Deal," and headed toward his pickup.

"Max," she called after him. "I went into Uncle Martin's room earlier and sat in his old chair by the window just looking at my land." She'd actually called it *her* land. She kind of liked the sound of that.

He stopped and looked back at her. "What do you think about it?"

"It's breathtaking. I think Wyoming was showing off for me."

He smiled over at her. "That's been known to happen."

"I'll see you at the bank."

"Call me if you're there before I am," he said, then got in behind the wheel of the truck and drove off.

As she watched him pull onto the highway and drive in the direction of town, she wanted to kick herself. Why had she pushed for another hour just to make sure she had the last word? That was a knee-jerk reaction, courtesy of her dad. She was letting him affect her even when he was nowhere around.

She sighed and went back inside to her uncle's room. She went directly to the chair and sank down in it, rubbing her temples with her fingers.

She barely knew Max Donovan, but she called his motives wrong every time. The poor man couldn't win with her, but she'd change that. He wasn't Walter. She had a gut feeling that Uncle Martin was a very good judge of people, and he and Max were close friends. That ought to be good enough for her. She closed her eyes and breathed deeply, feeling her muscles relax. This wasn't Las Vegas, and she wasn't known as Walter Bennet's daughter anymore. She was Marty's niece, which suited her just fine.

CHAPTER SIX

GRACE FINISHED AT the general store with ten minutes to spare to get to the bank across the street. She put her bags in the Jeep, grateful for the fleece-lined denim jacket she'd found at Gabby's, which had been her first stop in town. She'd also bought a new pair of thermal boots from Farley's, and she had worn them out of the store. They looked cute on her feet, and she already felt warmer.

After locking up the Jeep, she took the stairs back up onto the walkway. As she turned in the direction of the bank, she spotted Max talking to an older man with a short gray beard. He was using a cane to lean on as he engaged in what looked like a serious conversation with Max.

She didn't want to interrupt, so she walked slowly, taking her time approaching the two men. As she got closer, she caught a few words from the older man: "…should know about it."

"People are people, even in Eclipse…not fighting them," she heard Max say.

"Dang it, someone's gotta…ain't right… take him on."

Max shook his head, and now she could clearly hear what he was saying. "It's one man who's got a burr under his saddle."

Grace didn't go any closer, pretending to admire the window display in the bakery next to her. But she heard the older man because his voice was rising.

"He's runnin' around like a chicken with its head chopped off, but his voice is reaching ears out there." He leaned in toward Max. "I'd be right happy to have a little come-to-Pappy meeting with Big Albert, if ya want. There ain't nothing to lose, and it might turn out aces for ya. I'm old and slow, but I got a lot stored up about Al in my thick head that he'd never want to see the light of day."

"Freeman, no, don't. That would just be fuel for his fire. If I lose the vote, then I'll step away. I could go back to the ranch and be okay."

The old man chuckled roughly. "I know. You're a good man. Ain't no meanness in you. I'm right proud of ya. Now, I gotta hitch up and get back before Beulah comes hunting for me."

He moved back and looked surprised to see Grace standing there. "Oh, ma'am, are we blockin' your way?"

"No, not at all. I saw Max…and I… I don't mean to intrude," she said as Max turned. For a moment, his expression appeared blank, but then he smiled.

"Right on time," he said and flicked his eyes over her. "New jacket and boots?"

"The jacket's from Gabby's place, and Mr. Garret had the boots."

The older man was smiling at Grace. "Max, don't you have no manners? Introduce me to your friend."

"Freeman, meet Grace Bennet, Marty's niece. Grace, Freeman Lee."

"It's downright wonderful to meet you, Miss Grace." His voice was raspy, but his blue eyes were bright. "I'm glad the Lodge ain't empty no more. Marty'd be pure happy about that. If you need help, ya'll tell Max to round me up."

"I appreciate your offer, Mr. Lee. Thank you so much."

"Yes, ma'am," he said, touching the brim of his hat. Then he turned to Max. "Hang on, son. It's going to only get rougher the nearer you get to the end of this ride."

"I know. Tell Beulah I'll be by to visit soon."

Freeman nodded, then limped off down the walkway, using his cane.

"He seems very nice," she said to Max.

"It was his barn that I told you about being burned down then being rebuilt by the town. It's still standing."

"If I'm out of line asking, just tell me, no hard feelings, but I couldn't help overhearing. What's going on with Big Albert?"

He ran his hand roughly over his face. "It's no secret around here. I told you Big Albert never forgave me for beating him at the ballot box last election. He's a talker, and a lot of his cronies are still around and want the good old days back when Al did favors for people around here that were right on the border of being illegal. Freeman's ready for a showdown, but I don't want that. If I'm the one knocked off when the voting comes along, it is what it is. If I'm not doing a good enough job for the majority, I'll walk away."

"Do you think Freeman would really do anything?"

That brought a rueful smile to his face.

"Freeman might look old and slow, but if you get him started, he'll tan a hide or two."

"Maybe the cane would come in handy if he did decide to do something."

He shook his head. "I want to pull the reins in on that visual. Freeman's protective of the people he cares about, and he's lived here all his life. He's protective of the town, too."

"Is he family?"

"Close enough." He glanced down the street. "The bank?"

"Oh, yes," she said and as he started off, she fell in step beside him "Maybe if the bank gets robbed while we're in there, you can catch the robber and save the day. You'd be a real hero. That would certainly help you get reelected."

He laughed, an easy sound as they kept going. "There's only been one bank robbery while I've been sheriff. Lyndon Briggs was drunk and thought he was breaking into his brother's store not the bank. So, I guess technically it wouldn't be considered a robbery."

"What happened to him?"

"Jackie Sykes, the bank manager, didn't press charges, but he did make Lyndon pay for repairs and banished him from the bank forever. That ban ended up lasting for all of two months before Jackie lifted it, but Lyndon got the idea."

"No Old West justice, huh?"

"Not on my watch, pardner," he said, then stopped just before Gabby's store and pointed out a brick-and-wood structure directly across from them. The sign by the door read "Eclipse Community Bank." A smaller sign on the door read "Closed."

"But it's only four o'clock."

"Jackie also does real estate and sometimes he has to shut down temporarily to show a prospective client property."

Grace could wait a day. "Okay, I'll get it tomorrow."

He nodded. "Are you heading back out to the Lodge?"

She'd forgotten one of the things she wanted to buy. "I need to get some new linens for the bed in Uncle Martin's room."

He pointed back the way they'd come. "Two stores past Burr's office is a shop called Heavenly Dreams. Laurel May, the mayor's wife, owns it."

"Okay, I'll try there."

"You need to hunt down a hat, too," he said out of the blue.

"Excuse me?"

"You've got the boots and jacket, but if you don't get a good hat, you're going to be cold no matter what you do."

She swallowed the impulse to tell him she'd get a hat if she wanted to, but she'd promised herself that she would chill out when it came to Max and his bossiness. She was being petty, and she cringed inside, thinking of her reaction to his innocent comment. "I'll get one. Anything to stay warm."

"I need to get to the station. Safe ride," he said and touched the brim of his hat with his forefinger. He took the steps down to the street, stopping at the bottom to look up at her. "Don't forget the hat."

WHEN GRACE DROVE back into town three days later, she was more than ready to take Max's "suggestion" and find a warm hat. She'd tried going outside to explore the property around the Lodge and get a better feel for her surroundings, but all she got was cold—very cold. She only managed to get as far as an old stable set back from the Lodge to the south. Its wooden walls and roof were silvered from age, and the stalls were all empty. Outside, two holding pens held nothing but dried grass and weeds.

She drove to Gabby's store, but it was closed, so she continued on to the general store, where she hoped they'd have a warm hat and maybe a scarf she could pull up over her chin and mouth.

The bell that tinkled when the door opened got Farley's attention and he came out from the back area to greet her.

"Well, howdy there, Miss Grace!"

It kind of tickled her that the older men she'd met called her "Miss Grace." She liked it a lot better than "ma'am."

His voice rose over the country music that played in the background. "What are you searching for today?" he asked. The silver-haired shop owner was wearing an orange-colored Western shirt with fringes, white jeans, a belt with a horseshoe-shaped gold buckle and dark green studded boots with two-inch heels. She liked him. He was good entertainment when he showed her around the store, and a bit of a gossip about what was going on in town.

"I'm looking for a warm hat."

"Oh, my. Well, come on with me. I've got the best hats in town." He winked at her. "The best everything in town."

His hat section had a rack devoted to Flaming Coop D merchandise. Farley caught her looking at a poster on the wall beside it. "That's Coop Donovan. I watched that boy grow up to be the best of the best on the rodeo circuit."

She saw the price tag on a beautiful women's hat that was branded with the Flaming Coop D logo on the inside liner. It was pricey. "He's a local hero?"

"You bet. All the Donovan boys used to be on the rodeo circuit, just like their dad, Dash Donovan. Coop's the one who stuck it out and made it big."

That was interesting. "Quite a family," she said. "So, the sheriff was in the rodeo?"

"For a while, then he left to enlist in the army and got into one of them special units. A few years ago he came back here and took over as sheriff. Hope he gets reelected."

She saw a chance to ask something she wanted to know. "I'd think him getting elected again would be a slam dunk."

"It probably is, but you never know when you have someone running against you, some-one willing to do whatever it takes. Sometimes it's not about character—it's about greed and politics. Even around here it can get messy."

"That's too bad."

"Sure is," he said. Then he asked her, "What kind of hat did you have in mind?"

"A warm one."

Grace walked out of Farley's wearing her new hat—a soft gray knit beanie with earflaps—and carrying a bag with a scarf, some flannel shirts, thermals to wear under her clothes and a jar of jellybeans. A second bag had some cleaning supplies in it. She went down to her Jeep and put the bags on the passenger seat, then her cell phone rang. Max was calling.

"Hello, stranger," she said when she answered.

"I like your new hat, and the earflaps were a good idea, but turn your collar up. That helps keep you warmer, too."

He liked the hat? How could he…? "Where are you?"

"Turn around, then come on over."

She turned, and there he was standing on the walkway in front of the leather-tooling store across the street. She pushed her phone into her jacket pocket, then crossed the empty street. As she got closer to him and he flashed a smile, it struck her that she'd actually missed him the last three days, a man she barely knew.

"I haven't seen you for a while," she said,

her voice slightly breathless even though she hadn't exactly hurried across to him.

"I've been chained to a desk." He didn't look very happy about that. "Did you ever get to the bank?"

"No, I was just heading over there now. I've been busy at the Lodge, cleaning and trying to explore the property without freezing to death."

"The hat should help, but putting up your collar will keep your neck warm."

It was surprisingly easy for her to say, "Thanks for the suggestion. I actually bought a matching scarf, too."

"Good. I'm going down to the bank to make a deposit for Lillian. You want to come with me, and I'll introduce you to Jackie this time?"

The bank manager. "Sure," she said.

"How's the Jeep?" Max asked as they walked side by side down the walkway.

"It starts right up, and the heater works. Not as well as the one in your truck, but it's nice. So, are you done sitting at your desk?"

"I hope so. It's the worst part of my job. I was actually down at headquarters in Two Horns working. A new hire screwed up big-time, and I had to fix his mess before it got out of hand."

"What did he do?"

"I really can't tell you, but it's over and done with, and I'm short a deputy for a week." He hesitated, then added, "Do me a favor and keep this between us. I don't need it to get around, especially not now."

"Of course." Grace grimaced. "I'm sorry it happened."

"Me, too, but it's part of the job—the messy part. Marty always said that if you go through the mess, pain and all, you'll appreciate the peace at the end of the road."

Grace knew all about the messy parts of life. She was just crawling out of one, finally putting it behind her, and she would embrace the peace when or if it came.

"My uncle was pretty smart, huh?"

"MARTY WAS SMART about a lot of things," Max said. He still felt the loss of his friend. As they approached the bank, he realized how much ease there was between him and Grace. It wouldn't be a chore for him to be her friend. Marty had asked him to be there for her and he would be.

Before he could reach for the door to pull

it open, a local teen, Oscar Warring, the oldest of five Warring kids, slowly passed by riding an old quarter horse and holding up a car stuck behind him.

"Hey, Sheriff Max!" Oscar called out,

The kid was strong looking in his scruffy clothes that weren't keeping up with the growth spurt he'd obviously had.

"How's your mom doing, Oscar?" he called back to him.

The boy pulled his horse to a stop in the street, seemingly unaware of the car right behind him. "She's doing lots better and was pure happy with the cord of wood you sent over last week. It'll help a lot until Pa's back on his feet."

"You tell her to let me know if you get low again, or if you need help with grains and hay."

"I sure will."

Oscar nudged his horse to get going at the same time the driver behind him sounded his horn. The old horse reared at the sound, and Oscar barely kept in the saddle.

Max jumped off the walkway and landed between the luxury SUV and the horse. Seeing Oscar had regained control of his ride,

Max headed directly to the vehicle before the driver did something else reckless.

He rapped on the window and the glass slid down to expose a middle-aged man who was wearing Western-styled clothing that Max knew set the guy back a good amount of money.

"What in blazes were you thinking doing that?" he demanded, trying very hard to keep his anger at a minimum.

"The kid's riding as if he owns the street and blocking everyone else on the road. Then he stops traffic completely." The man's face was flushed with anger. "This is none of your business, buddy. Get out of my way."

Max undid the front of his jacket and pushed back the right side to make sure the driver saw his badge and his gun. "Wrong. It is my business as sheriff in these parts. But I'm feeling charitable today and I won't cite you for reckless endangerment, if you head out of town and keep going."

The driver looked like he wanted to say something else but had the good sense to keep it to himself and rolled up the window.

Max went over to Oscar. "You okay?"

"Yeah, I'm okay, Sheriff."

Max looked back at the SUV, then up at Oscar again. "Where're you going?"

"Up to the blacksmith to get a halter he fixed for us."

"Okay, get going but don't rush."

The boy understood. "If you say so."

Max patted the horse's rump. "Safe ride," he said, then went back to where Grace was still standing by the door to the bank.

"You really do love this town, don't you?" she said with a soft smile.

"It's my home," he said as he reached to open the door for her. Grace stepped past him into a small room with only one of three teller cages open. There was a jarringly modern-looking ATM to the left of the door.

She reached into her jacket pocket and took out a red wallet, from which she retrieved a black credit card. "This won't take a minute," she said, crossing to insert her card in the flashing green slot on the face of the machine. Max turned to talk to the teller to make Lillian's deposit.

"Hi, Rose," he said to the bank manager's daughter. "Lillian's account for deposit." He handed the envelope over to the girl with the short brown hair and pierced nose, ears and eyebrows. "Is your dad in today?"

"No, he's out looking at a ranch for someone from the Jackson Hole area who wants a quieter location."

The transaction was simple, and as Rose handed him back the receipt for Lillian he was surprised to see Grace was still at the machine taking a silver credit card out of the slot this time. The machine beeped as "Card Declined" flashed on the screen.

"I don't believe this," Grace murmured.

"Problem?" Max asked.

She stared at the machine. "Yes...no, um, I must be getting my PIN numbers mixed up." She rubbed the silver card on the side of her jacket, then inserted it one more time. It beeped and flashed "Card Declined." She took her card back, then tried a gold card. That card was declined, too.

Max could see she was embarrassed and avoided looking at him. "I don't know why it's doing that. I just bought stuff at the general store with my black card."

Rose spoke up. "Those cards mess up all the time. Bring it over here and let me slide it for you."

Max moved back to give Grace access to the teller cage. She passed her gold card to Rose. "I don't understand what's wrong."

He hadn't read Grace as wealthy; nothing

about her shouted it. "Maybe the machine's too low on cash," he said, a perfectly logical reason that could have happened with any card.

Rose smiled reassuringly at the two of them. "Don't worry, it happens. Let me run it again." She slid Grace's gold card through the machine in front of her and turned the pad toward Grace so she could put in her PIN. Rose's smile turned to a frown. "Can you put in your PIN again, please?"

Grace did, and even before the woman looked up, Max knew it hadn't worked.

"I'm sorry," Rose said. "I've never seen one of these cards refused unless it's stolen." Almost immediately, the girl realized whom she was talking to. Color flooded her face. "Of course, it's not. The screen would have alerted me." Quickly, she asked, "Do you want me to call it in and see if there's a hold on it or something?"

Grace nodded, her cheeks pink. "Yes, if you would, please."

Rose made the call, listened, then hung up. "I'm sorry. The card's been canceled by the company it was issued to at their request." She read the name off the monitor. "Golden Mountain Corporation. Maybe they went out

of business, or their account was hacked?"
Rose suggested.

"It didn't go out of business," Grace muttered tightly. She took the card back. "Thank
you for trying," she said as she slipped the
card into her purse.

"I'm sorry, ma'am," Rose said.

Grace nodded. "Me, too." She looked anxious to leave as she glanced at Max. "I'll be
outside."

She hurried to the door and out. Max thanked
Rose, then went after Grace.

When Max stepped outside, Grace was waiting there. "I never expected this, but maybe
I should have. Whatever, I'll get Henry's
money."

"You should have expected someone to
cancel your card?"

"No, I… It's just, it should have occurred
to me that he'd pull the cards."

"Who pulled your card?" he asked.

She looked around, then finally back up at
him. "The CEO, the founder and all-around
dictator of the company. He was upset with
me the last time we talked, and he has his
ways of making a point. He's particularly
good at making a point with the greatest impact possible."

"He didn't ask for the card back when you left, or quit, or whatever happened?"

"No, he didn't, but I can imagine him enjoying it when he finds out I tried to get money and was denied."

She didn't give a name to the man, so he asked, "This person, was he just your boss?"

She looked down and her shoulders sagged. "No, he wasn't, and he wasn't what you're thinking he was, either."

She'd read his mind, because he'd thought the guy was someone she'd been involved with romantically, someone who had decided he was done with her, or maybe she'd walked out on him, and what better way to get his revenge?

Max touched her arm to get her attention, startling her. "Listen to me. Don't even think about rushing to pay Henry. I can take care of him."

"No, you won't. I'll take care of it."

Her tone wasn't angry, but hurt and sad.

"Okay, but don't go smashing any piggy banks."

PIGGY BANKS? As Max said the words, Grace realized she had what could be called a piggy bank of sorts. Her father had set up a bank account in her name when she'd gone off to college, with automatic quarterly deposits as long as she kept a 4.0 GPA in her business and marketing courses. She'd only used the money in the account to buy her textbooks the first semester and to set up her dorm room. She'd left it alone after she'd started working at the college and had all but forgotten about it until right then.

It was *her* money, not her father's. She'd earned every cent of it. What was in the account wouldn't be a fortune, but it would help her right now when she needed it.

"I don't mean to be abrupt, but I need to go," she stated.

He looked down at her, his eyes shadowed by his hat, but she could see the concern in his expression. "I don't care about the money," he said.

"But I do. I'll call you soon, okay?" She hurried off to get back to where she'd left the Jeep. She didn't realize Max was right by her until she stopped to cross the street. There was no traffic in either direction and she hurried over to where her Jeep was parked. Max stayed beside her until she had climbed into the Jeep and started the engine.

"Max, I need to go," she said.

"Sure, of course." He took a step back. "Go and do what you have to do. We'll talk later."

"Yes, later." She put the Jeep in reverse and eased back out onto street. When she neared the highway access, she knew she had to stop before she threw up. Just the two miles to the Lodge seemed impossible for her to drive right then. Turning off onto a side street named Longbow Trail, she pulled to the curb and took out her phone.

She looked up a number and held the phone to her ear, her hand shaking. There was one ring before an automated voice gave her options regarding her bank account in Henderson. She pressed the number to hear her balance and barely breathed until she was given an answer. There was more in her account than she'd thought there would be. Relieved, she sank back into the seat. Walter hadn't gotten to it yet.

When given the option of hanging up or staying on the line to speak to a representative, she chose the human being. Half an hour later, she had arranged to have the account put on hold until she could personally sign for an electronic transfer of the remaining funds to an associated bank in Cody. She agreed to be there at ten thirty the next morning. Things would be okay. She'd beaten Walter to the punch. It wasn't a victory for her, but it was the final cut of her connection with Walter Bennet.

CHAPTER SEVEN

MAX WOKE IN his house on the ranch at the crack of dawn. He'd had scattered dreams throughout the night that he really didn't remember beyond being left with the sense that they were sad. It was probably better he didn't remember, especially if they were anything like the dreams he'd had when he first got back from the army.

He quickly got out of bed, showered and dressed, then left to go check in at the substation. As he drove down the highway, the sadness from the forgotten dreams dogged him. Then he thought of Grace Bennet. It had bothered him more than he liked to admit, thinking about what some guy had done to her. She was alone. No parents, no uncle and apparently no other family. Maybe that had filtered into his dreams.

His stop at the substation lasted longer than he'd anticipated, and he didn't get out of there until eight forty-five. As he drove along Clayton Way nearing the bank, Rose stepped down off the raised walkway and waved at him to stop. He pulled over and she hurried up to the driver's window. As the glass slid down, she smiled up at him.

"I'm glad I spotted you. I was just on the way over to the station to give this to Lillian."

He saw her hold out what he recognized as Grace's red wallet.

"Marty's niece left this on the shelf by the ATM and forgot to take it with her. Maybe you can get it to her."

He took the wallet and laid it on the console. "Sure, I'll drop in and give it to her."

"That's great, Max. Thanks."

"No problem," he said.

"Have a good day."

As Rose headed back toward the bank, he took out his cell to call Grace to let her know he had her wallet, but an incoming call stopped him. "Hey, Lillian. What's going on?"

"You're free for the day. That second recruit passed the firing range with flying colors, so he's eligible for duty. He'll be with Jimmy Jay in the cruiser. You don't have to worry about covering the eastern border."

He almost didn't know what he'd do with himself for a whole day. Taking the wallet back to Grace was a start, but after that he figured he'd play it by ear. He drove away in the direction of the Lodge. When he went through the gates and up to park, he found Grace's Jeep idling, the exhaust rising up into the cold air. It looked as if Grace was getting ready to go somewhere. He got out and found the door to the Lodge was open, so he stepped inside.

The place seemed fresh again: the dust was gone, and the front desk had been polished to a mellow sheen. Sitting on top of it was an older landline phone and an old-fashioned cash register. They'd been stored in the cabinet under the desk after Marty had computerized everything and stopped using them.

"Grace?" he called out as he closed the door behind him. "You here?"

"Coming," he heard her say from somewhere in the back.

Then he saw her hurrying over from the direction of the kitchen, and she looked different. Her dark hair was slicked back from her face and tucked behind her ears, and she'd traded her jeans and flannel shirt for tailored black slacks and a white cable-knit sweater.

"Don't stare," she said with a slight grimace as she did up the front of her leather jacket.

"I was trying to look more professional, but I think the motorcycle jacket ruins that impression. I'm not good at dressing up."

He thought she looked incredibly attractive. "Why are you dressed up?"

"I'm on my way to meet with a banker in Cody to sign some paperwork." She crossed to the door. "I don't want to be late." She stopped before pulling it open. "I'm sorry, Max. Did you need something?"

Could she be going to sign sales papers for the Lodge already? His stomach sank. "Something to do with the Lodge?" he asked as casually as he could manage.

"No. Burr's taking care of all of that. This is personal business for me." She gave him a rueful smile. "I'm sorry. I need to make sure I'm not late for my appointment."

She opened the door and motioned for him to go ahead of her, and then she locked up and took the stairs down to the drive. Max walked beside her, over to where he'd parked by her Jeep. She turned to him before she opened the Jeep door. A light breeze teased her hair where a few errant strands had already started to curl at her cheekbones.

"What time's your appointment?" he asked.

"Ten thirty."

He suddenly knew exactly what he'd like to do on his free day. "Strange coincidence, but I'm on my way to Cody, too."

"You aren't working?"

"No. I came by to give you something you might have been missing."

"What?"

He took her wallet out of his pocket and held it out to her.

"Rose found it by the ATM machine. You must have left it there by accident."

Her eyes widened with surprise. "Oh, gosh, I didn't even know it wasn't in my purse." She took it from him. "I can't believe I did that. Thank you so much for bringing it out here."

"Which bank are you going to up there?"

"The Reliance Community Bank."

"My brother's business, CD's Place, is only two blocks from there. I don't have to work today, so I'm going to see Caleb and have lunch." She looked impatient now, and he quickly finished with, "How about we go together, you do your bank business and meet me at Caleb's place for lunch afterward? The food's great and it's on the house." He smiled at her. "I promise to get you there by ten thirty."

"You must have something better to do than hang out with me on your day off."

He'd told himself he was doing it to help Grace because of Marty, but in fact, he realized he wanted to spend time with her. "I am painfully available for the day. How about we flip to see who drives, then get moving so you aren't late? I'm not supposed to use the truck for personal reasons when I'm not on duty, so I'd just have to stop by the ranch on the way and pick up my own truck there."

"No, we can take the Jeep," she said. "But could you drive? You know where we're going, and I can't be late."

"Sure thing," he said. While Grace went around to climb into the passenger seat, he got behind the wheel. The Jeep was old, but it ran well, and they were soon heading up to Cody on the highway. "Don't worry. We'll be there on time. Trust me."

She nodded and said, "I slept in Uncle Martin's room for the first time last night."

"How was it?"

"It was nice. I had been contemplating turning that whole space into a big office, but I'm not going to. I worry that if I change things too much, I'll lose that sense of Uncle Martin that I feel in there, especially when I sit in his old chair by the windows. It's not like a ghost thing or anything, but he's there."

He smiled to himself, grateful Marty was becoming more real to her. And who knew? Maybe she would change her mind about selling after all. "How long do you think you'll be at the bank?" he asked.

"I just have to sign some papers to close out a savings account I'd forgotten about until yesterday. It's not a lot of money, but I'm kind of lucky you're coming along so I'll have a bodyguard."

Max cast a quick sideways glance at Grace. "My rates aren't cheap for private work."

"How much?" she asked.

"I'll accept your company on this trip as partial payment."

"What about the rest?"

"That's where things get iffy."

She seemed puzzled when he looked quickly over at her. "Iffy? Why?"

"I'll introduce you to Caleb when I go by there, and you have to promise me you'll ignore anything he says about me unless it's good."

She chuckled softly at that. "I never had siblings, but I made up an imaginary younger sister who was sweet and fun and always wanted to do whatever I was doing. I called her Poppy, for no reason I can remember, but she kept me company...sort of."

"Caleb's very real, and he can be fun. He's a genuine people person and very social. He's never boring, but he's only recently become what you could call 'sweet.' And that's because he has a wife now, Harmony, and a little girl named Joy."

"I'm looking forward to meeting him, and I bet he'll only say good things about you."

He laughed ruefully. "Easy to say when you don't know him."

When her phone chimed, she took it out of the leather shoulder bag resting in her lap. "Just a minute," she said to Max and took the call. "Hello. This is Grace Bennet." She listened silently while Max kept driving. Then he heard her inhale softly before she spoke in a slightly panicked voice. "No, no, no, no, no. That's my account. Mine. I was promised the money would be there when I got to the bank today."

Max glanced at her. She was nervously rubbing at her slacks with the flat of her free hand. Her eyes were closed tightly. Something was very wrong. "Yes, please, call me right back."

The call ended, but Grace didn't say anything. Finally, Max flat out asked her, "Is there a problem?"

"Just something I thought was settled." She cleared her throat and said, "I'll figure it out."

His promise to Marty mixed with the tension he could feel radiating from Grace wouldn't let him give up easily. "Talking it over with someone can help, and if you want, I'll listen. It won't go any further than your Jeep. I promise."

She didn't answer for what seemed an eternity, then he sensed her turning toward him. "I thought I had things settled with the bank, but it looks as if it's falling apart. The man said he'd call me back, but I'm not sure he's going to be able to help me. I think you should probably take me back to the Lodge."

Maybe she'd been trying to do more than just close an account. Perhaps she'd been looking to borrow money and been denied. A sheriff didn't make much, but Max and his brothers all owned part of the ranch that had been incorporated years ago, and they received quarterly payments. Last time he looked, he wasn't wealthy, but he was well-to-do. "How about you tell me exactly what happened, then if you still want to go back, I'll take you." He slowed, pulled over to the side of the road and turned toward her to give her his full attention.

She looked down at the phone she clenched in her hand. "There's a demand that's going to be filed against the account—like a lien, I think. If that happens, the funds will be unavailable with no time frame for them to be released to me, or else seized by the person filing against it."

"This person doing it, is he the same one you mentioned yesterday?"

She was silent for a long moment, then nodded and spoke in a low voice. "Yes, and I don't know what he'll do. I gave up trying to figure him out. For a long time I thought he did what he did because he knew best and I trusted him. But it's always been about him, and he doesn't care about anything or anybody else." He saw her bite her bottom lip, then say, "I won't let him do this to me now."

Max couldn't stand the thought of someone out there trying to hurt Grace. There was no way to get the guy, but he would do whatever he could to keep him from taking what seemed like the last of her money. "Who just called you from the bank?"

When she looked at him, there were no tears in her eyes, but that lost expression he'd seen at the diner. "Norbert Brown, the manager."

"Good, good," he said. "I've known Bert for years, and he's a reasonable man."

Before he could suggest she call Bert back, her phone rang and she jumped at the sound, dropping the phone to the floor by her feet. She reached down to retrieve it and looked at the screen. "It's the bank," she said.

"Let me talk." He held out his hand for her phone.

"I can do—"

"Please, allow me."

She shivered slightly, then dropped the phone in his hand. He answered it. "Hello?"

"I'm calling for Ms. Bennet."

He recognized the voice. "Bert, you're talking to Max Donovan."

"Max. What's going on?"

He didn't want Grace to hear their conversation. "Hold on, Bert." He hit the mute button on the phone and told a small lie. "The reception's not good in here. Be right back." He got out and walked to the rear of the Jeep, then went another ten feet just to make sure Grace wouldn't hear him. He unmuted the call. "Bert, why is Ms. Bennet's money not available for her?"

"I received a notification of intent to file a lien against the full funds held in the account."

"We're on our way to see you. When we walk out of the bank, I want her to have the money that's in her account with her. If you can't make that happen, tell me how much money's involved and I'll cover it."

"Max, you know I can't give you that information, not without her permission. Put her on the line, and I'll ask for it."

"No, forget I said that." He knew she wouldn't go for that, but it had been worth a try. He glanced back over his shoulder and saw Grace watching him. "Bert, she's Marty Roberts's niece, and she needs help. She's inherited the Lodge and she came up here alone and is trying to deal with everything by herself. I'm not asking you to break the rules. I'm just asking if there's any way you can help her to get her own money legally."

Bert was silent for a long moment then said, "Hypothetically?"

"She needs real currency, but if your answer has to be hypothetical, go ahead."

"If a hypothetical account is to be closed, but a hypothetical lien was going to be put against it, the demand wouldn't be legal and binding until the documents for said lien had been wired to the target bank and they'd been accepted. The manager would have to sign off on it. If that happens before the owner of the account can close it, the action is irreversible."

Max frowned. "In this hypothetical situation, how long does it take between the notification about the coming lien and the actual filing?"

"If the notification of intent to file came across the bank manager's desk from an out-of-state bank, it could take around fifteen minutes to be approved and finalized." Bert cleared his throat. "However, if this hypothetical bank manager at a small regional bank is in an important meeting when it arrives, that could push the time it would take up to half an hour, but not any longer. Remember, this is all hypothetical, but if the legal owner of the account is there before that time, they'd get the payout."

Max checked his watch. Twenty minutes to get to Cody if there was no traffic. "Okay, Bert, we're on our way now." Bert was willing to do what he could within his means and that was all Max could ask for.

He got back in the Jeep and gave Grace

her phone. "We need to get there as soon as possible. There's a good chance that you can get your money."

She just stared at him for a moment before she asked, "What do you mean?"

Max knew he couldn't make any promises, but as he drove back onto the highway he explained some of it to Grace. "Bert knew Marty, and you're benefiting from that. It's still a fifty-fifty chance you'll get the money, but that's better than no chance at all." He reached out to touch her hand, which was clenching her phone. "Relax, Grace. It'll be okay. Trust me."

Unexpectedly, she laid her free hand over his. "I'm really glad you showed up this morning," she said just above a whisper.

He felt her touch on him tighten for a fleeting second, and then she drew back. He wanted nothing more in that moment than to see her get her money and be smiling when they left the bank.

GRACE SILENTLY WATCHED Max on the drive to Cody, wondering where his suit of shining armor was stored. He was always coming to her rescue, and even if she couldn't access the money in her account, she knew he'd done his best to help her.

"I'm sorry I got so upset. I've had a lot of stuff happen lately, and I'm trying to figure things out. Finding out about Uncle Martin and the Lodge came completely out of the blue, and since then other things have kind of gone sideways."

"That's all we can do in this life...adjust," he murmured.

As the miles slipped past, her nerves started to get to her. Finally Max pulled off the highway and onto Cody's main street. His phone rang and he handed it to Grace. He didn't want to stop again. "Could you put it on speaker for me?"

She took it and did as he asked. "Lillian, I'm not working today," Max said.

"God bless you, I know, but I have a message for you from the bank manager in Cody. Bert said that you have fifteen minutes to walk through the door."

"Got it," he said, then motioned Grace to end the call.

"What does that mean?" she asked as he took his phone back and put it in the slot on the dash.

"We have to be there in under fifteen minutes, or you won't be leaving with the money."

"Can we make it?"

"We'll be early," he said and turned off the street into a parking spot in front of a brick structure that had "Reliance Community Bank" written in blue letters on the facade.

Grace grabbed his right arm. "I can't believe we made it! You're wonderful!" She hadn't meant to say that last sentence, but it was true. The man had taken away a weight she wasn't sure she could have carried much longer.

His hazel eyes were touched with teasing. "Dang, I was going for awesome!"

She let go of him and laughed. "Well, surprise, Sheriff, you've officially achieved awesomeness."

Too late, Walter, too late, she thought but without any real sense of joy. She was just thankful that she had at least some money to keep her afloat.

CHAPTER EIGHT

HALF AN HOUR LATER, Grace and Max were back in the Jeep, the papers signed, the account closed and her money in a plastic bank pouch she'd put in her purse on her lap. They were waiting for an opening to get out on the street into traffic that moved at little more than a snail's pace. Grace felt as if her world had steadied again.

"If you hadn't brought my wallet back when you did, and if you didn't know Mr. Brown, I don't think I'd have the money now."

"Bert really came through."

Max came through, too. "How long have you known him?"

"We went to high school together."

"I would have thought he was older than you."

Max glanced at her. "I guess you're so young that anyone over thirty seems really old."

She chuckled at that. "No, of course not. I

just meant Mr. Brown seemed more like he was in his forties than his thirties."

Max answered his cell phone when it rang. "Hey there. I'm close by and I need a table for two for lunch. I also got the background checks on the band members." As he listened, Grace saw a frown emerge on his face.

"Nah, if you aren't there we'll head back, but I can read off the background checks if you need me to." He tapped the screen on his cell and read through some data. "The backgrounds came back clear except for a Randy Lawrence from Slater's Yahoo Four. A drunk took a swing at him when he was playing at Overboard in Cheyenne, and he decked the guy. Claimed self-defense. He was released with no charges." He listened. "No problem there... No, we're fine." He put his phone in the slot on the dash.

"No free lunch?" she asked.

"No Caleb—he's visiting friends up near Sheridan. Are you real hungry?"

She hadn't eaten anything because of her nerves and was starting to feel vague hunger pangs. "I'm in no rush for food."

"Well, I do need to eat, and I know just the place."

"Where's that?"

He didn't reply but put in another call on his cell. "It's me. I have a friend with me, we're heading back from Cody and we're hungry. We should be driving by you in thirty or forty minutes. I was hoping we could stop by, if that's okay. Text me back."

"Who's going to get back to you?" Grace asked.

"Oh, my mother," he said as he finally found a gap to pull into traffic and drive toward the highway. He glanced at her and that crooked smile that he had lit up his face. "She'll be incredibly pleased to meet you once I explain to her about your connection to Marty and the Lodge. Marty had an open-ended invitation to our family meals. He loved my mom's cooking, especially her tamales."

Family meals were foreign to her—at least meals made in her home by her parents. On the rare occasion that they ate together, it was always at some fancy restaurant. Most of the time, they just ordered room service from the hotel where they lived in the penthouse.

Max's phone chimed, announcing a text. He opened it and handed the phone to Grace. "Read it to me, please."

"'I'm sorry, Max,'" Grace read. "'But Dad and I are on our way to meet up with Lance

Burke and his family. He was hurt on a ride in Arizona, and he's decided to retire. You go ahead and stop at the house and help yourself to some chicken and tamales in the fridge. Just reheat them. They taste even better on the second day. Let Lawson take some with him so Evelyn won't have to figure out how to feed him and take care of the new baby. Stay safe. Love you lots.'"

Grace handed the phone back to him and he slipped it into his jacket pocket. "Who's Lawson?" she asked.

"A deputy and a friend of mine. We ride double off and on, so Mom must have assumed that's who was with me." He chuckled to himself. "Maybe it's better she doesn't know."

"Why?"

"Both of my brothers are married or engaged, and she sees me as a bit of a lost cause. Frankly, she tries to set me up with available women she comes across every chance she gets."

She kept her eyes on Max's profile and decided that the man had to be single by choice, because he had no bad side. He'd be a magnet for single women wherever he went, even while doing his job. "You poor thing. You have a mom who cares. Must be tough," she said, with deliberate sarcasm in her voice.

He glanced over at her, and she hoped she hadn't been too harsh. "You're right. She cares, a bit too much most of the time, but she does care, and I appreciate that. She raised us boys, and we didn't make it easy for her. My dad's an easygoing guy, the kind who rarely got angry, and then you only knew it when he called you by your full name. A normal dad. Together, he and my mom were—and are—a formidable duo, and very happily married. So, she thinks that's what I need. She sees that kind of life as normal."

"That's lovely, but marriages can also be cold and indifferent and end up with no one being happy."

He glanced at her and their eyes met for a brief moment before they both turned away, him to focus on driving, and her to wish she hadn't opened the door to any personal discussion.

MAX'S FIRST THOUGHT was that she had been married and it had ended badly with her ex-husband, the card canceler. "You sound as if you're speaking from experience."

She didn't respond right away, and he waited.

Then she finally said, "Yes, it's personal. My parents' marriage was…just a relationship, at least what I remember about it. It sure wasn't a good marriage, maybe a passable one at best." She actually chuckled at that, but there was no humor in it. "You know, it made me mad, and the way I showed it indirectly was by choosing the worst men to date."

He hadn't expected that, but reconsidered the credit card man and decided he probably was her last bad relationship, in spite of her implying that he wasn't. "How did that work out for you?"

"Not very well. My parents were so busy with their lives, I'm not sure they even knew about my dates. They definitely didn't show much interest in Bubba."

That caught his attention. "Bubba?"

"An old boyfriend who was, let's say, less than perfect. Bubba Ralston. Big mistake. Big, big mistake."

He wanted so badly to ask why it had been a mistake but didn't want to push too hard. "Not a nice guy?"

"He was pretty boring, actually, but he had a massive Harley, and we went on some great rides. He was a tattoo artist and really good at what he did. Basically, he was the kind of guy who would have really bugged my dad, but my dad was never home when Bubba was there. My mom met Bubba once—but she was headed to New York for a shopping spree, so she didn't say more than two words to him."

"So, it was all for nothing?"

"I learned I'd rather ride a horse than be on a Harley with a man who tattooed his own name on his chest in big black letters and showed it off to everyone."

"What happened to Bubba?"

"Last I heard he opened up a tattoo parlor just off the Las Vegas Strip and had most every part of his body covered in ink."

"One question?"

"Sure."

"Did he tattoo you?"

"Now that's personal, Sheriff," she teased.

"Oh, so he did…"

"No, but he wanted to. I'm not into pain, and tattoos are pretty much there forever. I didn't want that. Since you asked me, I'll ask you. You were in the army, right?"

"For eight years, most of them in Special Ops."

"So, what tattoos do you have?"

He glanced at her. "I have no tattoos."

"Come on, you have to have tattoos."

"No, I don't," he said. "I couldn't think of one thing I wanted to carry around with me for the rest of my life."

"You could have had your name tattooed somewhere on your body. I mean, you'll always be that person."

He kept his eyes on the highway. "I sure will be me."

"If you had your full name tattooed, what would it say?"

"Maxim—after my dad—Little-Hawk—after my grandmother's maiden name—Donovan."

"Little-Hawk. That's a pretty cool name, isn't it?"

"It means a lot to Mom."

"Okay, so since you won't admit to having a tattoo, I'm going to change the subject," she said. "Do you know anything about legal things? I've heard a lot of police want to be lawyers."

"I never have, but I can see it might help—and I don't have a tattoo."

"Yeah, okay," she said. He was about to protest, but she cut him off. "I'm just wondering, if I get a safety deposit box, and I put my money in it, can anyone else find out I have one and what it contains?"

"I don't think so, with privacy laws and that sort of protection. But anything's possible in this day and age, I suppose."

She sank back in the seat. "Maybe I should just stuff the money under my mattress," she muttered.

"Why not simply put it in a private safe?"

"Just assume that I don't have a safe, okay? Because I don't."

He cast her a look. "How about I assume that you do?"

She turned to face him more directly. "You can assume what you want, but I still won't have a safe."

"You do. Marty put in a safe at the Lodge."

"You're serious?"

"I told you I'd let you know when I'm joking by saying, 'I'm joking,' so we can both laugh. I'm not joking."

"Wow, I'd have thought Burr would have told me."

"I thought he had, and the safe isn't in sight. Marty made sure of that. When we get back to the Lodge, I can show you where it is."

"It's behind that meteor-night-sky painting over the bed, isn't it?"

"Nope."

"I guess I've watched too many movies

where the rich guy exposes his safe behind a Rembrandt or a Picasso. So, where is it?"

"In the tall wall cabinet that's between the desk area and the kitchen."

"I opened that, and it was empty. Are you sure?"

"Very sure."

"Okay, then all I have to do is call Burr and ask for the combination."

Max glanced at her; her expression now was nothing like it had been on the drive up. Now, she looked relaxed, her features soft. He liked that. "No, I can tell you what it is. He gave it to me and made me memorize it."

GRACE DIDN'T ASK why her uncle trusted Max Donovan so much. She—who basically trusted no man—was getting closer to trusting Max. He seemed to be a good person. It was that simple. She'd trusted Walter for a while when she was young but found out the hard way that he was the very kind of person he'd warned her about, someone always with a self-serving agenda. It had been painful for her to realize that it was all about him, all the time.

"We're here," Max said. The entryway to the ranch came into view. It was fancy, set off the road and surrounded by white rail fencing. A carved gold-lettered sign swung from the massive brick archway above a wooden gate. It announced, "Flaming Sky Ranch—Welcome!" Under that was the logo of a black horse with its mane and tail fanning out behind it and a burst of red-and-yellow flames shooting out of its hooves. Under that sign was a smaller one that swung in the light breeze: "Everything Rodeo."

"They just had the arch built and installed a new calling system." Max entered a code in a keypad by the gate and it slowly swung back, giving access to a broad driveway with a rise ahead that blocked whatever lay beyond it.

They drove past more rail fencing until they reached another sign carved to look like a huge golden saddle. It held a list of several locations with arrows pointing visitors in the right directions. The list included everything from the ranch offices to a rodeo arena, food sales, deliveries and even a first aid station. It almost reminded her of a sign at an amusement park.

"This is it," Max said as they crested the rise, and Grace saw Flaming Sky Ranch appear in front of her: a mix of buildings and livestock enclosures dotted the landscape, and rolling pastures stretched into the far distance, up toward the foothills.

"Wow, I thought a ranch would be a...a ranch, but this looks like a resort of some sort or a Western theme park."

"It is a ranch, but it's grown a lot over the years. My grandparents started with cattle, then horses, then my dad took over and he kept expanding it." Max drove slowly ahead. "When he had sons who fell in love with the rodeo, he decided to give us and other kids around here a real rodeo experience. We hold junior rodeos three times a year. The next one is in a week, over the Thanksgiving weekend. My dad has been building the ranch piece by piece—it's been his main focus since he retired from the rodeo. It's been an ongoing project for as long as I can remember."

Grace blinked, taking it all in. The view ahead of her almost rivaled the one from the Lodge deck. Among the buildings, one stood out: a long white structure with a weather vane on top of a steepled roof and holding pens out front. It had to be a stable. Not far from it was a big parking area next to an impressive outdoor arena. She could see men inside painting the bleacher seats.

"That's where the kids have their rodeos

and where my brothers and I learned to rope and ride," Max said as he pointed to the arena. "It's used a lot." He slowed and turned onto a dirt road just before they would have passed the stable. Massive trees arched over the road, their fallen leaves making a crunching sound as the Jeep drove over them. A tenacious few still clung to the mostly naked branches.

"Both houses down here can't be seen from the highway and are out of sight from any of the public areas."

They drove past a scattering of outbuildings— one looked like a much smaller version of the big stable, painted the same in white with black trim. A couple of paddocks were situated by double barn doors.

As the dirt road changed to inset brick, Grace asked, "How big is this ranch?"

"Just under four thousand acres, mostly flat land 'til you hit the foothills."

"That's huge. How many horses are here?"

"That varies so much that I couldn't make a good guess. The stable up here is for our horses. There's seven in there now."

"I saw an old stable at the Lodge, but it was empty. Did Uncle Martin have horses?"

"He did, a couple, but after he got weaker,

working hands from here took care of them. Do you ride?"

"I did one summer when my parents sent me to camp while they went to Florida for some business thing. They didn't know it was a riding camp, and I was in hog heaven for ten days. I never got to do it again."

"So, I take it that if you were staying here, you'd want that stable at the Lodge to have at least one horse in it?"

"Maybe two or three, if that were the case."

"Let's get some food, and then I have someone I want to introduce you to. Rebel was a real close friend of Marty's, and I think it would do you both good to get to know each other."

"Who is he?"

"That's a surprise for after lunch. As for now, we're here," he said as he pulled into a semicircular driveway that led to an impressive portico framing the doorway of a sprawling, single-story house that blended perfectly with the land. From the aged clay tile roof to the sandy adobe block walls, arched windows and dark wood trim, the Spanish-style structure wasn't what she'd expected at all.

Max got out and came around to her side of the Jeep, opened her door and smiled in at her. "You're going to have the best tamales and salsa you've ever tasted."

For a day that had started with Grace being so nervous, even upset for a while, she now found that she couldn't stop smiling. "Wow, this is beautiful," she said as she stepped out of the Jeep. "You grew up in this house?"

"The one I live in now. We lived there while Dad had this house built for my mother after the ranch started really taking off. My dad had just retired from the rodeo. I was ten or eleven when we moved in just before Christmas one year." Max touched the small of her back. "Let's go inside."

He leaned around her to push open the unlocked door, and as she stepped into the foyer, she half whispered, "Wow!"

HE LOOKED AT HER, at the smile and wide violet eyes, and he thought *Wow*, too. But even *wow* didn't adequately describe Grace Bennet in that moment. He felt some spark in him, and he almost laughed, but couldn't understand it. What he did know was he was kind of relieved his mother wasn't there to read whatever expression was on his face right then. She was way too good at that and inevitably jumped to conclusions.

"I'll start the food," he said, walking through to the great room, which had views of the ranch through a series of sliding glass windows. He led the way to the kitchen, which was the room in the house that got the most use. He'd get their lunch together, then take Grace down to meet Rebel, and concentrate on that and not on his reaction to the woman smiling at him.

"This is quite a setup," Grace said.

He exhaled, figuring it might take time to stop having that reaction when he was looking at Grace. It made no sense. She'd be gone soon, and he'd always be here. That was a deal-breaker. That was reality. His reality.

CHAPTER NINE

GRACE ENJOYED THE food that they heated up, and the company. Max told wonderful stories about the three brothers who wreaked chaos on the ranch. He told her about the pond at the original house in the foothills, about hot summer days spent swimming and exploring. Rodeos held for kids that were as exciting as any professional rodeo. His dad retiring so he could be with his family, and how that had been one of the best days of his life.

As Max gathered up the dirty dishes, he asked Grace, "What was one of the best days of your life so far?"

She had to think, then finally said, "I'm not sure. Those tamales were the best I've ever had, though."

Max loaded the dishwasher, then came back to the table. "Dessert? There are a couple of pieces of my mom's apple pie left."

"No, thanks. I'm stuffed, but happy. So, who is this Rebel person?"

"Let's go find out," he said.

"I want you to know your refusal to give me instant gratification amounts to cruel and unusual punishment."

"Ma'am, I know the law, and I don't agree. It builds character to have to wait for something rather than getting it right away."

"Okay, Sheriff," she said with a smile and went with him back into the foyer to retrieve her jacket and purse.

When they stepped outside, Grace quickly pulled her hat out of her jacket pocket and put it on with the earflaps down, then flipped up her collar. When she looked at Max, he had a smug expression on his face.

"Okay, so you were right about the hat and the collar thing," she said.

"I appreciate you saying that I'm right. In my business I don't hear that very often from the people I'm dealing with."

"I bet you don't. No apologies and no admission that you're right."

He grinned at her, then crossed to the Jeep and opened the passenger door. She followed, expecting to get in and go and meet her uncle's friend, but that wasn't the case.

Max said, "Let's leave your purse here. We're gonna walk."

She hesitated. It held literally all the money she had in the world. If it disappeared, she'd be lost. "I don't know…" she said.

"It'll be there when we get back. If it isn't, I'll give you the money you lost. How about that?"

It wasn't easy for her to just trust what he said, but she could try because it made sense. When it came to Max, she was gradually seeing the man he was, and that included a man with a deep need to help people, and a man who seemed real, not as if he was playing a part like a lot of the men she knew.

She pushed her purse under the seat. Standing back, she said, "I'm anxious to meet Rebel."

"I think you two will get along great. He knew Marty very well. They spent a lot of time together at the Lodge. I promised Marty that I'd find a place for him when Marty was gone. He likes it here, but losing Marty was hard on him."

"They were that close?"

"For almost ten years. We're going to take a shortcut. The ground's rough but it's a lot faster to get to the stable this way."

"I'm open for a walk. It's beautiful."

She was surprised when Max reached out to take her hand and firmly hold it in his. He met her eyes with that twinkle in them that she was beginning to notice gave away when he was joking or teasing.

"I don't want you to fall again," he explained.

She almost made a joke about no brochures and no wooden floors, but instead she let him hold her hand. She kept pace with him as they started across a mown grassy area toward a stand of trees. They walked in silence to the tree line, a mixture of old pines and deciduous growth. Soon, Max veered off to the left where there was a clear path through the stand.

He never let go of her, and she thought that it had been a long time since anyone had held her hand protectively. She liked the connection as they walked together over the ground that was spongy with layers of fallen needles and leaves.

When they cleared the trees, they stepped out into a wide open area. About a hundred feet ahead, she saw the smaller stable they'd passed on the way to the house. Two other buildings looked like double garages and a fourth was more of a lean-to with hay stacked under it. A man was pitching hay from a side pen into the bed of an old truck. When he saw Max and Grace coming toward him, he waved.

"Howdy there!"

His skin was weathered and lined, and she could see snow-white hair poking out from beneath a beat-up old brown Western hat. The hair matched a full beard. His clothes were familiar: boots, jeans and a heavy coat. He could be sixty or eighty, but he looked pretty spry.

Max let go of her hand as he moved closer to the older man. She thought she might be looking at Rebel, until Max said, "Chappy, I thought you were going to visit your brother in California."

So, he wasn't Rebel. With a pitchfork in one hand and the other on the side of the truck bed, he shook his head. "Naw, he's heading down to Mexico to look at some breeding stock, and I had no hankering to go with him."

Max turned and motioned Grace closer to him. "I want you to meet Marty Roberts's niece, Grace Bennet. She's staying out at the Lodge."

The man smiled. "Oh, real nice to meet you, ma'am. I sure was worryin' some idiot would tear it down or let it rot away. My heart'll rest easier knowin' it's not empty no longer."

Grace wasn't going to say anything about selling the Lodge; she couldn't do it. "I really like the Lodge. The setting is just beautiful."

"Marty loved it. He rode around his place all the time." He looked at Max. "What're y'all up to?"

"I wanted Grace to meet Rebel."

He pointed a thumb back over his shoulder. "He's inside being lazy." He shook his head. "He's missing Marty somethin' fierce. We all are, but work don't wait."

"That's for sure." Max motioned Grace toward the open stable doors. Grace walked with him into a ten-stall stable replete with the fragrance of leather and fresh hay in the cold air. Max kept walking to the last stall, which housed a beautiful pinto. The brown-and-black markings on its pure white coat were stunning, and a midnight-black mane and tail set off the coloring.

The horse crossed to the half gate. "Rebel, I brought a visitor. Grace Bennet, Marty's niece."

Grace stared at the man, then the horse. "Rebel?"

As if the animal understood, he tossed his head and whinnied.

Max reached out and stroked his neck. "Yes, this here's Rebel. This guy knows all of Marty's secrets and where he liked to ride. He's a living encyclopedia of knowledge when it comes to Marty Roberts."

A horse was the last thing she'd expected. She stepped closer. "I thought…" She shook her head, then cautiously reached to touch the horse's muzzle. It felt soft and his exhaled breath was warm on her hand. "Uncle Martin gave him to you?"

"I just promised to make sure Rebel always had a good home and was appreciated and treated well. I think, legally, you're his new owner since Marty left everything he had to you."

Rebel moved closer and pressed into her hand. "He's mine?"

"Yep, and he seems to like you." Max moved back a step to give her more room against the stall's wooden rails.

"Oh, my gosh," she breathed as she looked into his soft brown eyes. "I've wished for my own horse for years and years. I mean, since I was old enough to know how to wish."

"He's all yours if you promise to do what

Marty wanted for him, give him a good home and treat him well."

She looked at him and the thought came to her that Max had made her wish come true. After some twenty years, she finally had a horse, a beautiful horse. She'd figure out how to best take care of him back in Tucson. "I promise I'll give him a good home and treat him well."

"Then he's yours."

She was so happy and excited, she had to resist hugging Max. "Thank you," she said. "I wish I could take him with me to the Lodge."

"Why not? The stable there was his home for ten years or more. I'll have it checked out to make sure it and the hay barn are safe to use. The weight of snow can be destructive to old wood. Once we know it's solid, you can take Rebel down there whenever you want to."

This only got better and better. "How long will it take to check it out?"

"A couple of days. But if there's a problem it could be longer before you can take him back there, maybe a week or more. While you wait, you can come up here and ride him around the ranch. Get to know each other."

Now Max was offering his ranch for her

to ride on. "That makes sense, but I wouldn't know where to go for a ride around here."

"Don't worry. Someone'll ride with you at first."

"Would it be okay with you if I came back tomorrow for a short ride just to make sure I remember how to do it? Although I've heard that riding a horse is like riding a bicycle— you never forget after you've learned."

"I guess you'll know if that's true tomorrow. Early morning's best for riding."

What a day, Grace thought as she reluctantly left Rebel with Chappy while she and Max walked back to the house. Max took her hand when they got to the trees, and she cast him a sidelong look. Holding his hand could be addictive, and trusting him was becoming easier and easier. Yet, she barely knew him.

When they got closer to the house, she was prepared to ease out of Max's hold on her, but he beat her to it by abruptly letting go and waving to someone ahead of them. A lady was standing in front of the house, and Grace was pretty sure she was going to meet Max's mother. She was tall and slender, her dark hair streaked with gray and confined in a long braid. She hurried over to them and pulled Max into a hug.

"I'm glad I got back in time to see you today," she said, then turned to Grace.

"Grace, my mom, Ruby Donovan," Max said. "Mom, Grace Bennet, Marty's niece. She's staying at the Lodge."

"Yes, I know. Not that *you* told me about it, Max, but Elaine was by a few days ago and filled me in." Her dark brown eyes went from looking pleased to being touched by sadness. "Grace, I am so sorry about Marty's passing. He was a dear friend of our family. One of the nicest men I've ever met. I'm thankful he had family after all, and you're at the Lodge now."

Grace felt so good at what Ruby Donovan said about her uncle. "I'm glad I came," Grace said truthfully. She never would have known anything about the man who had lived here for so long, and who had made so many dear friends, if she'd done what Walter had ordered her to do that day on the jet.

"Elaine said you weren't sure if you're staying or selling."

"I need to settle my uncle's estate, then I'll figure it out, one way or the other. But even if I do leave, I won't forget where Uncle Martin called home or all the great people I've met."

"I was hoping you'd stay on and possibly

reopen the Lodge, but you have to do what's best for you in the end."

"All I know right now is I want to honor Uncle Martin no matter what I end up doing."

"Thank you for that," Ruby said.

"Oh, and by the way, your tamales are fantastic."

Ruby smiled. "I'm glad you liked them."

Max spoke up. "Mom, Grace is coming over tomorrow to ride Rebel and get used to him before she takes him back with her to the Lodge."

"Well, you come over anytime you want to ride here. You're always welcome, and Rebel needs love," Ruby said.

"I was thinking, when Grace comes to ride, how about you ride with her on Jiggers?" Max suggested. "He could use the exercise, and you could get away from work for a while."

Ruby started to say something but seemed to think better of it. "I would love to," she finally said. "But I can't right now—I'm in the middle of getting the tax papers organized. I'm sure one of the boys would be glad to get a reprieve from painting the grandstand seats."

Ruby walked over with them to the Jeep and Grace decided to ask her something. Stopping by the passenger door, Grace turned to Ruby, very aware of Max standing close by. "Can I ask you something about your son?"

Ruby nodded. "Sure."

Grace leaned closer and whispered, "Did Max get a tattoo while he was in the army?"

Ruby looked surprised before she said, "I don't know. I don't think so... Why?"

"Oh, we were just talking about tattoos, and I didn't quite believe him when he said he didn't have any."

"What are you whispering about?" Max asked as he came closer.

Grace glanced at him. "Does he always hide things?" she asked Ruby, smiling.

He shook his head, a grin teasing his lips. "What things?"

"Tell me honestly, with your mother as a witness. Sheriff 911, do you or do you not have a tattoo?"

Ruby folded her arms and looked at her son. "Well, cows and horses."

Max shook his head. "Oh, no, you don't. I plead the Fifth."

"What's that mean, 'cows and horses'?" Grace asked.

"It's something we did with the kids when we wanted the truth. If we called cows and horses, they had to tell the truth. If they lied, their punishment was to not get to ride for a week or longer. They had to work the cattle for a week instead."

"Oh, interesting," Grace said.

"No, it's not." Max was smiling. "We're leaving."

"Thank you, Mrs. Donovan. And thanks again for the tamales."

Ruby hugged her again and whispered in her ear so only Grace could hear this time. "Thank you for making my Max smile."

That touched her heart. She couldn't imagine a Max who didn't have a smile for people. "Thank *you* for everything," she said, then got into the Jeep. She reached under the seat and the purse was still there. She tugged it out and put it in her lap, then looked at Max as he settled behind the wheel. "You were right again."

He glanced over at her, then down at her purse. "I'm on a roll," he said and with a wave to his mother, he drove around the semicircular drive and back onto the dirt road the way they'd come. At the main gates while they waited for the barriers to swing open, Max asked, "What did Mom say when she hugged you?"

Grace shifted to see him better. She liked the smiling Max. "Tell me the truth about your tattoos. Cows and horses. Now you have to tell me."

"You have that wrong. That's only between my brothers and my parents. Not just anyone can use it."

She waved dismissively. "I'm kidding. Your tattoos are none of my business. I don't care if you have a full-color picture of Santa Claus on your stomach."

"Sure you don't," he murmured and pulled through the gates and headed toward the highway.

"I really don't, but I'd love to hear the story behind your middle names. I remember you told me your full name is Maxim Little-Hawk Donovan."

"Little-Hawk was my grandma Eagan's maiden name. She taught at a rez school south of here. Grandpa was helping repair their small schoolhouse when they met. Her full name was Martha Ray Little-Hawk, and her family was Eastern Shoshone. My mom wanted to keep the names of her ancestors alive, so she gave one to each of us as a middle name."

Now she saw where Max's looks came from, the high cheekbones, the tan skin, and Ruby was tall and slender, so maybe his height came from her, too. "That's a wonderful thing to do for her family."

"At first I hated it," he said as he stopped at the highway. "But I'm pretty proud of it now."

"Proud enough to get tattooed with it?"

He gave a low chuckle and shook his head. "You're relentless, you know that?"

She grinned back at him.

"Now what did Mom say to you back there?" he asked.

"If she wanted you to know, she wouldn't have whispered it to me."

"I'll remember this," he murmured with fake gravity in his tone. "That means I'll never tell you if I have tattoos or not."

They both laughed at that, and as they drove south, Grace couldn't remember any man in her life who was so easy to talk to and laugh with. When the Lodge finally came into sight, she was still smiling. Today had been pretty great, and she owed most of it to Maxim Little-Hawk Donovan.

WHEN THEY ARRIVED at the Lodge, Grace went straight to the office and opened the tall cabinet where the safe was stored. She had to stand on her tiptoes to see the top shelves, and even then she wasn't quite tall enough.

"Barely warm," Max said, going across to her.

Grace looked over her shoulder at him. "It's nice and warm in here."

"But you are barely warm looking for the safe way up there. Clue—it's at eye level, or at least, Marty's eye level."

"I looked there. It's empty."

Max hadn't been in the room since Marty passed, and it seemed almost the same except for the bed, which was decidedly more feminine-looking now with a comforter in shades of blue and lavender. One other thing was the windows were sparkling clean now; all the dust and grime were gone.

Grace said, "This cabinet is empty."

"It's there."

She turned to Max. "It's not. Look for yourself."

"Let me show you how something can disappear then be there again."

"Please do," she said and stepped to one side to give him room.

He could feel her eyes on him as he peered into the cabinet. Marty had done a good job making something that was there appear almost invisible. But he could see it beyond the shelf: a very fine gap existed between the wood at the back and the edges around it.

When he reached in, Grace leaned toward him. "There's nothing there," she said, so close to him now that he felt the heat of her breath brush his cheek.

He pressed a small spot at the back close to the right side where the white paint had been worn away. There was a soft click right before a twelve-by-twelve piece of painted wood swung silently forward to expose a wall safe that looked like an antique. Its burnished brass front had a heavy leverage handle and a combination lock.

Now Grace was leaning against him to get a better look. "I never would have found that." She moved back, put her purse on the kitchen table, and he got out of her way so she could have access to the safe. She reached inside, and he could see her running her fingers over the dial.

Grace turned to him. "I'm almost certain I can open this."

"What are you, a safecracker?" he asked, liking the way she blinked at his ridiculous question.

"Like I'd tell you if I was," she said with an expressive roll of her violet eyes. "I've only opened one before. I was nine years old and with my father at one of his offices. I hated being there and Sawyer knew it, so he gave me a challenge. He said if I could open the safe with one number missing from the combination, he'd give me a prize.

"I did it, after around thirty failed attempts and two clues from Sawyer. Inside it, Sawyer, who obviously knew how to open it, had left me a 1935 first edition of *National Velvet*." Her expression was almost wistful. "He knew I'd love it. I mean, I was obsessed with horses."

"Who was this Sawyer?"

"He was my father's assistant back then, and part of Sawyer's job was to keep me from annoying my father and the rest of the staff."

"That book must have cost a lot of money."

"I never even thought about the money until I was told the book had to be put in some protective display box and not touched by human hands because it was so valuable."

A nine-year-old had a book she was obviously thrilled with, and someone told her not to touch it, to keep it in some sort of protective case? "So you never got to read it?"

"Sawyer told me he'd take care of it for me, but he winked when Walter wasn't looking."

That brought an almost mischievous glint in her eyes. "So, he put it in the box it came in and left with it. When I went to my room, I found it under my pillow and the box was on the top shelf of my bookcase." She giggled at that. "I read all night under my blankets with a flashlight, and most nights from then on. It was wonderful, and I cried and…" She shrugged. "The ending was so bittersweet."

"Who's Walter?"

Her expression changed in a flash from the softness in her eyes at the memory to a faint frown. "Excuse me?"

"You mentioned someone named Walter."

Grace looked away from Max and back to the safe. "Oh, yeah…my father. He was hard to be around." She cut off any other questions he might have asked. "Let me see if I can open this safe." She moved closer and spun the combination dial. Taking a breath, she aligned the mark at the top of the dial with the start arrow, then exhaled. "First number?"

"Twelve," Max said.

She turned the old dial three rotations past the top point and stopped on twelve. "Next?"

"Twenty-two."

For the second number, she went two full turns left and stopped on twenty-two. When

Max gave her the third number, she went one full rotation right and stopped at the number. "Okay, here it goes," she murmured.

Her hand was a bit unsteady as she reached for the brass lever by the dial and pulled it down. Nothing happened.

"Shoot," she muttered and spun the dial.

She tried again, and she echoed each number under her breath as she lined them up. The lever didn't move.

"You're sure that's the right combination?" she asked over her shoulder, her eyes fixed on the dial as she repeated the number Max had told her.

"I'm sure."

"Okay, old dials can shift from use. Let me try it one more time." She repeated the combination out loud as she turned the dial, then whispered when she stopped at the last number, "It can't be."

It had hit her suddenly: the combination was the same as her birth date. She didn't believe much in coincidences, but it had to be a coincidence in this case. Her uncle wouldn't know her birthday. Then she knew he had known. "The picture."

Max was quiet, probably thinking she was losing it, and maybe she was. She touched the lever, then tugged down on it hard. There was a click, then the safe silently swung open. Just three tries, but she didn't feel victorious. Uncle Martin had known her birthday, used it for the combination yet never tried to contact her. She felt as empty as the safe looked inside.

When she turned to Max he seemed uncertain. "I thought you'd be happy you conquered the safe," he said.

"Oh, I am. I'm just overwhelmed. I want to lock the money up and figure things out from there."

Max leaned over, picked up her purse and held it out to her. "Here you go."

She took it, reached in for the bank pouch, then dropped her purse to the floor. She opened the pouch to remove a thin stack of bills that she'd had Bert separate from the other thicker stacks. She handed it to Max.

"That's Henry's money and your money." Then she turned and closed the pouch with the rest of the money and put it in the safe.

She almost closed the door but stopped when she realized something was already there, lying at the bottom almost out of sight. She took out a single blue envelope that was identical to the other two Burr had passed out. The same unsteady hand that had written her name on the first envelope had written *"Leave in safe for Grace"* on this one. She shut the door, then spun the dial before she held her find up for Max to see.

"Just one this time," she said, then reached to lay the envelope on the table. "Thanks again for all you've done for me, Max, and thanks for taking me to meet Rebel and trusting me with him." She knew she was starting to babble, and she stopped herself then added, "Let me know when I can get him down here."

"Of course."

She moved past him toward the door. She didn't want to be in the room any longer. She needed to breathe and digest what had just happened.

When she'd passed through the reception space, she went into the great room and sank down onto the couch. Max came to stand between her and the fireplace. She looked up at him when he spoke. "I wasn't going to say anything, but... I need to."

She hoped it wasn't about the new letter she'd found. "What is it?"

He sat down next to her and shifted to meet her eyes. "What happened in there when you were opening the safe?"

She wasn't actually surprised that he'd noticed the moment she'd recognized the combination. She wanted to tell him nothing had happened, but she couldn't because he might have answers for her. "You're too good at your work, Sheriff," she said.

"What does that mean?"

She shrugged. "I'd hoped you didn't notice, but you obviously picked up on the fact that something surprised me or bothered me."

"So what surprised you or bothered you?" he asked patiently.

"The combination to the safe. I recognized it." She reached for the original envelope she'd received from Burr that she'd left on the coffee table. Fumbling, she took out the small picture and, ignoring the unsteadiness in her hand, offered it to Max. "Look on the back," she said once he took it.

He turned it over, and she caught the moment he realized what the numbers on the back were. He took another look at the picture, then his eyes lifted to hers. "It's your birth date?"

"It is. He knew it when he set the safe's combination." She bit her lip, then said, "You knew him. Tell me why he'd do that and never try to meet me in person."

"I honestly don't know." He looked more closely at the picture. "These are your parents?"

"Yes, at my sixth birthday party when I'd wished for a horse, and I got a fashion doll modeled after my mother."

When he lowered his gaze again to the picture, she knew what he was probably thinking: that no one was smiling, especially not the birthday girl.

"Where was it taken?"

"At a restaurant on the top level of…a hotel in Las Vegas."

He handed the picture back to her and she slipped it into the envelope. "I want to show you a picture I have," he said and undid his jacket to get to his jeans back pocket. He took out a tooled leather wallet, flipped it open and handed it to Grace. "It's from five years ago, the day we finished the extension on the back deck. Chappy took it."

Grace looked down at a five-years-younger version of Max in the photo, with longer hair and a grin on his face. Then she saw Uncle Martin, who looked very much like Walter, but more tanned, with more gray hair. Where Walter was very refined, his brother was rougher looking wearing a red plaid shirt and jeans, and he was grinning like Max. Only five years ago he'd looked healthy and strong. Then she realized she'd never asked what illness he had.

"What did he die from? No one's said."

Max hesitated, then exhaled as he took off his hat and laid it between them. "Kidney failure. He'd had problems off and on, then it got worse."

"He wasn't…you know…alone, was he?"

"No, I was with him, and Burr and Elaine were there. Most of the town had visited him over his last week. He knew he was loved, and he was peaceful."

She closed her eyes. "I should have been there," she said.

She was startled when she felt Max touch her cheek for a fleeting moment. "Don't do that to yourself. That's a black hole that is hard to climb out of. Marty had an easy heart."

"An easy heart," she whispered, wishing her heart didn't ache. She felt overwhelmed by everything. The world was unpredictable, and she was exhausted. She had to open the second letter, but she had to do it alone in case she bawled like she had after she read the first one. She cleared her throat with a soft cough, then looked at Max. "Thanks for showing me that picture. He…he looks a lot like his brother.

Now, you should go and take what's left of your day off to do something for yourself for a change."

He glanced at his watch, then said, "I need to check in with Lillian before I head home."

"Don't waste any more of your free time."

He stayed seated. "One thing you'll learn about me is I only waste my time when I want to."

She felt drained. "I'm just really tired."

He put his wallet in his jacket pocket. "I wish I had answers for you about Marty. But just know that he always had a reason for what he did."

By that logic, Grace felt even worse. Then she remembered the anger in Walter when he'd spoken about his brother. Maybe he didn't make any contact because he wouldn't face his brother again. No matter why he did what he did, it was over.

"Even if I had answers, it wouldn't change the past," she said softly.

CHAPTER TEN

MAX KNEW HOW true her words were. The past was done. It never changed. There was no way to edit anything. And he could see how much it bothered Grace to not understand why Marty had done what he'd done. He couldn't give her answers to her questions, just guesses.

"If you'd like, I can change the combination on the safe or find someone to do it."

"No, thanks. It is what it is."

"Maybe an early night will help."

"Maybe so," she said on a heavy sigh.

He almost told her he'd make tea, but he knew she wanted him to leave. She was too polite to tell him to go away. He'd promised Marty to help Grace, not smother her. He eased to his feet and put his hat back on. "I'll be heading out."

Grace stayed sitting as she crooked her neck to look up at him. "Max? Can I ask you something? If it's too personal, I understand completely, but I was wondering if Uncle Martin mentioned me at all in the letter he left for you."

He didn't know what answer she wanted: that he'd mentioned her, or that he didn't mention her at all. Then he thought of one mention that he should have told her on the way back from the ranch. "Yes, he did. He wanted me to make sure you got Rebel, if you really wanted him. A cowboy always takes better care of his horse than himself, and he always took great care of Rebel."

That seemed to distract her. "Cowboy? Uncle Martin?"

He liked the idea that her emotions were so easy to read. Happiness when she found out about Rebel. Surprise, happiness, a bit of sadness having to leave him there, and now, disbelief that her uncle would be considered a cowboy.

"You didn't think Marty was a cowboy out here?"

"I thought he did all of this. I never thought he'd have time to do cowboy things."

He chuckled at that. "What do you consider cowboy things?"

"You know, taking care of cows and horses and plowing."

"He didn't own any cows, but he plowed

and cleared land, and he rode Rebel every chance he got. He loved riding."

"I've always loved the idea of a horse, and when you're young anything seems possible. It didn't matter that I lived in a hotel suite." Thankfully, she was almost smiling now, even if her voice was tinged with sarcasm when she said, "I would have settled for a stuffed horse."

"You finally have a horse."

She stood slowly and looked up at him. "Because of you," she said and unexpectedly reached out and hugged him.

He froze for a second, and when he finally realized he wanted to hug her back, she was moving away. "What was that for?"

She actually blushed. "I'm just happy and you made it happen. I can't wait for tomorrow to go to your ranch to ride him."

What he needed right then was to leave, to go out into the cold air and think straight. To be a friend to Grace was his goal, but he wasn't stepping over the line. He was there to try to show her the Lodge as Marty saw it; with the hope she'd end up staying. He knew the odds of that happening were low to nonexistent.

"Get some rest and come by in the morning when you're ready to ride."

Grace followed him, talking quickly. "I can go down and check out the stable. I saw it, and it looks okay, I mean, old and weathered, but it's not tipping to one side, and I didn't notice any holes in the roof."

He got to the front door and reached for the handle but paused before he opened it. "I'll be in touch as soon as Chappy checks it out."

"I just don't want to be a bother," she said.

She wasn't a bother—only when she hesitated every time he offered to help and called herself a bother. He wouldn't do that again, unless it was really important. He'd figured out that she didn't like feeling as if she wasn't in control. "You have my number," he said.

"Max, I finally have an answer to your question about the best day of my life."

"What was it?"

"Today was the best day of my life."

He was speechless. "Good…good, I'm glad," he said, feeling as awkward as a teenager. He quickly opened the door and headed out to his truck.

Between the hug and what she'd just told him, he felt confused as he took deep breaths, then got behind the wheel of the pickup. He figured Grace was kind of a spontaneous person, and that was why she'd hugged him. It was that simple. What wasn't so simple was his confusion when she'd smiled at him and said she'd just had the best day of her life. What stunned him even more was the day he'd spent with her was now in the running to be the best day of his life, also.

GRACE WAS UP most of the night thinking about the second letter. As dawn broke, she sat in the big chair looking out at the coming day. Finally, she retrieved the envelope and opened it when she sat down in the chair again. It contained a single sheet of paper with only one side written on.

She took a couple of breaths, then read the unsteady script.

Dear Grace,
You have found the safe and been given the combination. Hopefully Max gave it to you. I wanted to let you know that every time I opened it, I thought of you and I smiled. Life sorts out in odd ways, but there is always a plan, a reason for everything. I found that out the hard way, but I hope you're a better student of patience and fate than I've ever been. But at the end, all fell into place, and

I saw how perfect a life I'd had, that the peace I'd hoped for became a reality. Don't give up, never stop, and know that you became a very important person in my life even though I couldn't be with you. I hope you'll forgive me for my choices if they hurt you but know that I always loved you.

The tears were soft and not harsh and cutting, the way they'd been after the first note.

"I could have loved you, Uncle Martin," she whispered into the air. "I could have been with you when you needed me." She blew out air and swiped at her eyes. All she could do for her uncle was to make sure nothing he left was destroyed. This wasn't about her anymore, but all about Martin Robert Bennet's legacy.

She stood and hurried to get dressed for the ride. As she pulled on her new thermal boots, she looked up at the ceiling and said, "Thank you for Rebel, Uncle Martin. I love him." For some reason she felt her uncle would know that, and she actually smiled.

Dressed for the cold, she pulled on her hat and felt almost giddy, like her nine-year-old self had felt when she'd conquered her fear and found that being high in the saddle on an old brown horse at the camp was about the best thing she'd ever known back then.

She stepped outside into a deep chill in the air. Hurrying down the steps to the Jeep, she stopped when she saw a red pickup truck coming up the driveway. She couldn't see the driver until the truck slowed at the curve and came to stop at the foot of the steps. The window slid down and Chappy smiled out at her.

"Mornin', Miss Grace. I come to check out the stable and hay barn for Max."

"Oh, thank you so much."

"No need for thanks. Are you taking off?"

"I was going to drive up to Flaming Sky and ride Rebel so he can get used to me."

"That's aces. I'll take care of everything here."

"Is Max still there?"

"I don't think he got back last night. But Ruby's there. She'll let you in. We'll get Rebel back home as soon as we can." With that, he drove off toward the gravel access road beyond the end of the Lodge and headed down to the stables.

Grace climbed in the Jeep and went in the opposite direction to the gates.

When she arrived at the entrance for Flaming Sky, someone buzzed her in, and she continued to drive up to the main house. She parked in the driveway in the same spot Max had parked the day before; no other vehicles were in sight. Before she even got out of her Jeep, she heard an engine getting louder. Then the county sheriff's truck came into view. She had been excited before, but now she felt downright elated.

Max pulled up beside her Jeep and the passenger window slid down.

"Come on, get in," he called out to her.

She did as he said, closing the truck door before she turned to look at him. "I didn't expect to see you here. I thought you'd be on your way to work."

"I have to go down to headquarters at Two Horns to have a one-on-one with the fiscal adviser for the county about expanding the size of the substations. But I have some time before I need to leave. I thought I'd go with you for a short ride and see how you and Rebel do together, then head south."

That was perfect. She'd been worried about riding with a stranger when she didn't even know if she could get up in the saddle by herself. "If you can, that would be great."

"Aces," he said and drove around the top

of the half circle and back onto the dirt road. When they neared the smaller family stable, he kept going. Before she could point out the obvious, Max said, "Rebel's down at the main stables being checked out. He had a tender foot when he came up here from Marty's. He's been fine, but I figured checking it before we left wouldn't hurt."

"He's okay, though, right?"

"Sure, he's good. Chappy asked one of the hired hands to saddle him and Thunder up since I don't have a great amount of time."

She sank back in the seat. "Thunder?"

"My horse. I've had him going on six years. When Marty and I rode, he and Rebel got along just fine."

"Friends, huh?"

"I don't know if that's what you'd call them, but they never got snippy with each other or acted up when they were together."

They came to the main drive and Max turned left toward the busy part of the ranch, where all kinds of activity were taking place around the stable. Horses were being led toward the arena, and several trucks were parked in the area.

Max came to a stop near the open double doors and glanced over at Grace, who was trying to take everything in. Red, white and blue bunting hung from the fascia of the stable, giving it a festive feel. "We'll leave the truck here for now."

No sooner had they stepped out than a man called out, "Max! Perfect timing."

Grace looked in the direction of the voice to see a tall man with longish graying dark brown hair showing under a white Western hat striding toward them from the stable doors. His broad shoulders tested the fringed suede jacket he was wearing, and he looked as if he was used to hard work. When he smiled, Grace knew without Max having to introduce him to her that the man was his father. They were so much alike, from the long strides to the strong build and sharp features. Then as he came closer, she saw hazel eyes that mirrored Max's. She figured she was seeing how Max would look in thirty-plus years.

Max moved over to Grace by the truck. "Hey, Dad, I want you to meet Marty's niece, Grace Bennet, all the way from Arizona. Grace, my dad, Dash Donovan."

He stopped in front of them, touched the brim of his hat and his smile really did remind her of Max. "Right pleased to meet you, Grace."

"Nice to meet you, Mr. Donovan," she said.

"Around here, I'm either Dad to my three sons, or recently Papa to my new granddaughter. I'm Dash to everyone else. No formalities, okay?"

"Dash it is."

"I thought you were going back up to Cody, Dad."

"The contracts are signed. Burgess was generous this year and signed right away."

"Good for you." Max seemed impressed. "We're going riding. Do you have time to come along?"

"Oh, son, I wish I could, but I've got a lot of prep to do for the rodeo," he said on a rough chuckle, then nodded to the two of them. "Ride safe," he said before heading off.

Max touched Grace's arm to urge her toward the stable doors. When they stepped inside, Grace realized it wasn't just a stable. There was a large indoor training ring that took up one full half of the space, with seating on the outside of the low wall that ran around it. The other half of the structure was taken up by stalls.

Grace spotted Rebel right away, saddled and ready to ride, standing with a second horse at the hitching rail by the training ring gates. The other horse was waiting patiently. Its coat was unique, at least to her—a pale gold color set off by a deep brown mane and tail, along with identical stockings on all four legs.

"Hey, Chance," Max said to the man standing beside Rebel. "Thanks for saddling them up for us."

Chance was short and stocky with smears of white paint on his jeans, khaki jacket and worn work boots. "Chappy asked me to do it, and I was stoked to get a break from painting the bleacher seats." He glanced at Grace and smiled. "Howdy, ma'am," he said.

Max made the introductions. "Chance, Grace Bennet, Marty Roberts's niece from the Lodge."

"My, my, my," the man said. "I'm right honored to finally meet Marty's family and know Rebel can go back home. He's been grieving hard over Marty's passin'."

Grace turned toward Rebel, her eyes starting to burn with tears that she didn't want to show up right then. "Can I take him now?" she asked, thankful her voice didn't betray the crushing sadness she was feeling. She thought it was Max who handed her the reins, but she didn't turn toward him. "Thank you," she said and led the horse toward the open doors to get outside.

Max followed with Thunder and stopped

beside her. "Do you need help getting in the saddle?"

"No," she said as she turned to Rebel.

Grab the saddle horn, then get my left foot in the stirrup and pull hard and push with my right foot.

In her thoughts that sounded so simple, but when she was actually positioned for what she hoped would be a successful mount, it eluded her. She pulled but couldn't find the leverage to get even close to sitting on the horse's back. Rebel was patient, and Max wasn't rushing in to boost her into position.

All he said was, "Grip the saddle horn with your left hand, the back of the saddle with your right, then push off with your right leg." After two attempts, she was safely on Rebel's back. She exhaled with relief. "This is higher than I remembered."

"Don't worry about that. Look up and around and enjoy the view. You'll do just fine."

Grace looked away when a slow smile touched his lips. Max Donovan was a man she was starting to like being in her life, a man who she figured would make a very good friend. She could use that while she was here. But she knew that depending on others had cost her with her father, maybe even with

her mother. She took a deep breath of cold air
and tried to clear her mind so she could concentrate on riding.

IT WAS A peaceful ride for Max, enjoying Grace
taking it all in and talking to Rebel as if he was
going to answer her. That further cemented in
him the feeling that he'd done the right thing
by giving the horse to Grace. As they neared
the foot of the switchback that led up to the
original ranch house on Donovan land, his cell
rang to let him know he was needed at headquarters as soon as possible. They rode at a
faster pace coming back to the stables, and
Grace was able to keep up.

After asking Chance to look after the horses,
he drove Grace back to the house so she could
get her Jeep, and Max let the truck idle while
Grace was getting out.

She turned to look back in at him. "I can't
believe how much I remembered once I was
up in the saddle."

"You did a good job with Rebel," he said.
"I'll see you later."

"Okay," she said, then reached to close the
door, but stopped. "Max?" He glanced back
at Grace who met his gaze. When she spoke

again, he almost lost his breath. "I think I'm falling in love."

That blindsided him, and he tried to figure out what to say, but Grace threw him a lifeline.

"I just feel as if I've known Rebel forever. Silly, I know, but he's so great. I can't tell you how much I wish… I'd come here before. I wish…" She shook her head. "I wish I could tell Uncle Martin that I love Rebel."

She was talking about the horse, and he'd immediately thought she was talking about him. That was ridiculous. He managed to say, "I think it's mutual."

She smiled at him. "I hope so."

She swung the door shut and he drove off around the curve in the drive to get back onto the road to the gates.

CHAPTER ELEVEN

WHEN GRACE GOT near to the Lodge, she didn't slow down, but kept going to town. The day had been perfect so far, and she'd meant it about loving Rebel. Without a thought, she'd told Max the truth; a man she barely knew was the one person who would understand her instantaneous connection with the horse. He'd looked surprised when she'd said it out loud, and then he'd hurried away to get to his meeting. She understood: he was in work mode. But she was glad he'd been there for her first ride even though it was cut short.

She wanted some really great riding boots and remembered a pair she'd passed over the first time at Farley's. They were a deep mahogany leather with silver studs and images of shooting stars tooled into the sides. Farley had told her they were about the best boots she could buy for warmth and riding. She was going back to try them on and hoped they'd fit.

After she'd parked in front of the general store, she hurried inside. Farley was right there to greet her, talking nonstop while she tried on the boots. She left the store wearing them and had to admit they were incredibly comfortable. Her other boots were in a bag along with a couple of flannel shirts and more heavy socks. As she was putting the bag inside her Jeep, her phone chimed, but she didn't recognize the number except for the area code being local.

She answered and a lady's voice asked, "Ms. Bennet?"

"Yes, this is Grace Bennet."

She was surprised when the caller introduced herself. "Lillian Shaw. I work at the substation in Eclipse with Sheriff Donovan. Would it be all right if I came up to the Lodge to talk to you about something important?"

"Sure, of course." Her imagination went to the worst reason the woman would want to talk to her, that Max had been hurt or... She stopped right there. "I'm in town now at the general store."

"Perfect. Do you know where the substation is?"

"Yes, I do."

"Do you want to just meet me there instead?"

"Sure," Grace said. "I'll be there in ten."

Grace left the Jeep by the store and walked to the station. When she stepped inside the door, she came face-to-face with Lillian Shaw. From what she'd heard about Lillian, she'd expected a bigger woman, stern and firm in her duty. Instead, the lady who stood behind a large desk was barely five feet tall, with graying brown hair in a tight knot, wearing a neat uniform shirt and sharply creased black slacks. She smiled warmly at Grace, motioning her to a wooden chair in front of a section of the front desk that formed an L-shaped workspace.

"Thank you so much for coming here. Please sit down."

Grace fumbled with her jacket buttons, feeling a bit warm after the brisk walk to get there, then took off her hat and pushed it into her pocket. She didn't wait to ask, "Is something wrong with Max… Sheriff Donovan?"

"Oh, no! I'm sorry, I guess it might have sounded like that. I apologize, dear. He's in Two Horns at a meeting."

She didn't try to hide her relief while she wished her imagination didn't always go to the worst scenario first. "That's great," she said. "Now, why *am* I here?"

"I need to ask you one thing before I explain that to you."

"What thing?"

"I know the sheriff trusted your uncle implicitly and from what he's told me about you, you're a lot like Marty. I need to trust you to keep what I'm going to say between the two of us."

She had no idea what this was about, but if Max trusted Lillian so much, she would, too. "You have my word."

"Thank you," Lillian said. "This is the thing. That so-called meeting at headquarters turned out to be a meeting with internal affairs at the request of one of the citizens in town. They sucker punched Max with a complaint against him brought by a concerned citizen." She put air quotes around *concerned citizen.* "The man claimed Max was repeatedly squandering county money during work hours on personal business. He requested an investigation. He never mentioned you by name, but insinuated enough so anyone would assume his personal business was with you."

Grace was dumbfounded. "Was the man serious? I've been here mere days, and all I've seen is Max working all the time and helping people. Why would the man do that to Max?"

"Bluntly put, Albert Van Duren is running against Max to be sheriff, and he's trying to stir the pot any way he can to beat Max in the vote."

She understood why Lillian was speaking to her about it. "Max told me about Mr. Van Duren being sheriff for a long time and how he wanted to be back in office."

"Albert is what I call a snake in these parts, a truly low human being even if he was sheriff once. He wants to win, and the trend around here leans toward Max. I guess he's going into full gear now there's only a few weeks left before the election. It's two Tuesdays after Thanksgiving, you know. Albert's claiming Max is tarnishing the office and that he's making overworked deputies cover his shifts while he's off having fun with a new resident."

"Wow," she whispered.

"Yes, that's how I felt when I got the call from a friend who was there. Albert knows Max is relatively young, and there are pretty women around. Some men can get lost that way, but he's not on the prowl. He almost got married a few years ago but it blew up in his face and he's pretty much all about his family and work now. And he's darn good at what he does. But if people get the wrong idea, they can go after you. We have our jerks around here, and Albert seems to cultivate that circle of townsfolk."

"That's horrible. There's nothing between…" She stopped herself when it occurred to her that someone thinking that something was going on between her and Max wouldn't be that far off the mark. "I'm so sorry. I knew he was helping me, but it took time away from his family, not his job. That's garbage. What can I do to stop this?"

"Be careful if you're approached by some good old boy who tries to pump you for information. These people tend to show up at a few town locations—the diner, the general store, any rodeo-linked event, the Golden Fleece Saloon, the One Q-Ball Pool Hall. If you're ever at one of those places and someone starts talking about politics, don't take the bait."

"Everyone around here seems so kind and neighborly. I could tell them how great Max is, and how kind he's been to me, but I won't even say that, if you don't think I should."

Lillian smiled. "You shouldn't. Thank you so much for coming over and understanding the situation. Max didn't seem to think it was going to be an issue, but I'm afraid he's wrong. The truth is Max has been kind of like a son for me and Clint, my husband. I've seen him graduate from high school, go on the rodeo circuit, then to the army. He came back home six years ago and fit right in with this job. He's had a few rough patches here over the years, but he's solid."

"I know how solid he is. Thank you so much for the warning."

Lillian glanced past her, then said quickly, "Max is coming. He can't know we had this talk. He'd be embarrassed."

"I don't know what you're speaking about, Ms. Shaw."

The older woman smiled conspiratorially. "Call me Lillian, please."

Max pushed the door open and stepped inside, turned, and saw the two women. "Is this business?" he asked. "Grace, you didn't have trouble, did you?"

She could smile easily about that question. "No, I… I came to meet this Lillian person you talk about so much, and we got to chatting, and…" She glanced back at Lillian. "I'm sorry I took up so much of your time, but I'm glad I got the chance to meet you. Well, I should get on the road."

When she looked back at Max, he had his jacket off and had hung it on a hook on the wall by the door. His hat, too.

She would have loved to have lunch with Max if he asked. She was starving, but she figured the diner wasn't a good place for her to be seen with him right now.

"How did your meeting go?" she asked.

"It went. They refused our request for funding to expand the space in county substations. It was my third try, but I don't give up easily."

She looked around the long narrow space that served as the sheriff's office in the town. From what she could see over a half wall that separated the reception area from the business area, they could have doubled its square footage and it still wouldn't be enough.

"Can you put it on the ballot?"

He shrugged. "I think that's my next step, but I wanted to save the expense of a special election."

"Yes, of course," she said. "I should get back. Chappy was there when I left for the ride."

"Maybe I'll stop by and see what he's done."

"You don't have to. I know you're busy."

He narrowed his eyes slightly but didn't answer.

Lillian stepped in. "Not so fast, cowboy. For

now you're needed at the Grange Hall to talk about security. They're opening soon and need things to be signed off." She looked at Grace. "You come on back anytime, Miss Grace."

"I will," she said, pleased to find another resident who called her Miss Grace as if she actually belonged. She liked it. Then, as she stepped back to leave, she saw a stack of election signs leaning against the wall. Her first impulse was to ask for a few to put up at the Lodge entry, but that probably wasn't a good idea, either.

With a glance at Max, she left and walked back to the Jeep. Just when she was getting used to him and was actually starting to trust him and his motives, she had to stop being seen with him in public. Maybe the Lodge would be safe ground, and the Flaming Sky would be safe, too. But even then someone could pull up and see his truck parked at the Lodge or her Jeep at the ranch.

She smiled ruefully at the way things had to be from now on. Clandestine meetings between the newcomer and the handsome sheriff, planned impeccably to never be seen together. At any other time she would have laughed out loud at her thoughts, but not then. She'd just left Max at his office, and she already hated the thought of eating lunch alone.

She had just parked in front of the Lodge when a text came in. After turning the Jeep off, she got out her phone and saw it was from Max.

Chappy says weak cross beams need to be reinforced before heavy snow. Water line needs replacing and insulation. A couple of days if supplies are available locally. Could be a week, possibly two, if they have to be brought in.

She had enough to do around the Lodge, so a couple of weeks wouldn't be lost time. She sent a text back.

Thank Chappy for me. I'll be at Flaming Sky early tomorrow to ride Rebel again. Thanks for going with me today.

She waited for a response, but as the Jeep got colder and no text came back, she gave up and went inside. Max was probably at the Grange Hall, whatever and wherever that was, doing his job.

MAX WAS IN no mood to see Big and Little Albert at the Grange putting in their two cents on how security at the event hall should be set up. He looked down the long expanse of the narrow building, which had all recently been redone, from the newly painted dark beams overhead to the wood plank flooring underfoot. A food area was off to one side, a bar to the other, and in between were tables arranged in a ring around a greatly expanded dancing area. With a stage for live bands and caged lamps providing the lighting, it looked nothing like the old building had before.

The new owners were overseeing the final touches and doing potential employee interviews. Max was stuck at a large table by the bar across from the two Van Durens, Big and Little Albert. There were no overt mentions of that morning's meeting, just sly digs here and there at Max.

"A little late for this meeting, too," Big Albert said when he arrived.

His laboriously irritating son nodded in agreement. "Time's money, you know."

Yeah, Max knew, and he wasn't going to rise to the bait dangled in front of him. He turned to the owner, Preston Clayton, the great-great-grandson of the first Clayton to have settled in the area. The middle-aged man had the build of a former bull rider and the patience of a saint, until he was crossed. Max had suggested that they didn't need heavy security every minute they were open if Preston was around. He was a deterrent just by his size.

"Yeah, you're right. I'll be dogging people," Pres said.

"The only other thing is you might want to have someone monitoring the cameras during your busiest hours to stop things before they can escalate."

"I'd say that's a good idea."

"Maybe rethink that, Pres," Big Albert interjected. "I've done a lot of security layouts, and it's wasting money paying someone to sit for hours watching the cameras."

Max shrugged. "That's up to you, Pres. You're smart and I'm leaving. If you need anything else, you know where to find me."

"Where would that be, Max?" Big Albert asked and Little Albert smirked. "Just north of town?"

He'd have to be foolish not to catch the meaning in that jab, but he simply stood, held out his hand to Pres to shake, then with a touch to the brim of his hat, headed to the door and outside. The sky was gray, and he could almost smell snow in the air. Once he was in his truck, he drove to town. He didn't know where he was going until he passed the substation and kept driving until he was out of Eclipse and approaching the Lodge.

He turned off the highway onto the cobbled area that led up to the gates. After putting in the code, he drove to park by Grace's Jeep. Once out, he took the steps two at time onto the porch, then crossed to knock on the door. There was no reply and he rapped again. Finally he heard something inside and the door swung back to show Grace facing him.

"Oh, Max, I didn't expect you to come here. Is there a problem?"

"Does there have to be trouble for me to stop by?"

"No, of course not," she said, but he sensed she was uncomfortable with him showing up unannounced.

"Are you okay?"

"Sure, just a bit sore from riding today. But I'm going to stand under a hot shower before bed and hope my muscles relax."

There was something different about Grace that hadn't been there that morning. He'd noticed it at the substation, and now he really felt her backing off for some reason.

"Good. Keep riding and that should clear up pretty soon. You just have to get through it."

"I had no idea that I'd have to suffer to ride, but I'll do it."

"You're a real champ."

She chuckled at that. "No, but now that I finally have my own horse, I'm not going to let anything stop me from riding. Did you need something?"

"Can I come in for minute?"

She hesitated, but said, "Of course. I'm sorry."

She closed the door after Max stepped inside. He took off his jacket, tossed it on the desk, then did the same with his hat. When he turned, Grace was close and the ease he'd felt with her, riding or driving or just talking, seemed to be fading.

"Do…do you want to sit by the fire and warm up?"

"I could use the heat," he said, and she led the way.

They settled on the couch and the fire did feel good. "I was on my way home and stopped to tell you there's a storm coming soon. The clouds are dark and angry and the air smells of snow."

She curled her legs under herself and sank back into the soft leather. "You can *smell* snow?"

"The air's different and the cold's sharper. Just wanted to make sure you're prepared for it."

"If it snows, can I still ride Rebel?"

"You shouldn't until you're more seasoned with him. If you went off alone, it could be a mistake."

His phone rang in the pocket of his jacket out in the reception area. "I'll be right back," he said, then went to answer the call.

GRACE KNEW SHE shouldn't have asked him in, but she wanted to. And it was a safe space. No one would know he was here. Maybe she could ask him to stay for a late lunch or an early dinner, so she wouldn't be eating alone. She glanced through the archway and saw him leaning back against the desk, intent on his conversation, then he stopped the call and came back into the great room.

"That was Lillian. Her husband Clint's sick with food poisoning. He ate something on a trip out of town and barely made it home. She needs to be with him, so I've got to get to the substation as soon as possible to cover for her until nine."

There was no point in asking if he wanted to eat with her. "Seems like you work all the time," she said.

"It feels that way to me, too, sometimes."

He went back to get his jacket and hat, then turned at the door before he left. "I'll see you when I see you," he said, then was gone.

As soon as the sound of the truck engine had faded into the distance, Grace felt the emptiness settle around her.

CHAPTER TWELVE

AFTER MAX LEFT, Grace started reading through ledgers that she'd found in her uncle's office space. She learned that the Lodge had brought in some good capital over the years, until eighteen months ago when the money began to dwindle down until the entries stopped.

She glanced out the back windows and decided she didn't want to eat her dinner alone in front of the hearth. Eclipse might be a small town, but she was almost sure that it wouldn't be a scandal for a single lady to be seen eating by herself at the diner. She bundled up, then grabbed her shoulder bag and car keys, and hurried out to the Jeep.

When she walked into the diner, the door had barely shut behind her before Elaine called out, "Hey there, Miss Grace!" and hurried over to meet her at the end of the counter. The diner was half-full, with people talking and laughing and country music playing in the background. The effect was very welcoming.

"Any special seat that you'd like?" Elaine asked.

Grace glanced at the booth she'd shared with Max, but a couple with a baby were seated there. "How about the counter, if that's okay?"

"Sure thing. Choose your stool," Elaine said.

Grace took one close to the door and swiveled to face Elaine, who had gone behind the red Formica counter and offered her a menu. The minute she saw the picture of the French dip sandwich, she knew what she wanted. But before she could order, a phone rang and Elaine went to pick it up at the end of the counter.

Grace smiled to herself when Elaine answered with, "It's a beautiful evening at the Over the Moon Diner. How can I make you smile?" She liked Elaine.

Then she heard the restaurant owner say, "Oh, I can't. I'm short-staffed. Maybe if it slows down in a bit, the cook could run something over for you." She paused. "I'll make it happen," she said and put the phone down before she came back to Grace. "Poor Max is covering for Lillian. Her husband got awful food poisoning and Lillian's at the clinic with him. Max is stuck at the station and starving, apparently."

Grace changed her idea about dinner right then. Max had brought her groceries when she was hungry, and she'd bring him dinner tonight. She owed him that much. "What's Max's favorite thing to order here?" she asked, leaning closer and lowering her voice some.

"That's easy. My beef stew, fresh rolls, cookies and coffee."

She lowered her voice more. "Okay. I'd like to order that and a French dip with fries for me. I'll deliver Max's dinner to him, but this has to stay between us."

That moment might have been the first time Grace had seen Elaine frown. "Oh, no. You heard about the meeting, didn't you? I swear that Albert is a miserable excuse for a human being. He thinks he's so smooth, but I heard he insinuated that you were involved with Max."

She nodded. "I don't know much about it, but I think Max deserves a good meal. I just don't want to make things worse for him in any way. He's been nothing but good to me."

Elaine leaned a bit closer, and her voice was only loud enough for Grace to hear. "I understand. Don't say any more. So, when you deliver Max's meal, park in the back lot off the side street, not in front. Use the back door. I'll let Max know he'll have a delivery soon, but I won't mention who's doing it."

This was getting really clandestine.

"Thank you so much."

"I'll get your orders. Give me a few minutes."

When Grace pulled into the back parking lot to the substation fifteen minutes later, there was only faint light coming from two back windows on either side of a low porch at the back door. Picking up the bag for Max and one of the coffees, she quickly got out and hurried over to the porch. Taking the single step up, she knocked on the door. At the same time a bright light came on outside, lighting up the whole area. It almost blinded her. She was tempted to leave the dinner on the porch and take off. But a bolt slid back, then the door swung open to reveal Max standing there.

"Grace. You…?"

"Delivery from the diner for Sheriff 911," she said.

He smiled at that. "You moonlighting for a delivery service now?"

"I offered to drop off food for you on my way

back to the Lodge." She held out the bag and his coffee cup, anxious to get it over with and out of the light. She obviously wasn't meant to ever have a career in undercover work. "Beef stew dinner with hot coffee."

He took his order from her. "Come on in out of the cold."

"Thanks, but no. You…have a good dinner and stay warm," she said and turned to leave, but Max stopped her.

"Hey, it's warm in here, and honestly, I could use the company."

"Oh, I don't know… It's, well…" She couldn't stand there much longer and hope not to be seen. "I… Sure, okay," she said. "I need to get my food out of the Jeep."

"You didn't eat at the diner?"

"No, I decided to do takeout."

"Great," he said and handed his order back to her. "I'll get yours from the Jeep and you put mine on Lillian's desk."

She'd hated him giving her orders when they'd first met, but now she was more than willing to take them and get inside. She stepped into a back room with a cot up against the wall on one side, shelves filled with files across from it and a credenza on top of which was a hot plate along with a coffee maker.

When Max came back with her meal, she was still standing there staring toward the front of the station at the large picture window that exposed the interior to anyone passing by. He eased past her in the limited space.

"The food smells terrific," he said. "Come on."

It had been a bad idea, unplanned and foolish. Max was at the front now, the food on the desk, turning toward her, frowning then calling to her. "What are you doing? The food's going to get cold."

She was relieved and surprised when he turned to lower a blind that covered the whole window, then snapped on a brighter light. She hurried to the desk and sat down in the wooden chair she'd used on her visit to Lillian. Putting his dinner down by hers, she waited while he went around the desk to sit in the computer chair, then reached for his bag and emptied its contents on the desk: a large container with the stew, two rolls and a small paper bag that held the cookies.

He looked up and smiled at Grace. "Wait until you taste Elaine's cookies."

She reached for her coffee and took the lid off. Taking a sip, she glanced across at him.

"I've heard they're legendary, just like her coffee."

He lifted his cup, took off the lid and sipped some. "Great coffee," he said with a sigh. He seemed to study her before he said, "I'm glad you're here. I hate eating alone, especially when I'm stuck here, but at least Clint's doing okay. Poor Lillian, she does love that man."

Grace took her wrapped sandwich out of the bag and opened the container of dip. "It must be in the water around here, or in the air."

"What's that?" Max asked as he took the lid off his stew container.

"Love, I guess. It seems this town has a lot of longtime married couples who know what love's really about. You know, soulmates, that sort of thing. Like your parents, or Elaine and Burr."

He smiled ruefully. "How long do you think Burr and Elaine have been married?"

"I don't know. Maybe thirty years?"

"How about just over a year."

"I never would have guessed that."

"Well, they've known each other for years but it took a while for them to acknowledge the spark between them. Everyone else saw it way before those two realized what was right in front of them all along."

"At least they figured it out."

"My folks were different. Dad says he knew from the first time he saw Mom barrel racing that he was going to marry her. What he didn't know was that she'd already decided to accidentally-on-purpose cross paths with the infamous bull rider Dash Donovan to see if he was as charming in person as she hoped he'd be. Two months later on Christmas Eve, they were married."

She sighed softly. "Soulmates."

"If you believe in that kind of thing, yes."

She wasn't sure if she believed in that for her, but some people seemed to find that one person they could love forever. "You don't?" she asked, dunking her sandwich into the rich beef broth.

"I went on that wild ride once before and was bucked off. I'm not doing it again." He speared a chunk of beef. "I'll leave that up to my brothers."

"It was that bad for you?" she asked.

"Did you ever get hit so hard you had the wind knocked out of you and you had to fight to breathe again?"

"No. Well, maybe. I fell on a volleyball once, and it hit my stomach. For a second I couldn't catch my breath. Like that?"

"Not even close." He slowly took a drink of his coffee before looking back over at Grace without a smile this time. "It took me a long time to be able to breathe again."

"I'm sorry. Was it someone from around here?"

"Yes, right here in paradise." The sarcasm in his voice gave her goose bumps.

"Have I met her?"

"No, but you met her father, Freeman Lee."

"The man who was going to square off against Big Albert?"

"That's him. Claire is an only child, and she always wanted to do something bigger with her life—in her mind, she deserved better than the small-town ranch life. We dated in high school, then went our separate ways. She got a degree in genetic research and seldom came home after that. I didn't come back much, either. I did two tours over in the Middle East with the Army Rangers, then I came home, became sheriff, and to make a long story short, Claire showed up here three years later. Something happened at her job and she'd walked away from it. We connected again, and I thought I'd found the one I'd be able to have a good life with. We made plans, seemed to want the same things, so I bought a ring and proposed."

"She refused?"

"No, she didn't. She put the ring on and said that we'd have the biggest wedding in town. She started running around, looking for her wedding dress, getting on bridal registries and getting a write-up in the largest newspaper in the state."

"Then what happened?"

"We ended up with a hundred guests sitting in their seats waiting for the wedding ceremony to start. I was standing up in front, expecting Claire to come down the aisle at any time. But she didn't. I finally went back to see what was going on, and she was in a room by herself on the phone. She was talking to a man she'd worked with, begging him to come and get her, to stop her from making the worst mistake in her life. She couldn't be tied down to the life she'd told me repeatedly she loved. She couldn't bear it that I was a cop. I found out she had broken up with the man on the phone. That's why she came back home. But she'd never stopped loving him."

Grace was stunned. "She... I mean, she played you."

"That's one way to put it. After I could think straight again, I realized that, on some level, she'd come back here to make the guy jealous. That's why she did everything she could to let everyone know she was with me, especially him. I guess he took the bait, and she told me she was leaving."

She was almost sick listening to Max and seeing the tension in his expression. "What did you do?"

"I guess you could say I broke down. I heard myself telling her to get out. Her big problem was she didn't have a ride until Russell, the guy on the phone, got there, and it would take him two hours to show up. She started crying, and I was numb, then Dad showed up wondering where we were. He figured things out and told her he'd drive her back to her parents' ranch so she could wait there for her boyfriend to come get her."

"What about you?" she asked, the remainder of her sandwich forgotten.

"I left by the back door, took off for two weeks, then came back to figure out my new life. I worked past it, mostly thanks to Marty, who was a great sounding board for me. We played a lot of chess back then." He cocked his head slightly to one side as if sizing her up. "Sorry about all of that. I never talk about it, and now here I am ruining our meal by talking too much."

"No, it's okay." She started to wrap up her sandwich. "I'm just so sorry you and your family…and her family…had to go through all that. That's so incredibly sad and hurtful. Did she leave?"

"Yep. Freeman said she's working in Texas, doing genetic research again. She's still with Russell."

"That's it?"

"Yep, that's it. So you see, when you think you've found your soulmate, don't count on it being true. I'm not even sure there really is such a thing."

"So, that's that? It didn't work out with Claire, so there's no point looking anymore?"

He sat back in his chair. "I was dead wrong one time, and I won't go through that again."

"But—"

"No buts. I just want my life to be simple and do something I like doing. That's it." He cut off the conversation. "What do I owe you for the food?"

"Elaine said it's on her because she appreciates what you do for the town. She also hated how miserable that meeting must have been for you because of Big Albert."

He grimaced. "This town has an impressively fast gossip chain."

She put the top on her broth dip and placed it back in the bag with her wrapped half sandwich. "Was it really awful?"

"Not any more than usual when Big Albert is involved."

"What did he say?" she asked, already knowing the answer from Lillian. She'd never let him know what the lady had told her.

He shrugged. "He insinuated that I was abusing my office by passing off my work to the deputies while I went out and had a good time."

"What does he consider having a good time?" she asked.

"You know, having fun when I'm supposed to be working," he said.

"I don't know what that man would consider fun," Grace muttered.

Max looked away from her for a moment, then met her gaze again. "Albert insinuated that I was spending way too much time with you. I'm supposed to have violated the rules by having you in the truck with me during work hours. But the way he's slanting it, it's not true, at least most of it isn't."

"I was in the truck when you had the sirens and lights going on that call. But you've done nothing but help me." She shook her head. "I shouldn't be here."

He frowned at her. "No, you have every right to be here. I told the board to do what they want, but I've been doing my job."

"But you can't give him any fuel for the fire."

"Hey," he said and sat forward, putting his hands flat on the table. "He's a bully, Grace. He's politically motivated to get this job, and most people that vote around here know what he is. I'm not worried."

She was very worried for him. "I'm going to go." She drank the last of her tepid coffee, then dropped the cup in a trash container by the desk. "I'm sorry."

Max stood and came around to Grace, then reached out and cupped her chin gently in his large hand. His eyes were intent on her. "I promise this is just bluster from Albert. He's making a good show of trying to prove how dedicated he was when he was sheriff, but everyone knows he sat behind the desk most of the time. Just ignore him if you stumble across him, okay?"

"Don't underestimate him, Max."

"If anything, he's underestimating me." His fingertips skimmed along her jawline, then drew away. "You need to get home."

"I guess so," she said and put her jacket on,

then picked up her bag with the leftovers in it. "When's Lillian coming back?"

"She's not. I'm covering until nine, then all calls will be rerouted. I told you how that happens. Someone will be available to take the 911 calls."

Grace nodded. She hesitated before asking him, "Can you make that light not come on outside?"

"No, I can't. Why?"

She shrugged. "For the same reason you closed the front blinds."

"Got me," he murmured, then reached around her to open the door but drew back when a beeping sound came from the front of the office. "Hey, hold on. I have to take this."

"Okay," she said, and she followed him back to the desk.

He clicked an icon on the monitor screen, then said, "Nine-one-one, what's your emergency?"

As Max SILENTLY listened to an agitated man on the speaker, he knew he had a solid chance of solving the irrigation thefts. When he had all the information he needed, he spoke to Dutch Gates, the rancher on the phone, to verify his location. "A mile past Green Valley Dude Ranch off of Running Bear?"

"Yeah, I'm watching them now."

"Keep watching, but you stay out of sight. Do nothing until a deputy or I get there." He hung up, then put in a call, still on speaker. "Lawson, we have an incident and you're closer." He gave him the information, then said, "I'm on my way. No lights or siren after the turn. Wait for me, but if you need to move, do it carefully and keep your holster open."

With Lawson dispatched, he turned to Grace and realized she'd heard the whole thing. He hadn't thought about that. Now she was staring at him hard. "Work calls." He grabbed his jacket from a peg by the front door. "Thank you for being here and for bringing dinner." He smiled at her, hoping she'd smile back, but she didn't. "I'm sorry you heard all that. I never use the headpiece when I'm here alone."

"This is serious, really serious, isn't it?"

He wouldn't lie. "Yes, it could be the end of the irrigation equipment thefts."

"You're in real danger, aren't you?"

He didn't like this at all, especially the concern in those violet eyes. "I honestly won't know until I get there. Probably they'll be gone by then, or they'll stick around and give up."

She came closer to him and pressed her hand to his chest. "You're lying. I can feel your heart racing."

He almost joked that maybe it was her being so close that was making his heart beat faster. But that would be hokey, even if it was true. "Now you're a human lie detector?"

"I'm sorry. Just be careful," she said in a soft voice. Then she reached for the door latch, opened it and went outside. Max followed her to her Jeep. She got in behind the wheel and reached to close the door, but he grabbed it before she could shut him out.

He leaned down to look inside, not quite understanding why she was so concerned about the call. "It's my job to take care of the problem and walk away in one piece. You don't need to worry about me."

"You need to go," she said. "Good luck."

She was right. "I'll see you when I see you."

She nodded, and he let go of his hold on the door so she could close it.

He turned away and hurried to the truck, got it going, then drove across the lot to the side street, before merging with Clayton Way. He looked back and Grace was still sitting in her car, more of a shadow now without the inside light on, but he could clearly see her head was in her hands.

He forced himself to keep going, but for the first time since he'd been elected, he wasn't rushing full tilt to the scene of the possible crime. As soon as he was out of town and on the highway, he turned on his lights and siren and forced himself to focus on what he was doing. He wanted to be able to call Grace when he was done and let her know he'd walked away from it unharmed.

CHAPTER THIRTEEN

AT MIDNIGHT, Grace was alone in the kitchen at the Lodge, thinking about possibly redoing the cabinets. She couldn't sleep and had finally given up. Now she was trying to keep her mind occupied by debating between painting everything a crisp white or staining the cabinets a dark oak. But she couldn't make that matter enough to distract her, because she kept hearing Max giving his deputy orders: *If you need to move, do it carefully and keep your holster open.*

She knew what that meant without having to be told—that he'd warned his deputy to take off the safety snap and make sure the gun was easy to get out. That made her skin crawl and she admitted to herself that she wasn't going to be able to focus on cabinet finishes, not as long as she hadn't heard from Max. As that thought formed, she turned and headed to the office.

The old chair by the window had become

her favorite spot in the Lodge. She understood why her uncle had put it there and why it was so worn. She settled and stared out the window at the darkness. She knew her concern about Max was more than what it should have been, and she couldn't deny that after just a short time of knowing him, she found herself liking him more and more. It had been hard for her to hear what Claire had done. Even harder for her to know he was out there with his gun that wasn't just for show. She closed her eyes and rested her head against the back of the chair.

The sound of her phone ringing startled Grace and she scrambled off the chair to hurry to the nightstand and pick it up. She didn't recognize the number, but it was local.

On the fourth ring, she answered it. "Hello?"

When she heard Max's voice say, "Grace?" she fell back on the bed and closed her eyes. "Yes."

"I know it's late, and I hope I didn't wake you."

"I'm awake." She was very awake now. "Where are you?"

"I'm at the clinic in town."

"Are…are you okay?"

"I survived," he said calmly.

She was gripping her cell so hard that she thought she might crack the phone case. "What happened?"

"I got there and one of the suspects resisted arrest."

She squeezed her eyelids shut. "Are you sure you're okay?"

"Yeah, I'm fine. He had bad aim."

"He shot at you?"

"He was way off the mark, but it distracted him enough that Lawson could get behind him and tackle him. The other guy, who'd been cooperating until that point, took off running. I went after him, and to make a long story short, he looked back to see how close I was and ran into a cistern shed. He knocked himself out from the impact. It was hard work dragging him to the truck. Lawson has an amazing black eye, and the suspect with the rifle broke his wrist somehow."

She didn't care about them. "But you didn't get hurt?"

"No, I didn't. I'm at the clinic to make sure they get medical, then I'm taking them across the Montana border to Twin Bridges tomorrow morning. They have warrants out there that take precedence over what I can charge them with."

"How? That man tried to kill you."

"He didn't kill me, and the warrant on him is for two counts of bodily injury to a female victim and her seventy-year-old mother. That's the one he should be saddled with. He'll be gone for a long time, and it's a solid case. So, I'll step aside after I file charges for assault, theft and resisting arrest on both of them as a backup."

"I guess that's a good idea. So, your cells will be full for the night," she said.

"Actually, they can share one and beat each other up if they want, as long as they're locked up and don't annoy me."

He was so calm about it she was finally calming down herself. "Were they the ones stealing the stuff?"

"You bet. They had a big load on the truck, and the weight sank the flatbed in an irrigation ditch. They were sitting ducks."

"Ducks with a rifle," she said and loved the rough chuckle on the other end of the line.

"That's a weird visual," he murmured.

She heard someone speaking to Max, a male voice, but she couldn't make out the words. Then Max said to her, "I have to go. They're ready. I'll see you when I see you."

She put her phone on the nightstand and got into bed. She closed her eyes but opened them quickly. A duck with a rifle was a silly visual, but a criminal with a rifle had shot at Max. At least he was okay. She told herself that over and over again as she looked out the window. It finally hit her that there were no stars in the sky, not even a sliver of moonlight. The night was pitch-black. She got up again to look out and peered up at the heavens. The clouds were roiling, dark and mean, gathering over the land.

She sank down on the chair and stretched out her hand to touch the nearest windowpane. The glass was beyond cold. When she drew back she saw large white snowflakes starting to fall close to the windows. Snow! She got up and pulled open the sliding door to the deck. Impulsively, in her bare feet and pajamas, she stepped outside and looked up. A growing breeze stirred the frigid air and the flakes swirled around her.

In no time at all, her feet were so cold they were numb, and she hurried back inside. Grabbing the throw she kept at the foot of her bed along with her phone, she went back to the chair to sit with her feet tucked under her. Then she called the number Max had used before.

A woman answered, "Eclipse Medical Clinic and 24/7 Urgent Care. How can I help you?"

"Is Sheriff Donovan still there?"

"Hold on. I'll see if he left."

The line went blank, then Max came on the phone. "Hello?"

"Max? It's Grace. I didn't want to bother you, but it's snowing."

"Yes, it sure is."

"Is everything around here okay? I mean the roof of the stable won't collapse, will it?"

"No, Chappy put props in the high stress areas until he could reinforce the beams."

"Good. This might be a dumb question, but you said I probably shouldn't ride Rebel in the snow."

"Yeah. Snow hides things that you won't even know are there unless you're familiar with the lay of the land."

"Okay, I'll wait to ride. I'm sorry to bother you, and I hope you get some rest soon."

"Won't be for a while. The plan changed, so I'm going to have to take the prisoners up to Montana now in case the snow ends up closing the roads. I'll be back tomorrow sometime, hopefully." There was yelling in the background, and Max said, "I'll see you when I see you." Then he was gone, and the line went dead.

Grace didn't dream that night and when she woke, the palest of light announced the arrival of dawn through the windows, which had frosted over completely. As the clouds diminished enough for the sun to finally find a route to earth, she got up and looked outside.

The land that stretched out in front of her was a sea of white with some morning shadows falling here and there. She'd thought there'd be more snow, but the storm had left a thin blanket covering the ground. The tree boughs were heavy with ice, and the sun glinted off everything, making it look as if diamonds had fallen from the sky.

She couldn't take her eyes off it; the land that was hers was beyond anything she could have imagined she'd ever own. Her father had always bragged about his hotels and casinos, often saying, "I can't believe I made all of this." Well, she didn't make this, but it was hers. Uncle Martin's gift to her was absolutely breathtaking.

She finally left the view to bundle up and go outside so she could experience the snow firsthand. First, she put on the thermals she'd bought at Farley's store, layering them with fleece-lined jeans and a pink flannel shirt. She smiled at her reflection in the small mirror in the equally small bathroom. She combed out her loose hair and caught it in a low ponytail. After putting on her thermal boots and her jacket, along with her knit hat, she headed outside.

She pulled down the earflaps on her hat and flipped up her collar as she crossed the porch to the top step. When she breathed in the cold air as she walked down to check on the stable, she felt alive, truly alive. The building was still standing, so all was well.

After she went back inside, she settled at the old desk in the office, and started looking at the ledgers again. As she checked them, she recognized the irony that her expensive business education Walter had demanded she get was helping her to find out more about her uncle.

After she'd pored over hundreds of hand-written pages, her stomach growled. When she looked up at the wall clock, it was just before eleven. She'd been going through the books for almost five hours, and she was starving. She hadn't tried to call around to find a contractor yet because she had no idea where to start, but she was eager to figure out what she could afford to do to spruce up the Lodge. Max had said to ask him for help if she needed it, and she'd do just that. But he was busy, and she knew someone she could ask to recommend at least a handyman.

She put on her jacket and boots again, pushed her wallet into her pocket, then went outside to the Jeep. She brushed the snow off the windows before she got behind the wheel. She'd never driven in snow, and when she reached the highway, she was glad that a plow had already been by and cleared one lane in each direction. The snow had been pushed onto the shoulder.

Her trip took more time than usual but was thankfully uneventful. When she drew up in front of the general store, Farley was bundled up and clearing the walkway with a straw broom. She got out and called to him. "Hello there."

"Howdy, Miss Grace," he said with his usual enthusiasm when he turned and saw her at the foot of the steps that he'd already cleared. "What brings you out in this weather?"

"I know you know everyone around here, and I need a handyman or a contractor for a couple of weeks' work out at the Lodge."

He stopped sweeping. "Yeah, I got a guy I use, and he can repair or build anything.

Name's Penn Falconer. He's one of the boys at the Falcon Ranch south of town. Do you want me to call him for ya?"

"That would be great," she said.

He started sweeping again. "Go on inside and get warm. I'll be in as soon as I finish out here and we can get Penn on the line."

By the time she got off the call with the handyman, he'd agreed to come by later in the day to give her an estimate. When Grace went back outside, the walkway was cleared as far as she could see. She went back down to the Jeep, intending to go to Elaine's for lunch. But as she arrived at the diner, she saw Max standing by the pickup, just closing the driver's door.

When he looked up and spotted her, he motioned for her to stop, and she pulled in beside him. As she put down her window, he came over and smiled in at her. "I was just thinking about you," he said. Despite what he'd gone through, he looked as handsome as ever. "Are you hungry?" he asked.

She couldn't walk into Elaine's with Max not knowing who might be inside. "I don't think that's a good idea."

"Why?"

"It's just… Not after that meeting and all. We can eat at the Lodge."

"We can eat here," he said. "I'd like you to come have lunch with me."

"I don't know, Max."

"Trust me, I do." He opened her door and stood back so she could get out. When he held out his hand to her, she hesitated, and he added, "Please, come on."

Elaine met them when they stepped into the busy diner. Grace glanced around and saw the place was almost full. Then she looked over at Max's favorite booth and her heart sank. Little Albert Van Duren was seated at the booth with a man who could only be his father. They had the same coloring, the same build and the same blond hair. They were both big men, but the father was at least fifty pounds heavier than the son. And there they sat, scarfing down huge steaks.

She turned away, quickly putting her back to them, and stood closer to Max. She could leave right then and hope they didn't see her, or she could stay with Max and hope he'd been right.

"I'm sorry it's so busy," she heard Elaine say. "How about sitting at the counter until a booth clears for you?"

Max glanced at Grace. "Maybe we should just go to—" she started.

He reached for her hand and held it. "We can sit at the counter."

He didn't have to say *Trust me*, but it was implied.

"If you want to," she said.

"I do." Still holding her hand, he guided her to two stools about halfway down the line.

Once they were seated with their jackets off and hanging over the high backs of the stools, Grace tried to casually glance past Max to the booth by the door.

When Little Albert had started her heaters for her and filled the propane tanks, he'd been a bit flirty, more or less inviting her to the grand opening of the Grange. She'd begged off saying she had too much to do at the Lodge and that was that. Now he was here, and she just hoped he wouldn't look her way.

Thankfully, both father and son were still focused on their steaks. Elaine drew her attention as she came up behind the counter. "How about drinks while you wait, then I'll bring your food when you get a table."

Before she could say she'd gladly eat right there, Max responded, "Sounds good."

"I'll get your drinks and if I come out with your food and you aren't sitting here, I'll find you."

"I appreciate that, Elaine," he said with that slow grin.

"And I appreciate you, Max," Elaine said. "I'm glad you're here."

When Elaine was gone, Grace swiveled toward him. "Max?" He looked at her. "Did you see who's here?"

"I figure you're talking about Little and Big Albert?"

She exhaled. "Good, I didn't know if you'd spotted them."

"They're in my booth. I couldn't miss them. I'm pretty sure they're going to ignore us, but if they don't, that's okay. Don't worry about it."

Elaine came with their coffees. "Your food'll be ready in ten minutes."

"Thanks," Max said, then turned back to Grace, his eyes narrowed on her. "What do you think's going to happen if they spot us?"

She shrugged. "I don't know. I just thought it might be awkward. You know, Little Albert might invite me to go to the Grange Hall with him."

"Would you go?"

She couldn't believe he asked her that. "No. I told him I was snowed under with work."

Max chuckled. "Nice pun."

"Thanks, but I'm worried if he sees me, he might ask me." Now, if Max had asked her, she would have jumped at the chance. As soon as that thought formed, she felt awkward. That time at the substation had changed things.

"Then tell him truthfully that you're busy on that Saturday. You have a date with me."

Grace could almost feel her jaw drop. "What?"

"Don't look so shocked. Mom told me to ask you to come to the junior rodeo at the ranch that day. I'm taking you."

"You are?" she asked, definitely giving away her surprise at his statement.

"Yep. Mom told me to pick you up around eleven, so you'll see the opening ceremony."

So, his mother suggested it. Even so, she'd take it. "Okay."

"I'm the sheriff, and I'm supposed to keep people safe. I'll keep you safe from those two. Remember, protect and serve."

She loved how calm he was. "Okay, but if our booth's way in the back, promise me you won't go past their table to get to it."

Max nodded to her. "Cowboy promise," he said, his deep hazel eyes holding hers. "You're safe with me."

When Max had taken off his coat, she'd noticed he was wearing a plain chambray shirt with his star pinned on the breast pocket and the gun holstered on his hip with the clip and a two-way radio on his belt. He'd obviously changed at the ranch, then headed straight back to town to work. She hoped the town appreciated what a good man they had as sheriff.

Elaine came out of the kitchen, looked around, then went over to them. "There'll be a booth in a minute, but I wanted to thank you for yesterday, Max. The irrigation thefts were hurting a lot of good people around here. You're my hero, and you don't even need a cape."

She hadn't been talking too loudly, and with the music playing over the speakers, Grace was surprised when she heard a male voice say, "You did a great job, Max." When Grace turned, Big Albert was standing behind Max, who slowly spun his stool to face the man.

"Hey, Elaine," the man said. "Two boxes and some cookies?" She went to get them, and Big Albert added in a loud voice, "You done good, Sheriff. You got them bad guys, and you didn't even break a nail." The sarcasm in his words grated on Grace but Max just sat there. "You need a big button for that shirt that says 'Hero' on it," Big Albert continued.

Unexpectedly, the other diners broke out in applause, and someone whistled shrilly. Grace watched Max nod to them, but she could feel his embarrassment. As the clapping died out, he spoke to the diners. "Thank you all. I'm just relieved it's over."

The townspeople obviously understood what was going on and were behind Max. She loved that. They appreciated him; he truly was their hero.

Big Albert leaned closer to Max and said in a lower voice, "Enjoy it while you can, *Mr.* Donovan." He glanced at Grace. "You, too, missy." Then he turned and went back to the booth.

Max swiveled around to face the counter again and cupped his coffee mug in both hands to take a drink. As he sat it down, Elaine came over to them with a coffeepot. Before she finished refilling his mug, Little Albert was there, laying a hand on Max's shoulder. His father remained at the table with the take-out boxes in front of him, watching his son.

"Are you okay now? No injuries?"

His voice held fake concern as Max swiveled again. "Yeah, all good. How about you, Al?"

"I'm great. But I heard that real dangerous criminal you arrested got knocked out when he ran into a cistern shack. Him crashing into it almost lifted it off its foundation… So's I heard." He laughed at his own words. "You got it easy, I guess." He slapped Max on the shoulder. "You keep safe around here."

"You, too."

But the son wasn't finished. He switched his attention to Grace. "So, can I pick you up around six on Saturday to go to the Grange with me? Put on your best jeans and we'll make the night memorable. Let your work go and have some real fun."

Grace felt sick, but even worse when she realized Max was going to stand up and face the jerk. She put her hand on his shoulder, and that drew his attention to her so she could say, "My work's done."

"Good, then we're on for Saturday," he said with a gotcha smile.

"I still can't go. I'm busy." Before he could argue, she went for it. "Max invited me to the rodeo out at Flaming Sky." She wouldn't say sorry to him, but she wasn't finished. "It's my first rodeo, and I think it's going to be memorable."

"Go to the rodeo. The Grange celebration doesn't start until later when the rodeo's over." He looked smug. "So no problem."

"I have plans for later, too," she said.

Elaine took that moment to speak up. "Have a good day, Al. Don't forget your boxes when you leave. Those steaks are too good to go to waste."

Grace could almost feel the man's anger, and she prayed that he'd at least have enough brains to walk away quietly. It turned out he did. He silently went back to the booth, picked up the take-out boxes, then he and his father left, the older man shaking his head at his son. The door shut behind them.

"Your booth will be ready in a minute," Elaine said and took off with a cleaning rag in her hand. Max picked up both their mugs, then nodded to Grace. "Can you grab the coats?"

She did and followed Max to his favorite booth, where Elaine was finishing wiping away all traces of the Van Durens. When she stepped back, they both slid into their seats. Grace put their jackets on the seat by her and

Max put their mugs on the table and murmured, "Well played, Grace. I'm impressed."

"You two make a good team," Elaine said as she came back with their meals. "I wish I could be there when they open their take-out boxes."

Max was smiling now. "What'd you do, Elaine?"

"Nothing serious. I just gave them pumpkin cookies."

Max laughed and Grace had to ask, "Why is that so funny? Those cookies are delicious."

"Thank you, Miss Grace, but both those jerks hate the pumpkin cookies."

Grace chuckled. "Then thank you for doing that."

"You bet. If there's anything else you need, just let me know!" she said and left them alone.

Grace looked over at Max. "You're awesome," she said on a chuckle. "You didn't let yourself get baited into punching him. You stayed calm."

"I'll tell you a secret. Just between you and me, if you hadn't been there, I probably would have done something I might have come to regret, especially to Little Albert."

"But you didn't. Good grief, both of them are just awful. I can't see how the dad was ever sheriff."

Elaine came by with the coffeepot for refills. "Albert Jr. thinks he's the world's gift to women. I'm glad you brought him down a peg, Grace. Very smooth."

"I didn't think anyone in this town could be so horrible."

Max chuckled at that. "You really need to get out more. We have some doozies around here."

"Amen to that," Elaine said before she straightened up. "Nice to see the two of you here. This man eats alone way too often. I used to like it when he'd come in with Marty. Two of my best customers. Now you're here, and I like that." She smiled at them both before she turned to move on to the next table. "Enjoy!" she called out over her shoulder.

CHAPTER FOURTEEN

Max watched Grace and noticed her eyes were glistening. "I'm sorry," she said. "I don't mean to get emotional, but it seems I'm prone to it lately. I mean, I never even met my uncle and here I am almost crying over him." She picked up her napkin and dabbed her eyes with it. "I'm sorry," she half whispered as she balled up the napkin in her hand.

He could see a certain lost look in her eyes, then considered that maybe her emotions weren't all tied to Marty. He was trying to figure out what else to say to her when his cell rang. He held up his forefinger, signaling that he'd get back to her in a minute, before he took the call. "I'm here."

Lillian was on the line. "Where is here, cowboy?"

"The diner."

"Just got an incoming from Windy Point Arena. Jed said someone's in there riding and won't leave. He wants you to get them out."

"Tell Jed to get them out."

"He says he's not going to do anything until you're there, because it's Bobby Joe Lemon, and he's drunk, and he's got a rifle. He's barefoot and bare chested, even with the snow."

"Log me in. I'm leaving now." Sighing, he hung up and looked at Grace. He regretted having to leave her there alone. "Got a call. Bad timing." Standing, she offered his jacket to him without him having to ask. He reached for his jacket, then looked over at Elaine, who was taking an order at a nearby table. "Elaine? Gotta run. Put this on my tab."

"Max, you're not paying for anything here today," she said. "Safe ride."

"Thanks." He turned back to Grace. "Got a half-dressed drunk with a rifle riding where he shouldn't be a ways south of here."

He knew instantly he shouldn't have mentioned the rifle, but it was too late to take it back. Grace looked concerned, but she spoke evenly. "Go ahead, and stay safe."

"Trust me, I will," he said as picked up his hat and put it on. "Maybe I'll see you later."

She nodded. "I'll be at the Lodge."

He couldn't leave without saying, "It's going to be okay. Bobby Joe Lemon is probably sixty years old, arthritic and has a penchant for riding half naked. He's not dangerous, just drunk."

She didn't look fully convinced when she said, "If you say so."

He wished he had time to spare to make her feel better, but he didn't, and his main priority was getting to Bobby Joe before he froze to death. "I *do* say so," was about all he could add.

GRACE WATCHED MAX leave and sat back in her seat. An armed drunk on a horse, and Max was heading off to deal with him.

"Excuse me," Elaine said as she came back to the table. "Do you mind if I sit for a moment?"

"Oh, no, please do."

Elaine took Max's place and pushed his untouched food away. "I should have boxed it for him," she muttered, mostly to herself before she looked across at Grace. "Burr and Marty were good friends over the years, and I wanted to ask if it was possible for me and Burr to be there when you scatter his ashes at the bridge over Split Creek? I know you can't do it until spring after the snow has cleared, but would it be okay if the two of us were there with you? If you don't want anyone else there, we understand." Elaine quickly added, "We don't mean to be pushy."

She hadn't thought about when she could scatter the ashes, but Elaine was right. "I'd like it very much if you two would be there with me."

"We'd be honored," Elaine said as she stood. "Please, just let us know when you'll be ready to do it. Do you want anything else to eat? I have the best cookies around, freshly baked, although I'm missing a half dozen of the pumpkin."

"So I heard," she said, and they both laughed.

GRACE KEPT HER phone with her all day, but it didn't ring until the handyman, Penn Falconer, called to arrange a later appointment to give her an estimate for the work she needed done. He couldn't get there until the following week. That was fine. She wouldn't rush it, because she wanted the Lodge to be in as good a shape as it could be before she left.

It was six o'clock, and a light snow that had been falling for the last couple of hours had deposited a fresh layer of white on the ground. There had been no word from Max, but she didn't have the nerve to call his cell. So, she sat on the couch facing the fire she'd just started and looked around. She was doing this all on her own without her dad forcing his opinions on her. It felt liberating to answer to no one and to do as she pleased. But there was a sense of loneliness in it, too.

She was surprised when headlights flashed through the front windows, then went out at the same time the sound of an engine died. She hurried to the door and opened it. Just like that, she didn't feel lonely anymore: Max was standing in front of her, wearing his suede jacket, black jeans and his ever-present black hat.

If she'd hugged him the way she wanted to right then, she knew it would have been really hard to ever let him go. "Are you okay?"

"Aces," he said. "And I'll be even better if you let me inside out of this cold."

"Oh, yes, sure," she said, stepping back for him to go past her into the warmth of the Lodge. She caught the scent of leather and freshness as his movement stirred the air around her. Then she swung the door shut and turned to him, barely a foot separating them.

"No shooting?"

He shook his head. "No, just a drunk on a horse with an empty shotgun." He was undoing his jacket. "He was so drunk he didn't know where he was."

"He's in jail now, right?"

"No, he's back home. I figured having to explain to his wife what he did and how he's going to have to pay a fine for public drunkenness and trespassing is a better punishment than a few hours in jail."

"But he didn't hurt you, right?"

"Not a scratch on me." He tossed his jacket on the desk, then laid his hat next to it. "But I had to have the truck's interior sanitized. The smell of an unwashed drunk's puke is enough to bring you to your knees. Henry has some magic potion that cleans and kills the smells that get in cars, and it seems to have worked this time."

"Oh, I'm sorry."

"Don't be. So, was lunch good?"

"I haven't eaten it yet." By the time she got home, she wasn't hungry anymore. "Elaine sent me home with our meals, and she said they can be reheated. Do you want me to turn on the oven?"

"Thanks, but no. While Henry was cleaning the truck, his wife fed me the best huevos rancheros ever, and her helpings are huge."

Before she could respond, the landline for

the Lodge rang, startling her. "First call since I had the phone set up," Grace said and reached over the desk for the receiver. "It's probably the wrong number," she quipped then said into the mouthpiece, "Split Creek Lodge, how may I help you?"

There was no response for a moment, then a male voice she didn't recognize said, "Hello there, Grace. You can help me by finding Sheriff Donovan. I was told he's been spending a *lot* of time with you, and I need to speak to him about that."

It took a second for what he'd said to sink in, and she quickly covered the mouthpiece with her hand. "Max, someone's trying to find you. He said he knew you were spending a lot of time here in a kind of sleazy tone."

"Can you put it on speaker?"

"Yeah, sure," she said. She pressed the speaker button, then uncovered the mouthpiece. "I'm sorry. You're looking for the sheriff?"

"I was told that if I couldn't find the sheriff he'd be with you…if you're Grace Bennet, that is. I wanted to talk about that with him, to let him know how a lot of people feel about the way he's doing his job—or I reckon I should say, not doing it."

Max touched his lips with his forefinger, then mouthed, *I'll take it.*

She nodded and was surprised when Max said in a matter-of-fact tone of voice, "If this is a life-threatening emergency, please hang up and call 911. If not, you can contact our office during our business hours of seven a.m. to seven p.m., Monday through Friday, and arrange for a meeting with Sheriff Donovan." When he'd barely finished speaking, the line went dead, and he put the phone back in the cradle.

"Who was that?" Grace asked.

"Sounded like Benny Mason, a good old boy who's part of the Van Duren circle. They never broke the law together, but they bent it a lot. I kind of think those good old boys are one of the reasons Marty pushed me to get on the ballot. He knew what they were and wanted them out." He narrowed his eyes on her. "Are you okay?"

She probably looked the way she felt—unsettled by what had happened. "Don't worry about me. What are you going to do about the call?"

"What I did. Let him know that what he says or does means nothing to me, except for the fact that it upset you. I'll take care of him and make sure he doesn't contact you again."

"But now he knows you were here. I should have never let you talk to him."

"You didn't let me do it—I did it."

But she was involved, and she couldn't be. "You shouldn't be here." That hurt to say, but Max was the one who would really get hurt if he lost the election.

"Hey, listen to me, Grace. I'm not going to let anyone tell me how to live, or who to have in my life."

When she went back to Tucson, she didn't want to leave Max with his life in shambles. His job meant everything to him. "You listen to *me*. You can't take the chance that they won't go even further to discredit you. Men like that never stop where power or money's involved. I lived with a man who was driven like that, and someone like you would never understand how horrible they can be and justify it every time. Money and power are their drugs, and they're not going into any rehab, believe me."

Max was stunned by the simmering anger and pain that he saw in Grace at that moment. He knew who she was talking about with such emotion: the credit card man. She lowered her eyes as she hugged herself tightly.

He touched her chin with his forefinger. "Hey," he said softly.

Finally, she looked up at him. "I'm sorry. I know I sounded extreme just there, but I only meant to say that you can't beat men like that. You can't. Good doesn't always win out." She shrugged weakly. "Believe me, it usually doesn't."

He drew his hand back as he shifted to her side and put his arm around her shoulders. He felt her stiffen, but not pull back. "Let's sit and talk about this." But she didn't move when he gently tried to urge her into the great room.

"No, no, no, no," she said and twisted to move away from his touch, leaving him standing there as she went behind the desk and headed toward the living quarters. She went inside without a glance back.

Max weighed his options and opted to go after her. Thankfully, she hadn't shut the door on him and when he stepped into the room, Grace was sitting in Marty's old chair, staring out the window. He crossed to get one of the chairs from the kitchenette and put it by her, angling it so he could look at her, before he sat down.

There was heavy silence as they both sat there until Grace sighed. "I think it's better if you leave."

"Who was the man you were talking about?"

She closed her eyes tightly. "No one important."

He couldn't let that go. "Whatever happened with that man, you can talk to me about it. It won't go any further than this room. I promise."

"I don't need to talk anymore, especially about him. You need to leave. Please."

He was used to talking to people who weren't in a good place emotionally, and he knew better than to push. So he sat there prepared to wait as long as it took for him to find out who the person was that she'd been talking about in her outburst.

She shifted and clasped her hands tightly in her lap. He couldn't stop himself from saying, "I need to know about him before we settle about me leaving or not. All I know is you look as if you're hurting, and I want to help."

GRACE CLOSED HER eyes and wished she could just sink into the chair until he couldn't see her anymore. She'd scared herself a little by being so emotional about something she kept thinking she'd left behind her. He was right about her hurting, remembering all the times Walter hurt people around him, good people he crushed.

"Talk to me, Grace," Max said. "Who is he?"

The room was silent except for the furnace starting up again. His voice was low and something in it almost broke her heart. A man who'd been nothing but good to her was only asking for the truth. She braced herself, then decided he deserved that much.

"Walter Bennet." Her voice sounded alien to her own ears, low and flat. "The founder and CEO of Las Vegas–based Golden Mountain Corporation, one of the best entertainment and hospitality businesses in the country. Or so he says."

When he didn't respond, she finally opened her eyes and glanced at him. Then she said the hardest part. "He's my father."

He stared at her, then asked, "How could he have canceled your cards or gone after your bank account when he's dead?"

She looked away and out the window. "You assumed he was dead when I told you my parents were gone and not in my life." She exhaled, then kept going. "I'm sorry I let you believe that. My mother passed, but Walter's still alive and fighting battles he almost always wins. He canceled the cards and tried to take the bank balance because he's a bully, a man who values money and power over everything else in life. He's a master of control and cutting people to their core with words and never blinking an eye."

Max stood up and went to the window. She looked up at him and saw him reflected in the glass staring at her. "I thought—" He shook his head, his face slightly distorted in the glass. "How could he do all that to you, his own daughter?"

She looked down at her hands. "I stopped taking his orders and caving in to his pressure. He finds that unforgivable, especially from his only child who turned out to be a girl when he wanted a boy to carry on his name and his empire. Then I received Burr's letter claiming I was the niece of some stranger who had left me everything he had and it was the last straw."

"The gender thing's just plain mean, but why would he cut you off because of the letter?"

"I asked him if the man was really my

uncle, and he verified it but didn't care that he'd died. He wanted me to get rid of whatever he left me and forget he ever existed. No hint of grief whatsoever. He just wanted me to turn my back, tell Burr to sell it all and never think about it again. I refused. Then he told me his brother was a total loser who had walked away from the family thirty years ago. He didn't care he died, Max."

She opened her eyes and saw Max's expression reflected back in the glass as he processed the horrible words about his friend. "When I said I was coming here, he cut me off from everything. The joke on him is, I didn't care. I don't want to be around him, or to be like him, and when I left to come here, I thought I was free of him at last."

Max exhaled heavily, his breath steaming up the glass. "What did Marty ever do to him?"

"I don't know and probably never will. When I was young, I'd wish for a sister or brother and a father who would just love me and spend time with me. I gave up on all of that and just settled for wishing I wouldn't disappoint him. Maybe I'm a coward for giving up, but the one thing I can't accept is his indifference to his older brother dying."

Max turned to her, a frown showing faint lines at the corners of his eyes. "Maybe he'll come to his senses."

She made a scoffing sound. "He lives the life he wants, and I'm building a life of my own that doesn't include him." She'd confessed her lie and that weight was off of her, but she still felt awful about what Max might be facing because of men just like Walter.

When he started a sentence with, "But, you never know—" she cut him off.

"I do know," she said far too abruptly. "I'm done with him. I'm not hoping for fairy-tale magic to take over. I'm okay. I've got my home in Arizona, and I'm learning about my uncle by living in his place, walking in his footsteps. I have a horse, a child's wish that finally came true, and new friends. It's all good."

He came closer and crouched in front of her. His eyes were soft when they met hers. "Yes, you have friends. And this friend is not walking away from you. That's ridiculous. I'm a very single man and having a woman for a friend is not against the law or in any contract I signed when I took over as sheriff. Not doing my job is the only thing that could be a problem, and that's just a lie to muddy up the waters. So, we'll stop the easiest smear first and make Big Albert and his cohorts look petty and foolish."

She looked up at him questioningly.

"I'll make this simple. I'm not walking away or pretending I don't know you when I'm out in public. I won't stop coming here or riding this land with you, and I'm sure not going to take back the invitation for the rodeo. So, forget that hogwash. Instead we'll be transparent and make it known to anyone around that we're good friends and like each other."

It couldn't be that simple. "And the Van Durens are going to give up and ride off into the sunset just like that?"

"They probably won't. But if they keep dishing swill out, the more petty and jealous they'll look. Believe me, everyone knows about the standoff at the diner between them and us, and from what Lillian's heard, we're on the good end of public opinion. So, we just keep that going while I do my job and Lillian takes care of logging my work hours and what I'm doing and where I am at all times. I think this will be as easy for us to pull off as a frog picking off a fly."

"Which one of us is the frog and which one's the fly?"

"That sounded better in my head. We, you and me, we're the frogs, and those good old boys are the flies. How's that?"

"Will I get warts?"

"No, you can only get them if you kiss a bullfrog. My dad told me that years ago. I don't intend to ever kiss a bullfrog."

"You're a wise cowboy," she said.

"I'll take that as a compliment and look forward to the rodeo, where we'll have a great time being good friends."

Grace sighed. "You're so calm about the whole election thing. I don't know how you do it, especially after that call. It hurts to see them causing trouble, trying to destroy decent people for their own agenda."

"Don't give them a second thought and get ready to have fun at the rodeo."

He seemed confident, and he was making her feel more secure. "I'm looking forward to it."

"Okay," he said, then slowly stood and looked down at her, more serious than he'd been moments ago. "You sure you want to go?"

She blinked at the question. "Would it be better if I didn't go?"

"No, I didn't mean that. I want to be sure you don't feel I'm pushing you in any way to do it if you don't want to."

She'd been pushed by Walter to do what he wanted her to do most of her life, and he'd never once asked if she was okay with it. "Yes, I really want to go."

"Then you get some rest and as soon as Chappy clears the stable, we'll take that ride for you to see your land and the bridge on Split Creek."

"I have good riding boots now and enough thermal underwear to hopefully keep the cold out. And I have my knit hat."

He moved back as she stood to walk out to the entry with him. They went around the desk and Max reached for his jacket. As he shrugged into it, he said, "I just remembered something. Wait here. I'll be right back."

He headed into the great room. He was out of her sight for a moment, and then she heard the squeak of a door or cabinet open and close. Max came back holding a hat in his hand. It was brown suede with silver threading around the crown and a star inset in a silver oval at the front.

"Where did you get that?"

"It was in the carved cabinet by the chess

table on the back wall. This is Marty's hat. I just remembered he put it away when he got sick and said he'd take it out when he could ride again. I'd forgotten all about it." He looked down at the hat and fingered the brim. "He made the band himself and he forged the star at the farrier's in town." He held it out to Grace. "Would you like it?"

She took it from him and felt the brushed softness of the suede. Her eyes burned, and she fought the tears that were close to surfacing. She honestly seldom cried. She'd learned early in her life that tears only annoyed Walter and upset Marianna, both things to be avoided at all cost. But another real connection with her uncle touched her deeply.

She looked up at Max and swallowed before she could speak. "On a list of the best gifts ever, with Uncle Martin leaving me Rebel and the Lodge being the top two, you finding this and giving it to me is a strong third."

He smiled that smile that never failed to make her heart beat a bit faster. "Being number three on that list is an honor."

When Grace carefully put the hat on, it was slightly too large, but she felt as if it was perfect for her. "I'll wear this to the rodeo and hope I look like I fit in."

"Oh, you'll fit in," he said as he reached for his own hat. "Do me a favor?" He took out his cell phone. "I want a picture of you in that hat. I know a few people who'd love to see you wearing it."

"Sure, I guess so."

She expected him to take the shot, but instead he came back behind the desk, got his phone ready, then touched her hat brim to push it back slightly. "I want to make sure you aren't hiding your face." Then he stretched an arm out in front of them, put his other arm around her shoulders and aimed the camera at them. "Smile," he said and took a picture. He checked the screen, then held it out to Grace for her to see. "You take a good picture," he said.

She had never liked being photographed, but this photo was different. Max was smiling, and she looked happy. She loved the picture. "It's nice."

"Yes, it is," he said. He put his phone in his jacket pocket, then went around to the door. He looked back at her. "Everything's good with us, right?"

When she nodded, he gave her a thumbs-up sign and then opened the door and left.

Grace stood in the entry until the sound

of the pickup died away. Taking off the hat, she ran her forefinger over the silver star and felt that if she looked up right then, she'd see her uncle walking into the room to get his hat back before he went to take Rebel for a ride. Foolish thinking, but it made her feel so close to him. She was slowly seeing the kind of life this place offered the right person, and she knew when she left, she'd miss so much of what she'd found.

Slowly, she walked back to her room, placed the hat on the bed, then settled in the easy chair again. She pulled her legs up, wrapped her arms around them and rested her chin on her knees. The view was so soothing, and she felt lighter after telling Max about Walter. He'd understood, and he'd figured out how to maybe make the Van Durens back off. He was amazing, and for the first time she let herself think a what-if. What if she stayed to see where this thing with Max could go? She knew it was sliding past just being friends, but she didn't know if she let go if she'd slide off a cliff or into something like love.

Her cell announced an incoming text. Reaching for it, she found two new texts, one from Sawyer and one from Max.

She made herself pull up Sawyer's first.

I thought you should know that your father is taking you out of his will completely. I know this is none of my business, but what he's doing is wrong, and you need to come home immediately to make peace with him. I will help you any way I can. Sawyer.

If she trusted Sawyer any less than she did, she'd think Walter had pressured him to contact her. Or maybe Walter had dropped that information, hoping Sawyer would pass it along to her. She quickly texted back.

Thanks for the heads-up, but it's his money and his empire, so he can do what he wants with all of it. I won't be coming back. I wish you well and want to thank you for all you've done for me over the years. You've been a wonderful friend. I'll miss you.

Sawyer wouldn't push her—he never did—so when she sent the text back, she didn't expect a reply.

Max had sent her the picture he'd taken. Then her phone rang, and it was Max. She took it. "Thanks for the photo."

"No problem. Lillian just called to tell me I have been instructed to have my gun safety certificate renewed tomorrow down in Two Horns, or I'll be riding a desk until I do. Apparently, I'm late doing it by six months. It looks bad for me, with the election coming up—it makes me look sloppy."

"You think Van Duren said something?"

"Maybe, but I'm going to do it. I'll miss Thanksgiving but I'll be back in time for the rodeo on Saturday. Chappy will be around your place. If you need anything, let him know."

"If I get another call, what do I do?"

"Hang up and call Lillian. Don't talk to them. Better yet, unplug the landline for now."

"Okay, I'll do that." Ruby and Dash had invited her to come over for dinner, and she'd liked the idea of a real Thanksgiving meal for once. She had never experienced a traditional Thanksgiving. But she wanted Max to be there. "If you won't be there for Thanksgiving, should I still go?"

"You're more than welcome to go without me and enjoy yourself. Burr and Elaine will be there. I can't let anything slide, so I'm going to have to go down now and get the certification over with. I've worked a lot of holidays, so I'm used to it, and so are Mom and Dad."

She'd go. "Okay, you do what you have to do, and I'll eat turkey and mashed potatoes with your family." She tried to keep a light tone in her voice and not expose her disappointment.

"I guess I'll see you when I see you," he said.

He hung up before she could say, "I'll miss you."

CHAPTER FIFTEEN

ON THANKSGIVING DAY, Grace woke to a sky with dark clouds but no snow. She went to the Donovans' and had a wonderful time. Their sons weren't home for Thanksgiving: Caleb was away with his family, Coop was still in Boston with his fiancée, McKenna, and Max was tied to his desk in Two Horns even though he'd passed certification with flying colors. So she had dinner with Ruby and Dash, Elaine and Burr, and Lillian and Clint.

She was so grateful for the invitation but missed Max. The food was traditional and delicious. The experience was novel for Grace, who had never had a meal like it, with people around the table who actually liked each other and made her feel very welcome in their circle. After dinner, they all went into Eclipse to put up some of Max's election signs, posting them along the main street where they would be seen by the most people, and near the town hall, where the voting would take place.

When she got back to the Lodge, she stopped by the gates to put up a couple of signs. Then she went inside and sat in Uncle Martin's old chair as evening fell, thinking about how she felt as if she belonged. She wasn't an outsider anymore. She fit right in with the townspeople and was going to an honest-to-goodness rodeo on Saturday with the county sheriff, who she had to admit was pretty great.

For what was maybe the first time, she saw that she had options. She could sell and go back to Tucson and her life there. Or she could start a completely new life, just like her uncle had done. There was so much here that she'd come to care about: the town, the people, the land, the Lodge…and Max.

She'd miss him most of all. A man who'd gone through misery to come out the other end with a stable, good life and had told her he wasn't looking to change that. That made her wonder if she could stay here and make a life with Max around, seeing him the way friends would see each other, and be able to pretend that was enough for her. She wasn't sure what she felt for Max, but she knew that every time she saw him her feelings got stronger. Maybe it wasn't love exactly, but probably as close as she'd get to the real thing. But it couldn't happen.

The next day she spent time helping Chappy in the morning, fixing the doors on the stalls in the stable. She enjoyed doing it with him, listening more than talking, learning how to replace rusted hinges on the stall gates with new ones that didn't squeak. When Chappy left around noon to go back to Flaming Sky to help with preparations for the rodeo the next day, she stayed down at the stable to oil the hinges. She felt a sense of pride at the job she'd done and knew how to make it even better.

Chappy had been using a black marker when he'd measured where the cuts would go in the wooden beams, and he'd left it behind. Five minutes later she'd labeled the two front stalls, one "Thunder" and the other "Rebel," in large bold letters. She stepped back to admire her handiwork and almost jumped out of her skin when she heard, "That's called vandalism, lady!"

She spun around, and Max was there smiling at her from the doorway. "You're back."

"I am for now." He came closer and looked at the new labeling on the stalls. "I never would have taken you for a graffiti punk."

She loved his dry sense of humor now that she understood it. "First a frog, then you call me a punk?"

He cocked his head slightly to one side, his hazel eyes studying her. "I take that back. You're a sight for sore eyes."

"It was that bad in Two Horns?"

"I'll tell you all about it as soon as I have a cup or two of hot coffee."

"You're in luck. I happen to have a fresh supply of Uncle Martin's grinds."

He reached to take her hand in his. "Then what are we waiting for?"

MAX BUSIED HIMSELF making a fire while Grace brewed their coffee. When she came into the great room and handed him his mug, then settled beside him, he felt an ease between them that made his heart happy. He'd missed her during the short time he was gone, and he'd come to the Lodge before he'd even gone to the substation.

He knew he'd missed her too much, and that he'd thought about her too much and he was in a precarious point in their friendship. He was wary of where it was going, but he didn't quite know how to draw back to a safe distance when he just wanted to be right where he was.

"So, what happened in Two Horns?" she asked, diverting his thoughts.

"I got certified on my first try, but then I had a whole other mess that I had to deal with—boring stuff, nothing you'd care to hear about. That took a whole day, then a deputy accidentally discharged his firearm by dropping it in the parking lot. No one was hurt but a cruiser windshield was shattered. That triggered an internal investigation that I had to authorize and monitor for twenty-four hours."

"How can a gun go off just by dropping it?"

He knew that look on her face, the same one he'd seen when he'd left to answer the call about the irrigation thieves and again with the Bobby Joe Lemon situation.

He quickly said, "It's never happened before as far as I know. It was his fault. He'd been rushed and hadn't secured his weapon. He's on leave for ten days, which is mandatory, and he has to take a safety firearms program. That leaves me short-staffed again."

"Can you still go to the rodeo?"

"I'll be here at eleven tomorrow morning

to pick you up, one way or another." He saw
her shoulders drop on a sigh of relief, and it
pleased him that she really did want to go
with him.

"So Big and Little Albert didn't cause the
certification action?"

"Oh, yeah, they did. Someone let me know
as soon as I arrived that Big Albert filed a
complaint that I'd deliberately avoided renew-
ing the certification because I was off doing
what I shouldn't be doing and putting the entire force in jeopardy."

"Max, that's horrible. What did you do to
him?"

"Nothing. I passed the firing range with
a perfect score, so it didn't do anything but
make him look like a petty jerk. Score one
for the good guys."

"He ruined Thanksgiving for you and took
time away from you to work on your reelection."

"Yeah, but I found out how much support
I have from my staff, and I had some time to
think about other things."

She shook her head. "You're a cup's-half-
full kind of guy, aren't you?"

"Most of the time." He finished the last of
his coffee, then put the mug down by hers,

which she'd barely touched. "That's Marty's influence. The man could always see the brighter side of life."

"He didn't get that from his brother," she said with no smile at all.

He wouldn't let her go in that direction so he changed the conversation. "I wanted to talk to you about something, and I'm not sure how to broach the subject." He'd known that sooner or later, he'd have to put everything on the table; he just hadn't expected it to be today. But he wanted to know her answer, no matter what it was, so he could figure out where to go from here.

His serious tone made Grace a little uneasy. "Sure," she said. "What's on your mind?"

"You know Marty asked me to keep an eye on you, to be a friend to you while you're here, and I've tried to do what he asked. The thing is I'm in a spot that I honestly never expected to be in again. I promised myself I'd never go there again. I couldn't. Now, it seems, I got there without even knowing where I was, and when I realized it, it was too late to backtrack."

Max was looking right at her, but she didn't understand what he was saying. All she knew was, whatever had happened or was happening, was important to him.

"I don't know where you're going," she stated.

He sat forward, his hands on his knees. "I know we only met a short time ago, and I know how you feel about relationships, and I know that you're going back to Arizona as soon as you can. What I also know is, I have feelings for you that I can't shake. Every time I see you, they're there. It doesn't make sense, but I can't let it go. I need to know that I'm not delusional to think there might be something between us."

Grace sat absolutely still, scared by what he was saying, but also relieved and happy. She was overwhelmed by the idea that what she'd been thinking about, all the maybes, might be changing to real possibilities.

"Max, I…honestly I've been thinking the same thing, but I can't figure out how it would work. I don't want to hurt you or be hurt myself if I'm wrong. And I don't have any idea if I am or not. But I need to know."

He shifted to face her and reached for her hand. "I do, too. But I'm not sure if I can give you what you need. I'm not sure if this is solid reality or a daydream. But one thing

I do know is this is about you and me. As far as anyone else knowing, I've been there, done that, and I don't want to be there again, but I won't let people stop me from seeing who I want to see."

She'd never hurt him the way Claire had. "I understand not wanting to be hurt, I really do, but I don't know how to find out what's real and what isn't by pretending to care less than I do. It would be a lie. I don't want that."

With his free hand, he touched her cheek, and whispered, "I don't either," before he leaned closer and kissed her. It was gentle and wonderful, and then he moved back, his hazel eyes holding hers before he said in a rough whisper, "So far, so good."

"Yes," she answered.

He stood still holding her hand. "I need to leave. Lillian's going to be swamped if I don't show up soon, then I'll go to the ranch and help them with last-minute details for tomorrow." He smiled at her, a soft expression that touched her heart. "I'll see you at eleven."

"Yes," she said, and he held her hand until they were in the entry, and he had to let her go to put on his jacket and hat.

They faced each other, then Max opened his arms to her and said, "I need a hug." She went into his embrace and didn't want to let go. Max was the one to step back first to kiss her on her forehead.

"I don't want to leave, but I have to," he said with that crooked smile. "Tomorrow. Eleven." He paused, then turned and didn't look back as he went out and the door swung shut behind him.

THE NEXT MORNING, Grace heard an engine in the distance and ran into the lobby to look out the window. Max was five minutes early. She was wearing her uncle's hat along with jeans, boots, a beige long-sleeved Western shirt and her denim jacket. She was so excited to see Max again after their discussion last night that she took some deep breaths before she opened the door.

He was pulling up at the foot of the stairs, and she hurried down, getting into the truck as quickly as she could. Before she could reach to do up her seat belt, Max leaned across the console and kissed her. Then he drew back grinning and said, "A very good morning," and with that he started driving.

As soon as they were on the highway, Max touched her hand where it rested on the console and laced his fingers with hers. What had happened yesterday hadn't been a dream or hallucination, but very real. She looked at him. *Yes, very real.*

"You're a punctual man, Sheriff. I'm impressed."

"One of my many attributes," he said, and his hold tightened slightly.

She smiled as she let herself look at Max in his black hat, black jeans and black leather jacket with silver buttons that looked like shooting stars. Then she saw his boots, red with tooling of more shooting stars.

"Are you staring at me?" he asked.

She was sure grateful his attention was on his driving. That way he wouldn't see her blushing like some silly teenager being caught staring at the football quarterback. "I was trying to figure out where the sheriff had gone."

"He's still here. Just no uniform, and my belt and gun are locked up in the glove compartment. I'm just Max today, taking my girlfriend to her first rodeo." He unexpectedly chuckled at that. "Mom said my first rodeo was when I was three months old, and she brought me with her for closing night when Dad was competing. He won, and I slept through it all."

"I promise I won't fall asleep," she said. "I just hope you don't get a call before it's over."

"I'm clocked out, but if Lillian calls I'll have to leave. There's an even chance she'll call."

"She's working?"

"Clint's staying with her at the station."

"Mmm," she murmured, not wanting to bring up what was worrying her, but thinking that she should, given their conversation yesterday. "Are you sure that this is all okay?"

"What do you mean?"

"Well, for one, you're driving me here in the county truck. That could be misunderstood, couldn't it?"

"Too late. We're in it, and we're almost at the ranch. I'm on call all the time. I need the truck for that."

"Oh, okay, I understand." His lack of concern made her feel better. "What do we say if someone asks if we're together, like really together?"

"That we're really together."

She waited, then said, "Okay. The tickets today, how much do they cost?"

"Nothing. It's free, but there are donation boxes set up at the food stands, at the souvenir booth and at the main arena gates. I'm hoping it does well, because all proceeds are being split between the Simply Sanctuary Horse Rescue that Coop and McKenna are involved with and the retirement home for former rodeo performers down near Cheyenne."

They arrived at the gates where a stocky man stood under the arched sign for the ranch, which had been embellished with gold, red and white streamers along with a banner that read "Welcome Future Champions."

"Hey, Boomer," Max said, sticking his head out the window. "How's it going?"

The man named Boomer beamed. "It's going real good."

"Great. See you up there." He then drove up the driveway and toward the rise. "We'll park on the private road to the house and not get tangled up in the traffic around the arena."

More streamers looped from post to post along the white wooden pasture fencing for as far as she could see. Then they got to the rise, and the transformation was even more jaw-dropping. Red, white and gold were everywhere. Horse trailers were parked in the closest pasture on dirt cleared of snow, and the arena beyond held a huge banner hung from a partial roof over the bleachers: "Youth Rodeo's Tenth Anniversary Celebration."

"Good turnout," Max said as he slowed, then drove onto the private dirt road to the main house. He pulled over, the truck wheels crunching the snow that had been cleared to the shoulder. "Dad's going to be walking on air. Every year the attendance grows."

He sounded proud of his father, and she envied him. She wished she could be proud of hers. "I didn't expect something this grand," she said, undoing her seat belt when the truck came to a stop.

"If I'm needed to help with the kids, you come with me. If we get separated, call my cell." He looked right at her, his eyes holding hers. "I don't want to lose you," he said before he opened his door to get out, and the expression on his face told her that his words held double meaning.

Grace didn't want to lose him, either. "I won't get lost," she said when she met up with Max at the back of the truck.

Seeing no one else around by the house, she reached for his hand and squeezed it.

"What was that for?" he asked.

"I just wanted to thank you for a good time today in case I forget to tell you later."

He kissed her quickly. "You're welcome," he said.

MAX WATCHED GRACE'S reactions to what was going on in the arena as much as he paid attention to the actual events. She was cheering and clapping just as much as anyone in the audience. So far, things had been easy, people saying their hellos, smiling, and talking about the weather or their stock. When the last competition was over, the presentation of awards was set up in the middle of the arena and Grace turned to him, her face glowing.

"That was great," she said. "I can see why your family's so involved in it. Do you miss being more involved?"

"Honestly, sometimes I do. If I'm not re-elected, I'll get more involved with the rodeos, both professional and the juniors here and in the state."

"I can't even imagine how exciting a professional rodeo would be."

"They're incredible. If I hear of one while you're still here, I'll take you to see for yourself."

His dad went up on stage, and the awarding

of ribbons to the winners began. When the last award was handed out, it went to Henry's oldest son, who took top scores in three different competitions. Everyone in the place was on their feet, cheering and clapping, and Henry was there taking pictures.

Dash announced that food and dancing were about to start in the main stable area and that the hay barn was ready for the kids.

Max leaned closer to Grace and said, "Let's sit here for a bit and let the crowd thin out." He slipped his arm around Grace's shoulders. "You're cold and I'm keeping you warm. I like that."

She looked at him, their faces so close she felt the heat of his misting breath on her cheek. "Protect and serve," she said, and he gave her a good-one expression as he pulled her closer.

When the crowd had diminished to a trickle, Grace asked, "What now?"

Max stood and held out his hand to help her up. "Food, dance, visiting with people and finding Henry to congratulate him." When she got to her feet, they started down the stairs.

BY THE TIME they arrived at the main stables, the fragrance of barbecue was in the air, and laughter and voices drifted out of the open doors. The interior had been completely transformed: a wooden dance floor had been laid out in the training ring, with a stage in the center of it where a band was already playing country music. People sat on hay bales inside the divider wall, and others sat on benches just outside the ring. Heaters strategically placed around the building kept real cold at bay.

Max leaned closer to her so she could hear what he was saying over the music, laughter and conversations. "The barbecue smells great."

Elaine brushed past them, followed by several men, all carrying what looked like large roasting pans with lids. People were filing in behind them, and Ruby was there managing a line for food that already wound out the doors.

Max drew Grace to one side. "Let's sit down and wait for the food line to thin out now." He motioned to some benches by the short wall of the ring. "The farther from the food frenzy, the better."

They had barely been seated when Farley came over, dressed in an all-red outfit with a gold-studded belt and white tooled boots.

The man never ceased to make a statement with his clothes. "You two hiding over here?"

"We're just waiting for a break in the food line," Max told him.

"Hey there, Miss Grace," Farley said, shifting his attention to her. "I wondered if I might find you here after seeing you two together lately."

Max quickly changed subjects. "Did you see Henry's oldest boy take three firsts?"

"That kid's gonna be something someday," he said, but got right back to what he was interested in. "So, are you two a…thing? I heard something along those lines from…someone. I knew the two of you would be a good match but didn't know you were sparkin', Max."

"Mom invited Grace and asked me if I'd bring her. This is all so new to her—she needs someone to explain things to her so she can enjoy it."

The man actually looked disappointed with those facts, and Max wasn't about to stick around for any follow-up questions. He just wanted to enjoy being with Grace.

"Now, we're going to go dance and have fun," Max said.

"You do that. I'm heading over to get my share of them ribs."

After Farley hurried off to get in line, Grace giggled. "Sparkin'?"

"Oh, yeah." He shook his head and stood. "How about dancing? I won't let anyone cut in—don't worry about that."

She hesitated for a second, then took off her hat and jacket and left them on the bench. Max guided her to the dance floor and once there, took her hand with his.

"It's smart you left your hat on the bench. If you get twirled, it could fly off your head and get stomped on by the dancers."

She looked at him, and her violet eyes were smiling. "Note to sheriff. Don't twirl me."

"Okay, but you don't know what you're missing."

"How about I twirl you instead?" she said.

"I don't think I'd mind that." Max moved closer to Grace, slipping his other hand down to the small of her back, and they started to dance to a slow song. Farley had nailed what was going on between them, and he'd given it a name: they were sparkin' all right. Grace shifted to slip her arms around his neck and leaned closer.

Grace hadn't danced in a long time, and when she had, it hadn't been to a country and Western song about love against the odds. At any other time, she might have snickered at the corny lyrics, but not then. When she was in Max's arms, she didn't care about odds.

"How are you feeling?" he whispered in her hair.

Without thinking about it, she said, "As if I belong right here, with you."

His hold on her tightened. "Me, too."

She closed her eyes, just letting the moment be what it was and wishing it would go on forever. The song flowed into another, a plaintive ballad about a rodeo cowboy finding love, but walking away because he could never settle down.

"Sad songs," she said as she looked up at Max.

He met her gaze and said to her, "Come on, give me a smile."

The warmth in his eyes was breathtaking and she saw his gaze drop to her lips. "You have the most beautiful smile," he whispered. Then he started to lean down, and she wanted the kiss she knew was coming.

Before that could happen, a heavy hand touched her shoulder and a voice she knew said, "Mind if I cut in, Sheriff?"

She felt Max tense, but his voice was level. "Actually, I do, Albert." And with that he expertly maneuvered Grace into a twirl, then back into his arms.

Albert was still there. "Let the lady answer for herself."

The song ended, and Grace said, more loudly than she intended, "I can speak for myself, and I don't want to dance with you." Nervously she took a step back and looked at Max. "Can we go and get food now?"

"I'm starving," he said. Without giving another glance to the other man, he put his hand on the small of her back and lightly guided her through the remaining couples on the dance floor, leaving Little Albert standing there alone.

CHAPTER SIXTEEN

GRACE SAT DOWN with Max after getting their food and was surprised to see Freeman Lee talking to Big Albert, who had stopped at the open doors to the stable.

"What's going on?" Grace asked Max and motioned to the men.

"I don't know, but Freeman can hold his own with Al."

"But what if they get into a fight?"

He chuckled at that. "Freeman talks a good game, but he wouldn't do anything to mess up today. He'd never do that to my parents."

The next time they saw Freeman, he was coming back into the stables alone and motioned to Max to come over to him.

Max stood up. "I won't be long," he said.

When he came back five minutes later, he acted as if nothing had happened. Elaine and Burr had stopped by to chat with her, and after they left to help with the cleanup, she expected Max to say something. When he still didn't, she gave up on waiting. "What happened with Freeman?"

He stood and put on his jacket and hat. "I'll tell you later. I think it's time for us to leave."

He reached down and picked up Grace's coat and hat, handing them to her. As she put them on, she said, "I should say goodbye to your parents and thank them for everything."

Max looked around and then smiled at her. "They're dancing. Trust me, you don't want to interrupt them."

She glanced over at the dance floor and saw them moving to a slow ballad. Dash said something to Ruby that made her smile, then he leaned down and kissed her forehead. Ruby cuddled closer to him and rested her head on his chest. Grace was entranced by the connection the two of them had after so many years of marriage.

"I'll thank them later," she murmured.

They stepped out into the cold night and walked side by side toward where the truck was parked. They'd just made it to the top of the private dirt road when Big Albert approached them with his son in tow. Grace barely controlled a groan. They looked determined.

"You got a minute, Max?" the elder Albert asked.

"We're leaving."

Grace wouldn't allow herself to look down. When she'd been confronted by Walter in the past, she'd learned never to show any sign of weakness. Maintaining eye contact was maintaining control. Now the two bullies were no more than a few feet from her, and she stared at them.

"I was just telling Pa how you two embarrassed me on the dance floor." He looked at Grace. "How about you make up for it now? The band's still here, and we can ask for a good song." His expression was smarmy, and she just kept looking at him without responding. She saw uncertainty creeping into his eyes, and then he actually puffed out his chest. "I can dance with any girl here, but I'm giving you a second chance."

HIM TALKING TO Grace like that put Max over the edge, and he figured it was almost time to put his cards on the table, if he had to. But first he'd try for a quick exit. He ignored Little Albert as if he didn't exist and repeated, "We're leaving," to Big Albert.

The older man came back with, "Sneaking

off, huh? Just like you. I'd bet you aren't on the way back to work, either." His laughter was almost a cackle. "Dumb, really dumb. Seems you have no respect for the office you hold. That's going to cost you big-time."

Grace was very still, and he didn't want to resort to name-calling. "Is that a threat?"

"Naw, that's a promise."

So much for a fast exit. He wasn't going to go any further with the blowhard. "Listen to me, Al, and listen good. I went down to Two Horns on a request that I renew my certification in weapons and accuracy. I got it first try, a perfect score on the written component and for the shooting range."

Al made a scoffing sound. "Am I supposed to be impressed, Sheriff?"

He ignored that. "Someone mentioned that you'd been down to headquarters the day before with a couple of friends on a tour of the place. One of them was Benny Mason. You were in your old office, which of course is mine now, and they saw you looking through my files. Then you went up to Internal Affairs carrying some files with you and left there with no files. Fifteen minutes later they were told an anonymous complaint had been filed against me for defaulting on being recertified in… Well, you know, and I had to show up first thing the next day."

The more Max said, the tighter Al's expression became.

"You're a—"

Max cut him off. "Donovan, the name's still Donovan. Oh, I almost forgot about the cameras that will verify what I'm saying and the fact that my old certification notice, which was a copy of an original, was missing out of my files. No one seemed to know what happened to it, but that didn't matter. A look through the county records, which had been archived, found the original that expires in six months. Seems you really entertained your cronies. I bet you all went for a drink after that to laugh about how you got me."

"You can't talk to my pa like that!" Little Albert said in a sudden burst.

His father said, "Shut up," then looked directly at Max while his son was turning red from anger. "What do you want?" he asked through clenched teeth.

"All I want is for you to back off and make this a clean election where the best man wins."

"What about…the other things?"

"No one except you two will know about

it unless you hurt anyone I care about. Then everything's on the table. Otherwise, this is over and done. And one more thing—stay out of my office unless you get to put your name on the door. Deal?"

Little Albert looked deflated when his father said, "Deal."

Right then the junior bully rose out of the ashes of defeat and sneered at Grace. "You ain't nothing special. I only asked you to dance because Pa made me. You're nothing but a dog."

Max took a step toward the idiot with the intent of breaking a few teeth. But his father got to him first and grabbed him by his jacket collar, jerking him back so hard that he landed on the shoulder of the road in the low pile of ice and snow.

"I told you to shut up!" Big Albert bit out, then turned to Grace. "Sorry, ma'am, I'll take care of him."

"He's all yours, Al," Max said.

As the two men walked away, Max and Grace got in the truck. Once the heater was running, Grace looked at Max and said, "I was wrong about something I told you before."

He couldn't guess what, except for things

he didn't want to hear. "What are you talking about?" he asked with some caution.

"The good guys do win sometimes."

He chuckled and leaned over the console as she did the same toward him and they kissed. When she sat back in the seat, she sighed softly.

"You're a very good guy, Max Donovan," she said. "But I did think for a moment you were going to hit Little Albert."

"Naw, I wasn't going to hit him."

"Oh, good," she said with obvious relief.

"I was going to crush him."

They both laughed as Max turned the truck around and started for the gates.

When they were on the highway heading to the Lodge, Grace said, "I need to get something straight between us."

He flashed her a look. "What's that?"

"When we first met, it was really annoying that you were always stepping in to save me in some way, as if I was helpless on my own."

"Heck, no, I never meant—"

She'd put that wrong, and she cut him off. "I know. I figured out what you were doing the more I was around you and saw how you dealt with other people, your family, your friends and now... Well, I've come to really like that about you. I appreciate that I feel safe with you, and that I can trust you. I don't feel that way often. I'm not used to it. Walter always had a security detail to watch over me no matter which one of his projects we were living in. They kept us safe, but they didn't make me *feel* safe. On top of that, I couldn't get away with anything because they always found me."

"You were a troublemaker?" he said with fake shock.

"I never did anything big. But I did slip out of the penthouse to meet one of the dealer's sons in the basement laundry room once."

"Wait—dealer's son?"

She amended that with, "Blackjack dealer."

"Ahh." He grinned. "How old were you?"

"We were both twelve, and I was sure he'd kiss me. I'd never kissed anyone before, and I didn't want to be uncool."

"No one wants to be uncool," he said.

"Right. So I managed to sneak out, he showed up and we ground our teeth against each other's for a minute. Our make-out session was cut short because Walter sicced Security on us. I cried for ages over that—I was so humiliated."

"He was just being protective," he said.

"No, he wasn't. He paid Sawyer to be protective of me. He was angry with me because he'd been embarrassed when Security found out the boy was a dealer's son. That didn't sit well with Walter at all. He never even talked to me about it. Neither did Marianna. But Riley, one of the security guys, told me that if I ever wanted to learn how to kiss, he was available. I'm not sure if he meant it, but I told Sawyer, and Riley disappeared without a trace."

"Good old Sawyer," he said, then turned off the highway and drove up to the Lodge. After he'd parked next to her Jeep, he turned to her. "I can tell you something that might make you feel better about being uncool and grinding teeth."

"You've got my attention," she said.

"I've kissed you a few times and all I can say is, you're very good at it. No teeth problems, no nose problems trying to figure out where your nose goes."

"Where were you when I was twelve and so uncool?"

"Let's see, you were twelve, and now you're twenty-six?"

"Yes."

"I was about twenty-two years old and had been in the army for a year and wanted to join the Army Rangers to go over to the Middle East."

"I guess you were really good at kissing by then," she said, wondering why she didn't feel any age gap between them. She'd never thought about it.

"I don't know about that," he said, grinning. "But I was cool enough."

"Cool enough to get a tattoo?"

He chuckled at that. "I was very cool by then." He didn't elaborate any further. "Now, I'll be cool and walk you to the door."

"Before I get out, I have a question, if it's not too personal."

"Ask me and I'll tell you if it is or not."

"What did Freeman want with you back at the ranch?"

"Oh, he told me that Big Albert and his son were miserable people, but no one seemed to be buying into their lies. I appreciated that, but that wasn't why he called me over, really. He just wanted to chat."

When he didn't elaborate, she decided not to push. He didn't look mad, but he sure didn't look happy, either.

"Oh, okay… Um, I guess I should get inside and let you go on your way. But thank you for the best time I've had in a very long time. It might have been my best day yet."

"I like being around on your best days," he said. She reached for the door handle, but Max stopped her.

"Grace, wait a minute, please."

"IS SOMETHING WRONG?"

Max hadn't expected to say anything about his meeting with Freeman, especially not to Grace; he didn't want to discuss Claire anymore with anyone. But something nudged at him, a thought that the only person he wanted to tell about that conversation was Grace, because she was becoming more and more important to him every time he saw her.

"Freeman told me he was going to Texas. Claire works at a lab there in research, and Freeman and Beulah are flying there tonight for Claire's wedding."

"She's marrying that Russell guy?"

"No, someone named Gregory O'Brian. Freeman says he has degrees on top of degrees. They work together and are going on a research grant trip to Central America for a year. So they're having a small wedding, then leaving the week after." Max couldn't read Grace's expression in the dull blue glow from the dash light. "Apparently, he's from a very wealthy family."

Grace was very quiet until he stopped speaking, then she asked softly, "Are you all right?"

That took him back. "Me? Sure. I'm okay."

"I just mean, you loved Claire for a long time and now she's marrying some guy and going off to be with him in another part of the world."

He saw sympathy in her violet eyes, and he didn't want that from her. "You think I'm heartbroken? Devastated?"

"Are you?"

"I'm not. I'm figuring out how I feel, but it's nothing like that. Claire liked to live life on her terms, definitely not around here. I guess she found what she was looking for with this O'Brian guy after she dumped Russell."

She studied him for a moment, then sighed. "So how *do* you feel?"

He took off his hat and tossed it back onto the second seat, then met her eyes again. "I think I'm feeling good about a lot of things. Three years is a long time to get over something, and Marty helped push me on that until I was in a better place and was on the right road. I'm not stepping off of that road again."

"No one could blame you if you were upset."

"Meaning *you* wouldn't blame me for being upset?"

"Why would I blame you for anything you felt? Emotions are emotions, and you deserve to be happy, and to have a family and find love like your parents did."

He couldn't explain to her how he'd felt when he'd heard about Claire, because he really hadn't felt very much except wanting to go back and find Grace and dance again without Little Albert ruining it.

"I need to go and see what's happening with the ranch cleanup, but before I leave, I want to do something."

"What's that?" she asked, but he was already getting out and coming around to her side of the truck.

When he opened her door, he held out his hand to her. She didn't understand but let him help her down to face him. "What did you want to do?"

"This," he said, and kissed her.

When he drew back, he tapped her chin lightly. "Now I'm leaving. I'll pop by and see you tomorrow. It's going to be a busy week, but I'm hoping after the election's over we can take the horses out for a ride anywhere you want to go."

"I'd love that," she said. "*And* we can celebrate you winning the election."

"Don't jinx it," he said, then got back in the truck and drove off, grinning the whole way down the dirt road.

AFTER DROPPING GRACE off at the Lodge, Max had gone to town instead of heading back to the ranch, partly to make sure Lillian and Clint weren't still at the station covering the phones, and partly because the weather service predicted snow to start falling by midnight, driven by heavy winds. He ended up sleeping on the cot to see how bad the storm would be before he headed to the ranch.

Now he stood before the big front window at the substation, watching people dig their cars and trucks out from under the snow before the snowbanks the plow left behind buried them completely. It was barely six o'clock when the calls about electrical outages had started coming in. Max had them redirected to the power company. He couldn't go anywhere until the plows started on the highway and he needed to get to the Lodge. He'd tried calling Grace as soon as he woke up and saw the snow. But the call to her cell went directly to voice mail, and the landline just rang and rang. He was worried about her and anxious to get out there.

When the plow finally arrived, Max drove out to the Lodge and parked his truck at the gate. The front gate was frozen shut and he had to jump over it; he'd take care of that later. He was relieved to see smoke coming from the chimney. Smoke meant a fire, and that meant Grace must be okay. He knocked on the door and when there was no answer, he tried the latch and opened the door. He stepped inside and was met with cold air. No furnace sounds broke the silence, just the snap and pop of a newly laid fire. He crossed to try the light switch in the great room, but the power was clearly out.

Blankets and pillows were on the couch, and a tray with a mug and a half-eaten sandwich on the coffee table. But Grace wasn't there. He went back into the reception area and walked behind the desk and over to the closed office door. Rapping on it, he waited, called her name then heard movement right before the door opened.

Grace stood there, barefoot, her hair sleep mussed, wearing pink pajama bottoms and a white T-shirt emblazoned with "This Isn't My

First Rodeo, Buckeroo!" under the silhouette of a cowgirl on a bucking horse. He read the shirt out loud and laughed. Grace crinkled her nose. "A gift from Gabby."

"Wear it to your next rodeo," he said, then switched tones. "Are you okay? I've been calling you for hours, and I got worried when you never answered."

"No signal," she said. "And it's cold in here. There's no electricity and I'm on my third fire."

"Come with me and see how awesome I am," he said, getting a grin out of her.

"I already know you're awesome," she said, "and I'm not dressed for the weather."

"We aren't going outside, but first, I need a hug. I'm so glad you're okay."

She nestled up to him and he closed his arms around her, needing to feel the realness of her against him.

"Mmm," she murmured. "Now, you were saying you can make the electricity come back?"

He shifted to brush a couple of errant curls off her forehead. "It never left," he said, then took her to the backup generator in a closet off the laundry. He hoped Little Albert had done his job right when he delivered the propane. Grace was watching when he started up the generator and a moment later the furnace hummed to life.

When they'd gone to the great room and settled on the couch, Max said, "Just say it."

"Thank you. I had no idea that there was a backup generator anywhere around the place."

He'd taken off his jacket and Grace was sitting so close to him that he could feel her heat through the denim shirt he was wearing. As much as he wanted to, he didn't put his arm around her. He'd been thinking so much about her and how everything between them now was wait-and-see. He didn't much like that now. He hadn't been enough for Claire, and he'd almost lost a part of himself in the process. He knew if things kept going the way they were, he'd either have to take a leap of faith or let Grace go.

"Do you have any idea when you'll be leaving, if you do?"

She was staring into the fire. "The only person who misses me is Zoey, my friend who owns the consignment store. I'm kind of on my own schedule for now."

He tried not to grimace at the thought that only one person would miss Grace being gone. He knew he'd miss her something awful. "Have you thought about staying here?"

She surprised him when she said, "I have. I wish you'd been there for Thanksgiving—it was magical. I felt so accepted by everyone there. I loved it."

"I heard you helped put up some election signs, too. Thank you for that."

"It was fun. Clint is so funny, and so is Burr. Gosh, I haven't laughed that much in a while. This town is pretty spectacular, and you're…" Her expression changed and she shrugged as she turned to look at him. "I can't stay to run the Lodge. My dad built his empire on buying and selling and building and destroying the past to make room for the future. I'm not like Walter—I don't want that life. It frightens me how much I don't want that.

"When I was young and didn't know anything about anything, I wished for a horse and new parents who would like me more. Then I just started wishing my dad would be proud to walk me down the aisle one day when I got married. I finally got a clue and started wishing I'd never be like Walter. So far I'm doing okay on that front."

Max did what he'd wanted to do when they first sat down and put his arm around her shoulders, pulling her against his side. He would have liked to be able to say he understood what she was feeling, but he couldn't begin to. "Hey, your horse wish came true, too, didn't it?"

"Dumb luck," she murmured.

"Maybe, maybe not," he said and thought, *What a brilliant response*.

She rested her hand on his chest. "I'd vote for maybe not."

"So, you won't stay and bring this place back to life just because it's similar to what your dad does? You'd rather walk away from all of this than follow in your father's footsteps, even the tiniest bit?"

She twisted to look at him. "Can we not talk about it? It's… I just don't want to. Please. I'm here, I'm not back in the Bennet kingdom in Las Vegas. I'm with a man who means a lot to me, and I'm so happy."

"I am, too," he said. "The Van Durens are off my back, the snow is a blessing after the years-long drought and you're here with me."

As he looked into her eyes, he was amazed at how clearly he knew that he loved Grace. What he felt was a real love. Not a convenient love, or the kind of love he'd almost settled for with Claire—he owed her for walking out on him. This was a deep-down love that seemed to wrap around him.

She looked at him quizzically. "What are you thinking?"

He wanted to tell her, but he was afraid it was too soon, too much, so he'd bide his time and when he knew it was right, he'd tell Grace that he loved her and hope she felt the same way. If she did, they could figure out the rest together. Right then, he needed to go back to work. He stood and Grace did, too.

"I have to head back to check on the situation in town and do some wellness checks on some of our seniors, to make sure they're okay."

She walked with him out to reception, where he put on his jacket and hat he'd left on the desk. "How do you feel about a second date?"

"You're counting the rodeo as our first date?"

"Sure. We can't ride too far for a while, but I want to go someplace where I can dance with you without being interrupted this time."

"You know a place?"

"Yep, a great place. Pure Rodeo. Caleb owns and runs it. It's right by the ranch and they have great live bands."

"I'd love that," she said.

"I'll check with Caleb to see when a good time would be to go. Actually, the family's going to have dinner there in a couple of days to welcome Coop and his fiancée back from their trip to Boston and talk about their wedding and things like that. Would you want to go with me?"

She smiled. "Absolutely."

"Okay, great! But in between now and then, how about a mini-date tomorrow? If the roads stay clear, you could swing by the ranch and visit with Rebel."

"That would be wonderful," she said. "I miss him. I just hope we can ride soon."

"We will, trust me," he said. "I'll call you tomorrow and let you know when I'm free."

"Sounds good," she said, and he left to trudge back to the truck on the other side of the gate. He was warming up the truck when he thought about what Grace had said about Walter Bennet. He decided to call Lillian to get a background check on the man. As he pulled onto the highway, he realized he was ready to make a leap of faith.

When he arrived at the substation a few minutes later, he relieved Lillian so she could go have lunch with Clint. She'd left the readout on Walter Bennet on the computer for him.

He scrolled through ten pages, stunned at the empire Walter Bennet had built. Yet, he'd lost his daughter. He saw a personal contact number for the man, took a deep breath and made a call. When a male voice answered, "Walter Bennet," he almost hung up, but didn't.

"Mr. Bennet, you don't know me, but I'm calling about your daughter, Grace."

GRACE WOKE THE next morning, her arms and chest aching from clearing the snow off the porch and her Jeep. She stayed in bed longer than usual, enjoying the view from the partially frosted windows.

She didn't know why she hadn't admitted to Max that she'd almost thought of staying at the Lodge despite what Walter did or didn't do. She was her own person and the idea of letting Walter still dictate her actions made her cringe. If she stayed and reopened the Lodge, she'd keep her promise; keep her uncle's legacy alive and protect the Lodge. She'd finally have a real home, something she'd never had before. She could hardly wait to see Max again to tell him she was staying.

She tried to stay busy, feeling restless now that she knew what she wanted, and she hoped that Max would be part of her future. As the hours ticked by she only heard from Lillian, who called to let her know that they were sending a smaller plow to the Lodge to free the gate so it would open and clear the snow from the highway through the gates and up to the building.

Max had no doubt arranged for it, and she appreciated him doing so. She bundled up in layered clothes, two pairs of socks, her heavy jacket with the collar up and her uncle's hat. She was going to walk down to the stable to make sure the roof hadn't caved in and see how far Chappy had gotten on reinforcing the top beams. The air was bitterly cold, but the sun reflecting off the snow made everything look so beautiful. When she reached the stable, she was relieved to see that the roof was intact, but the snow banked against the doors made it impossible for her to get inside.

She took her time going back. When she finally stepped out onto the driveway, she stopped dead in her tracks. A large SUV was parked at the foot of the porch steps and pounding echoed through the air. She moved closer and stopped again when she saw Walter at the entry door, banging on it with a closed fist.

"Grace!" he yelled.

She entertained the idea of just turning

around and going back to the stable, but her father spotted her before she could make her escape. Ducking her head, she went to the car, and saw Sawyer sitting in the driver's seat with a pained expression on his face. This was not good at all. She managed a smile for him that probably looked as pained as his. Then she turned toward her father, who was standing on the top step.

"What are you doing here, Walter?" she asked.

He was in an immaculately tailored gray overcoat and polished oxfords with snow clinging to his pant cuffs—completely inappropriate for this weather, and she was sure he was very cold.

"Can we take this inside?"

She didn't want him to ever go inside the Lodge, but she couldn't block him without things getting worse than they already were with him showing up out of the blue. She hurried up the steps past him, opened the door and went in. He followed her, slamming the door shut so hard it shook the glass in the windows next to it.

She was furious he was there, and her anger only grew when he took his time looking around before he finally turned to her. "It's a dump, as I expected. Just like Martin to let it go like this, then leave it to you." Walter looked disgusted. "I was glad when he left, and his wishy-washy way of looking at life. It was always incredibly annoying to me."

He was rambling bitterly, and she couldn't stand it. "Stop, Walter. Just tell me what you're doing here."

"Well, dear daughter," he said sarcastically. "I came to rescue you and take you home where you belong."

Her stomach roiled at his words. "I don't need you or anyone else rescuing me."

He ignored what she'd said with a dismissive flick of his large hand. "I'll send in my development team when the snow melts to get an evaluation of what this land is worth. Then we can contact the developers and make sure we get every cent of profit out of this fiasco."

Grace cut him off. "This is my place, not yours. Who do you think you are coming in here and acting as if you have any part in my decisions about the Lodge?"

"I received a call from a man who felt you could use your father's help and support to figure out what you were up against instead of throwing it all away."

Had Burr called Walter and inadvertently

said something to set him off? "Who called you?"

Her father had a smug smile on his face as he undid the buttons on his long overcoat. "He seemed very worried about you, so I take it you've not been doing too well on your own here."

"Who called you, Walter?"

"He said his name was Max Donovan."

Her heart dropped and she could barely catch her breath. *Max?* "No, no, no," she said. "He wouldn't do that."

"He did."

Her world closed in on her, sucking the oxygen out of the air around her. She'd trusted Max and told him things she'd never wanted to talk about before. He knew she didn't want Walter anywhere around the Lodge to taint it with his hatred for his brother. He knew she never wanted to be in Walter's orbit again, but he'd been the one to draw Walter here. That hurt her more than anything Walter had ever done. She had to fight to keep from screaming and giving Walter the satisfaction of seeing her totally break down.

"I don't want you or need you here. You really are a horrible father."

The smile was wiped off his face. "Don't you talk to me like that."

"Just go away," she said. She could feel her world starting to crumble and the idea of making a home at the Lodge crumbled with it.

"And you can either come home and let me clean up this mess or stay here, but don't expect me to come to rescue you the next time you need it. There's no more money, no more bank accounts you can clear out and nothing for you when they read my will."

"I don't want your money. I earned every penny you paid into that bank account."

He chuckled harshly at that. "When you get ready to sell this dump, call Sawyer and he'll pass on the news to me. Then we'll talk."

She knew that she would lose all semblance of control if she said anything right then. Instead, she just stared at Walter, and kept quiet.

"Okay," he said. "If you think this place is worth breaking up our family, then you deserve whatever comes."

"There is no family," she managed to get out. The closest she'd come to having a family was here, and Max had taken it away from her. She couldn't stay. She'd leave alone the way she'd arrived.

Walter stood very still, and Grace saw the glint of hardness in his eyes. "You've been such a disappointment to me."

She didn't break under his assessment. Instead, she asked him what she'd wanted to know since she'd found out about the Lodge. "Why did you hate Uncle Martin?"

CHAPTER SEVENTEEN

WALTER SEEMED TO age before her eyes. "I didn't come here to talk about that."

"Then how about this? Did you and Marianna ever love each other?"

He ran a hand roughly over his face, then looked right at her. "Yes, we did. I loved her until she didn't love me. I think she pretty much hated me, and that's why she stayed away as much as she could."

Grace could hardly bear to hear the words. "Why?"

Walter shrugged. "We'd been married for a year before Martin showed up in Vegas at the company offices. He was out of rehab again, and Marianna had the nerve to tell me she admired him for admitting to his failures and mistakes and doing something about it. She admired a total loser. She compared me to him, and I came up short. She called me egotistical and heartless."

"She loved him?"

"Marianna claimed she didn't, but there was something there."

"So you threw him out?"

"I let him stay in the smaller penthouse by ours, but after he admitted he wished he'd met your mother before I had, yes, I kicked him out. He told me he knew he could have given her a better life than I ever could."

His sharp bark of laughter startled Grace.

"I had him tossed and told him to get out and if he ever came back, I'd make sure he'd be sorry. He said he was only leaving because Marianna had asked him to. She told him she was married and took that seriously. But that didn't mean she loved me.

"I thought if we had a child things would change. They didn't. Marianna left me as often as she could and passed you off to your nanny. Eventually, there was no reason for me to be around for more than the occasional photo op or holiday. So I stayed out of her way."

"What about me, though?" she asked, her eyes burning now. "I was there, but you never were. Why?"

He grimaced at that. "You're right. I was as bad at being a father as I was at being a husband. That's on me." He exhaled, then appeared to diminish as he hunched his shoulders. "I'll be going. This is all yours." With those parting words, he walked out, closing the door behind him.

Grace slowly sank to the floor and leaned her back against the desk. She hurt so much she wondered if anyone could die of a broken heart. Max had drawn her to him, saying "Trust me," over and over again, and she had. She'd felt safe with him on so many levels, only to have it all pulled out from under her.

"Trust me," she muttered to herself and started to cry.

MAX HAD BEEN tied up all day with emergencies due to the storm and the power outages, and it was seven o'clock before he could leave town and head to the Lodge. He was sorry that he hadn't been able to keep his mini-date with Grace and go spend some time with the horses, but he was excited to see her again. He was smiling when he drove up the driveway and parked by the Jeep.

His knock on the door was unanswered until he heard stirring inside. Then Grace opened the door for him. But something was terribly wrong. She looked as if she'd been crying, and her face was very pale.

"Grace? Are you all right?"

She was in stocking feet, jeans and a lavender plaid flannel shirt, looking as if she might have slept in them. Her hair was mussed, and she wasn't smiling.

"No, I'm not."

He moved to come inside, but she stood in his way. "What's going on?" he asked at a total loss about what could have happened since he'd last seen her.

"I take back everything I said about you and me," she said in a low slightly hoarse voice. "I don't want to be anything to you, and you're nothing to me."

He felt dread wash over him. "What are you talking about?"

"I trusted you enough to tell you about Walter and what he did to me. But you ruined everything."

"How?"

She held up an unsteady hand. "You lied to me. I thought you were—" She stopped abruptly, her hand slowly lowering as it closed into a fist at her side. "This can't be my home. I had this ridiculous idea that I'd stay and that we could…you and me…" She shook her head sharply. "You ruined it."

He wanted her to stop saying that. "How did I do that?"

She swallowed before she said, "You called Walter. You told him he had to come and rescue me, like I'm too foolish to take care of myself. He came here to take me back to Las Vegas."

He understood what had happened, but not how she knew about a three-minute call he'd made last night. As soon as he got off the phone with the man, he'd realized Grace was right. Walter Bennet was a class-A jerk, and his call hadn't made any bit of difference. He'd asked Max what kind of mess Grace had made, then brusquely informed him that she was on her own. That had been it—followed by a click when he'd hung up on Max.

He'd been foolish to make the call in the first place, and when her father had said she was on her own, he'd ached for Grace and vowed never to mention her father again. Now it had exploded in his face in the worst possible way.

"He actually showed up here in the snow despite the bad road conditions?"

"Yes, because *you* called him. He came to take me back with him, and he wants to raze the Lodge and develop the land. He saw dollar signs and he came to claim the money through me." She pressed the heels of her hands to her eyes, then looked right at him. "You…you knew how I felt, but you ignored me. You have some delusional idea that you know what's best for everyone… You're like some messed-up superhero running amok, trying to save everyone in your path. You—" Her voice was rising, and she stopped abruptly.

Her violet eyes looked right at him, her lashes spiked with dampness, and he saw that lost look he had before. That hurt more than her words.

"I did call him, but I—"

"Stop, please. I can't do this. You're the first person I trusted in a really long time. I wanted to trust you, to feel safe with you, and…"

He was struck dumb, the same as he'd been with Claire when she'd told him she was leaving. The difference was, he'd been hurt by Claire, his heart bruised, but not broken. With Grace an ache deep inside of him was growing, and he could barely keep eye contact when he finally spoke, trying to ignore the feeling he'd lose part of himself this time.

"I can only say I'm sorry. It was silly of me to think I could do anything to help." He went closer to her, the cold air from the still open door settling in his bones. "I'm more sorry than you'll ever know." He made the only offer he could think of. "If you stay here, I'll leave you alone."

She exhaled with a shudder. "No, no, this can't be my home. I can't stay now."

Max could almost hear Marty speaking to him years ago. *Max, if you find a spot in life where your heart's easy, don't pass it by and throw away your chances that it's right where you belong.* He'd thought that he might finally be at that place in his life, as long as it included Grace. Now he'd never know.

"I guess there's nothing I can say to change that now, but maybe later we can talk."

She shivered and hugged herself tightly. "No, there's nothing left to talk about. Please, go."

He had no option but to leave, but before he thought it through, he stepped closer and cupped her chin before he kissed her on the forehead. He felt her flinch at the contact, and he whispered, "Goodbye, Grace," before turning and going back to his truck. He heard the door shut behind him. The world was cold and gray, and he was stuck in that world with no idea how to break out of it.

He was barely to the highway before he had to pull over. He sat in the idling pickup, trying to wrap his head around what had just happened. His cell rang and he glanced at the screen. Caleb. He ignored it. As soon as the ringing stopped, it started up again. This time it was his mother calling. He ignored it and would have turned the phone off if he could have.

He realized that what he'd had with Claire had been him settling for someone familiar, someone he'd grown up with, someone he liked. That had seemed like love to him, but with Grace it wasn't anything like that. It was complicated and layered and now it was over because of him. She'd been ready to stay at the Lodge and be with him, and he'd shattered her trust. He struck the steering wheel with the flat of his hand.

The phone rang again. It was his dad. He hesitated, then didn't answer.

Instead, he put in a call to Burr. He had to ask him a few things, then maybe he'd figure out what he was going to do from here on out.

THE MORNING OF the election, Max showed up at the town hall and was the first one to vote. After visiting with others arriving at the polling place, he headed to the station. Lillian hugged him when he walked in, something she only did on birthdays, usually.

"Good to see you, cowboy."

"Catch me up to date on things," he said and sat opposite her at the desk. He'd hardly been able to think straight over the week since he'd walked away from Grace. He tossed his hat, and it caught on the hook, then he undid his jacket. "You hear anything interesting lately?"

"No, I haven't seen Grace. She's been holed up at the Lodge most of the past week. Poor thing. She has to be so lonely."

Lillian read him like a book, and it annoyed him. "I didn't ask you about Grace. I was talking about work."

"Sure you were," she said, but he knew she meant, *And bulls give milk.*

He let out a sigh. "Okay, how's she doing?"

"Seems to be selling, leaving to go back to Arizona soon, but she's been sticking close to the Lodge in the meantime. Chappy's working on the stable. He hasn't said much about anything going on out there. How are you doing?"

He almost said he was fine but wasn't. He wouldn't lie to Lillian.

"I'm here." He sighed. "But I had everything I ever wanted, and I messed it up."

"So I heard. Have you tried simply apologizing?"

"Of course, and she cut me off at the pass. She won't answer the phone or open my texts. I was so close, Lillian."

"Then clear it up."

"Easy for you to say," he murmured. "Right now I have some business to do. Call me if you have to. Otherwise I'll see you when the polls close."

THE CELL PHONE rang and Grace rolled over in bed, tired of crying all the time and reliving Max walking out of her life. She was back to where she'd been when she'd first driven into town, alone and confused, but this time, she was also miserable. She reached for the phone, saw it was Burr calling and answered.

"Hi, Burr."

"Good morning. I have some good news, I think."

She sat up. "What good news?"

"I have a buyer for the Lodge."

Her heart sank. This made everything final, and she should have been thrilled, but she only felt more lost.

"Oh, really?"

"You don't sound too excited."

"Just woke up and I'm…wow, just surprised, that's all."

He explained the offer, and the money was right on the amount Burr had come up with when she told him to go ahead and sell.

"That's great. Do you know what they're going to do with it?" she asked.

"You'll like this. They plan on running it—living on the premises and reopening it as a family-oriented destination."

That was too good to be true. "Can you make it illegal for them to cut up the land and raze the Lodge by putting it into the purchase agreement?"

"No, I can't do that, I'm afraid. It will be their property, unless you'd rather make it a long-term commercial lease. If you did that, you could hold on to it for as long as you want. In perpetuity, if that's your preference."

In perpetuity. She remembered him using that term to describe how long Uncle Martin had no entry fees for tournaments at the pool hall he'd helped name.

"I'll have to think about that."

"Sure. Take your time. The buyer wants to come out and look around and he should be available after seven tonight, though it might be as late as nine. Is that okay?"

"Yes, I'll be here."

"Okay, I'll be around. It's election day, you know, and Elaine is hosting a celebration party for Max after the polls close."

She closed her eyes. She might never see Max again, but she hoped he'd win and that he'd be happy.

"What if he loses?"

"He won't, but if he happens to, then it'll be a support party for Max instead. Elaine wanted me to invite you. But I guess you'll be busy around that time. After you meet the buyer, if it's not too late, come by and either celebrate or commiserate."

She wouldn't be there, but she evaded a direct answer. "Thanks for the invitation, and for finding a buyer so quickly."

"You bet. I'm off to vote," Burr said.

When she'd hung up, she stared blankly at the ceiling. It was over.

GRACE WAS SO nervous about the buyer coming that she could barely sit still. In her jeans and red plaid shirt, she walked around the Lodge the same way she had the night she'd arrived. She went from guest room to guest room and turned on all the lights, thinking about the new linens she'd ordered for each room and wishing she'd be there to see how they looked when they arrived. Maybe she could ask the new owner to take pictures when it reopened for business.

She rejected that idea right away because she knew seeing it become everything she'd imagined would be too painful knowing that someone else had fulfilled her uncle's wishes. She'd failed and wasn't even sure that she'd go inside when she came to scatter his ashes. She ended up in the great room on the couch with the lights out but a fresh fire in the hearth.

Burr had told her when she'd informed him she was selling that she could leave as soon as she wanted to, and all the paperwork could be done online. Right then, she made up her mind that she'd leave the next day. Burr said he'd take care of getting Rebel to her in Tucson as soon as she had a place to keep him.

She saw the headlights approaching just before nine and was on her way to the door when the person knocked.

"Coming!" she called and opened the barrier.

Max Donovan stood in front of her, and she was thankful she was still holding on to the door handle. She literally could feel her legs weakening and she couldn't seem to catch enough of a breath to say his name.

"Good evening, Grace," he said with strange formality.

"What are… Why are you here?" She had been so close to leaving and never having to see Max again, and now he was there in front of her, close enough to see deeper lines at the corners of his hazel eyes.

"I'm here to look over the Lodge. Burr said you were expecting me. I'm sorry if I surprised you."

She took a huge chance and let go of the door handle to step back far enough to lean against the desk for support.

"You…can't be the buyer."

"Yes, I am. You asked me if I wanted to take it over when you first arrived. I've reconsidered your offer, and I'm making you one. Can I come in to check everything out?"

He was a different person, more controlled than she'd known him to be. He was serious. This wasn't a joke. When she nodded, he stepped inside and swung the door shut behind him. She just stood there, trying to get her mind around what was happening.

Max took off his black hat and laid it on the desk next to her, then placed his jacket beside the hat. *Just like he used to do*, she thought, and her heart ached. She knew it would be a long time before she could wake up in the morning and not think of Max and go to sleep not thinking about him. She wasn't sure how she'd make it through that, but she had to.

"So," Max said as he looked around, "all the light bulbs work. The place is definitely in decent shape." He slipped past Grace through the archway into the great room. "Nice fire," she heard his voice say from the shadows. Then the lights in the great room came on.

Grace didn't know what to do. Max was acting as if nothing had happened, and she was so aware of him and what could have been that she felt nauseated. She hesitated, then followed him into the other room. Max had planted himself on the couch where he always sat when he was at the Lodge. He motioned her to come over.

"Sit so we can talk about the deal."

She slowly went over and sat down, leaving space between the two of them. He looked more dressed up than usual, in a dark brown Western-style shirt with silver at the cuffs and silver stars for buttons. Along with his black jeans, he was wearing the red boots he'd worn at the rodeo. She knew she was staring, and she looked down at her hands.

"So, what do you need to know that you don't already know? You know this place better than I do." She was relieved that her voice sounded almost normal. That was a huge victory considering what was going on in her mind.

"You're right, I do. Do you have any questions about the purchase, or anything special you want to be done or not done?"

"Why are you doing this?"

He blinked at that. "I told you. You asked me and I'm willing to do it."

She stood, ready to leave him there so she could breathe again. "You can figure out everything that needs to be done with Burr. I trust him." She wanted to go anywhere that Max wasn't. But he stopped her from leaving.

"Wait. I'll tell you why I'm doing this as long as you hear me out."

She stayed standing, taking whatever advantage she might have. She felt cold even though the fire was blazing.

"Just do it and get it over with."

"Okay. I did it because I've been foolish, and it's cost me a lot, probably more than I'm figuring on in the future. I want to put this right." He looked up at her. "Sit down before I get a crick in my neck."

She didn't want to do what he told her to do, but she still felt a bit unsteady, so she took a seat making sure she didn't sit close enough to make any contact. "Okay."

"Thank you," he said and shifted to face her more directly. "When I called Walter it took me three minutes to see for myself what you told me about him. We spoke—at least, he did, then he hung up on me. I was so wrong, so arrogant that I thought I could make things okay for you. I underestimated what you'd told me about him, and I'm truly sorry for that. You knew what you were doing. You've been right most every time, and I am that superhero without a cape without any real superpowers who's just bumbling along, making a mess of everything."

He exhaled roughly. "I'll take good care of the Lodge and the land." He looked at her, then dropped his eyes to his hands pressed on his knees. "I won't ask you to trust me—just know that I'll do the best I can."

Grace didn't know what to think or what to do. She could feel the tension in him as he stood up and looked down at her with narrowed eyes.

"Grace, I wish you a great life." He shook his head, and she could see him giving up, ready to leave, and if he did, she knew he wouldn't be back.

There he stood so close to her that all she had to do was reach out and take his hand. The urge to make that contact was almost overwhelming. She knew right then what she wanted, what she'd always wanted, but she'd been too afraid to trust the man in front of her. That fear was still there, but this time she didn't tell him to leave. She couldn't. She had to finally talk to him.

"Max, I know you'll do right by Uncle Martin. I don't doubt that, but I don't want to sell to you or lease to you," she said, her heart racing so hard she thought it might leap right out of her chest because of the chance she was taking.

His hazel eyes held hers and his jaw clenched. On impulse she reached out for his hand and held on to him. He started to pull away, but she tightened her hold.

"Max, don't go."

He glanced at their connection, then at her and she saw it in his eyes, what she was feeling right up until that moment...fear, and the loneliness that was almost unbearable.

"I have to go," he murmured. "I'll tell Burr to tear up my offer."

"Yes, please tell him to do that." She didn't let go. "But you sit down and listen to me this time."

He shook his head. "I can't go through this again. I'm sorry, Grace. I regret what I did, and I always will."

She tilted her chin and looked up at him. "Cows and horses. Why did you really call Walter?" she asked barely above a whisper.

"Because I couldn't stand the thought of you being alone when Walter should have been there for you. He's your *dad*, Grace. I wanted him to know what an amazing person you are, and I didn't want you to be alone in this world, even if we couldn't be together. I called him because I really cared about you."

He cared, past tense. "You cared about me?"

"That's why I butted in when I shouldn't have. That's why I made you hate me. That's why I'm here now."

"In Uncle Martin's first letter he left for me, he said he hoped that I'd find an easy heart, that he wanted that for me. I started to feel I was getting close to it, the more I was around you and the town and the other people here. But it was mostly because of you. I loved that feeling. I wanted more, and when you said that you wanted to see where things could go with us, I was thrilled. I could have told you then…" She hesitated then said the truth. "I loved you then, but I didn't say it because I didn't know if you felt the same way."

She slowly let go of his hand, praying he wouldn't walk away. Hoping she'd been right to tell him the bare truth. She'd loved him then, and she still did.

Silently, he sat down by her. His eyes were on her, and she couldn't figure out if he was happy or terrified. Then he touched her hand, lacing his fingers with hers, and looked into her eyes. He cleared his throat, then asked, "And now you hate me?"

"Oh, Max, I got scared. I was so afraid when I thought you'd broken my trust, and I… just retreated. That's what I always did with Walter when he went too far. I never apologized to him for my actions when he was like that, but I want to apologize to you. You were caring and compassionate, and I was awful. I can't ever make that up to you, but I want to try. The second letter Uncle Martin left in the safe… He knew what I needed to hear even though we'd never met. He wrote, 'I hope you're a better student of patience and fate than I've ever been. But at the end, all fell into place, and I saw how perfect a life I'd had, that the peace I'd hoped for became a reality. Don't give up, never stop.'

"He was right. I was giving up, too afraid to try harder and maybe face more pain than peace. But I don't want to give up on you. You're the most important person who ever came into my life."

Her hold on him tightened as she said, "I never hated you. Never. The truth is, I love you. I'll always love you no matter what happens."

For a moment he just stared at her, then he smiled that smile that made her heart race. "Marianna Grace Bennet, I love you. I have since the first time I saw you, sprawled on the floor here."

She all but fell into his arms, holding on to him to make very sure she wasn't imagining the happiness he'd just given her.

"I want to be with you for the rest of my life. To make this our home and to spend every minute I can loving you." His voice was a rumble against her cheek pressed to his chest.

She eased back to look up at him. "That's what I want, too," she whispered right before he kissed her.

She met his touch and let herself get lost in a growing happiness that she'd never felt before. She never wanted to stop, but Max eased her back so his eyes held hers, eyes full of warmth and the hint of a smile.

"One hundred percent cool," he said, then leaned in to kiss her again.

Moments later, she was sitting curled up beside him, resting her head on his shoulder, her hand on his chest. His heart was racing matching hers.

"Thank you," she said.

"For what?" he asked, his warm breath brushing her skin.

"I made it to one hundred percent cool," she murmured.

"You sure did," he said. "Beyond cool."

She moved back when she remembered the election. "Oh my gosh, did you win the election?"

His low laughter was so nice. "You just kissed Sheriff Donovan version 2.0. I won and the Van Durens congratulated me. How's that for a win?"

As Max stroked her hair back from her face, he asked, "Horses and cows?"

"You said that backward," she said.

"It works either way."

"Okay. Ask me anything?"

"So, just to be clear, you do love me and want to share this place with me, and you're not going back to Arizona, right?"

"That's right, Sheriff," she said. Then she glanced past him and seemed startled.

"What's wrong?"

"Out the back! Come on," she said as she took his hand and hurried with him out of the great room, past the desk, into the office and over to the sliding glass doors.

"There!" she said, pointing toward the night sky.

"What are you—" He stopped when a shooting star flashed across the heavens, then another one right after it.

Grace was almost bouncing with excitement. "It's beautiful."

"Beautiful," Max echoed but was looking at her. He hated to think how close he'd come to losing her.

"Is there going to be more?" she asked as she glanced at him.

"I don't know," he said as he let go of her

hand to pull her closer to him. He felt every breath she took. "December's the best time for the storms. Maybe Marty's behind this, letting us know that this is what he wanted when he wrote the letters. He wanted us to be friends and figured it could lead to something even better. I told you he always had a reason for everything he did."

"I think he was awesome," she half whispered.

"Me, too," Max said, relishing her closeness and a feeling of being right where he belonged.

Grace met his gaze and smiled softly. "My turn for cows and horses." She shifted and lifted her arms up and slipped them around his neck.

"You don't have to do that. I'll tell you anything you ask and always the truth."

Grace smiled at him and repeated, "Cows and horses?"

"Go for it."

She grinned at him, and it almost took his breath away. "Tattoo or no tattoo?"

"Right now at this moment, you want to ask me that?"

"Tattoo or no tattoo?" she persisted.

"Okay, okay, if you have to know, well…"

He loved how excited she looked to finally hear the truth. "The truth is I don't have a tattoo, but I'm thinking of getting one on my chest."

"What?"

"One of you."

Her eyes widened, and then she smiled. "That's a joke, right?"

"What if it isn't?"

She hesitated for a moment, then shook her head. "No...you're kidding. I can tell."

"Okay, you got me. I don't have any tattoos and I'm not planning on getting one anytime soon."

"Wow! I've learned to read you, and I'm pretty darn good at it. So, no tattoo."

"What about you? Do *you* have any tattoos?"

"Me?" She laughed at that, and he loved the sound. "No, none. Cross my heart."

He laughed, too. "Well, now that's settled—" He sighed. "I'm so relieved that you want to live here. I have to admit, I wasn't too excited about moving to Arizona."

"You would have done that?"

"I'm glad I don't have to, but honestly, I'm at a point where I don't want to spend another minute without you. So I would have made the move…for you."

When Grace whispered, "I love you," then kissed him again, he knew without a shadow of a doubt, he'd found his easy heart.

IT WAS AN unusually balmy day in May when most of the townspeople joined Max and Grace to honor Martin Robert Bennet. Grace loved her uncle, a man she'd never met, and she loved the man beside her so much she couldn't put it into words. They planned to live at the Lodge after their mid-July wedding until they could build their own home close by on their land.

As the guests eulogized their dear friend, her father—an unexpected addition to the mourners—stood to her right on the bridge, his head down, his hands clasped together.

Max looked at Grace and his smile was slow and easy. He leaned down to whisper to her. "Marty would have loved to see so many people here, especially Walter."

"He would. I can't tell you what it means to me that he's here."

Grace saw the look in Max's eyes and knew what he wanted her to do. She reached to slip her hand in the crook of her father's arm. At first, Walter didn't move, but then he shifted to be closer to her. Max squeezed her other hand, as if to say, *Well done*.

The stream below them was flowing, and the day felt fresh and sweet when Burr came over to hand the urn to Grace. Max held it for her to open it, and she put her hands over his to share the moment. Then Grace felt a hand on her shoulder—Walter's hand. It was a perfect day to say goodbye to Uncle Martin as the ashes drifted downward into the clear water.

When the urn was empty, Grace turned to Max and kissed him. "Thank you for everything," she whispered before she looked at her father.

"I have to leave, Grace," he said in a low voice. "I'm sorry. Soon Sawyer will be calling the shots."

"He's a perfect choice to take over when you leave." Walter had shown up on his own to remember his brother, and she'd let him leave on his own, but before she'd do that, she did something she could never remember doing in her life. She kissed her father on the cheek and whispered, "I'm so glad you came... Dad."

He looked at her briefly as if he didn't know what to do. Then he said, "Me, too.

I'll call you soon." With that, he turned and walked off.

Grace spotted Sawyer waiting for him at the top of the trail. The man waved and she had a feeling Sawyer might have been part of her father showing up so unexpectedly.

She turned and saw Max handing the urn over to Burr to take up to the Lodge. He took Grace by her hand that bore the engagement ring that he'd given her. The ring was platinum with a beautiful amethyst gem, a soft purple color that glinted violet in the sun.

He looked around, then said loudly, "Okay, folks. Barbecue and music on the back deck. Marty would want to see you all have a fun time."

Burr spoke up. "Absolutely. Marty wouldn't have wanted it any other way."

The crowd began to disperse with Elaine and Burr leading the way. Grace held on to Max as they followed the rest. "I can't believe my dad came."

"I don't know if I should tell you this," he said as they trailed after the main group.

"What's that?"

"I called Walter a week ago, and I had a heart-to-heart with him, so different than the first time. I told him about us and said that you deserved his support doing what Marty wanted. And, I added, he was very welcome to be here. I told him that it would mean so much to you. I just didn't know if he'd show up or not."

She stopped to turn and look up at Max. He did it again, and again he'd been right. "I didn't think I could love you any more than I already do, but I was wrong. Thank you for making that call."

He smiled at her. "That's a relief. Now, about our wedding."

"I'll call him about that."

"Great idea," he murmured as they started walking again.

Off in the distance, Grace could see people already on the deck and hear music coming over the outdoor speakers that Chappy had installed for them. Today had been sad and happy all at once.

Max stopped before they reached the end of the trail.

"Just a minute," he said and took out his cell phone. She watched him glance at the screen, then frown.

"What's wrong?" she asked.

"I'm not sure." He hit the icon to take the call and said, "Hello?" He listened, his hazel eyes on her as his frown turned into a smile. "Absolutely. She's right here."

She took the phone. "Who is it?" she asked in a whisper.

"Take the call," was all Max would say.

She put it to her ear. "Hello?"

"Grace, it's Dad. I wanted to ask you something before we fly out."

"Okay," she said with trepidation.

"Max mentioned your wedding in our last call, said it's in July sometime, and I want to be there."

She felt her throat tighten, and she knew she was about to cry from happiness.

"But I'll only come if I can walk you down the aisle. It's a lot to ask, I know, but would that be possible?"

Now she *was* crying and smiling at the same time. "Yes, I'd… I'd like that a lot."

"Thank you, Grace. I'll call you later and get the details, okay?"

"Yes, Dad, that's definitely okay."

She handed the phone back to Max. He took it, then hugged her to him. "You all right?"

"He wants to come to our wedding, and he wants to walk me down the aisle."

"Awesome," Max whispered in her hair. "Another wish came true for you."

She swiped at the tears on her cheeks. "This is the best day of my life," she said.

Max gathered her safely in his arms and when she looked up at him, he kissed her quickly then asked, "Any other wishes you want to make?"

She didn't have to think twice about her answer. "No, how about you?"

He smiled that smile she so loved. "Nope. I have everything I want right here with me now."

"So do I."

He shifted to take her hand and she loved the feeling of her fingers laced with his.

"Let's go up to the Lodge and celebrate Marty's life, and the beginning of our new life together. He would have loved that," Max said.

As they walked toward the celebration, Grace felt her world settle around her in the most incredible way. Everything she'd missed in her life before was now falling into place, from her father showing up at the ceremony, then asking to walk her down the aisle, to finding a real home for the first time, and finding Max, who made Uncle Martin's wish for her come true. Max was the reason she'd found her easy heart, with her loving and being loved by him, her cowboy, her hero, her everything.

* * * * *

Be sure to check out the previous books in Mary Anne Wilson's Flaming Sky Ranch miniseries:

A Cowboy's Christmas Joy
A Cowboy Summer

Available now at Harlequin.com!